DAN LORD
BY THE DOWNWARD WAY

BOOK ONE OF THE
VON KOPPERSMITH SAGA

ISBN: 9780692318218

Interior map image by Dan Lord
Book design by John Herreid

Printed in the United States of America

SALVO
PUBLISHING

Thanks to all of you who gave me guidance and encouragement throughout the writing of this book, especially Tony Lord, and Daniel & Jack

To Daniel, Jack, Charlie, & Max:
this book is for you, my boys

Contents

Part 1 - The Protector and the Traitor. Leo Goes Grave Digging and Finds an Island.

Into the street the Piper stept,
Smiling first a little smile,
As if he knew what magic slept
In his quiet pipe the while;
Then, like a musical adept,
To blow the pipe his lips he wrinkled,
And green and blue his sharp eyes twinkled,
Like a candle-flame where salt is sprinkled;
And ere three shrill notes the pipe uttered,
You heard as if an army muttered;
And the muttering grew to a grumbling;
And the grumbling grew to a mighty rumbling;
And out of the houses the rats came tumbling.

-Robert Browning, *The Pied Piper of Hamelin*

One

Approximately twenty years ago…

When Leopold Von Koppersmith was four years old, his father died. His mother's heart broke as a result, and although she was always very tender to Leo, there was never any mistaking the absence of an intact heart. She had black circles under her eyes and, as if to complement them, she wore dark clothing that seemed even darker against her pure, milk-white skin.

"Anselm, bring the car around, please," she said one bright, cold morning to her head of housekeeping. Anselm had served the family for decades, and Leopold, who was now nine, had never known life without him.

Within a half-hour a long, black vintage Mercedes limousine rolled into the shadow of the august Von Koppersmith Mansion, breaking the chilly quietude of December with the crunch and snap of its polished tires over the gravel-lined driveway.

"Where are we going, Mama?" Leo asked.

Mrs. Von Koppersmith led her son down the sweeping front steps, gently ushering him into the limousine. After he buckled his seatbelt, she looked into his wide brown eyes.

"For a little visit."

The Mercedes whisked past two acres of wooden fencing once white but now peeled and delapidated, behind which sprawled gently rolling overgrown fields of shimmery green rye grass. Leo stared out the window and imagined the herds of cattle that his mother had told him were once part of the Von Koppersmith estate, long ago. In those days, great throngs of vigorous, well-paid workers tended the animals, raised crops, and maintained the grounds from the mansion courtyards and gardens to the millhouse and stables.

Things had changed since then. Old money, though still in abundance, had begun to dry up, due in part to strange, extravagant expenditures over time. The only permanent staff now consisted almost entirely of Anselm, who was both the head of housekeeping and the driver; other than him there was just Mrs. Jombley, a full-time housecleaner, and Leopold's tutor, Mrs. Winnipeg. The grounds were handled by an outside landscaping service that came around twice a month. Leopold had no brothers or sisters, and in a month like December on a Saturday he could wander until lunch and never talk to another living soul.

He knew what "a little visit" meant. The Von Koppersmith family cemetery was on the exact opposite end of the estate—all of the American Von Koppersmiths on his father's side had been buried there since 1642. Many members of the European Von Koppersmiths were there, as well, owing to the expensive (and some said "ridiculous") efforts of the family in the seventeenth century to gather as many ancestral remains as possible and relocate them to the United States. Of course, Leopold's own father was buried here, and it was his grave that was their destination.

Leopold did not mind. The cemetery was a lovely place, though it needed pruning. While Anselm strolled off to smoke his pipe, Mrs. Von Koppersmith took her usual seat on a stone bench in front of her husband's tombstone. She laid her delicate white hands in the folds of her long, dark skirt and closed her eyes. Her hair trembled gently in the breeze, like black harp strings. She looked peaceful, even prayerful.

Leopold sat with her, but the bench was too cold for sitting on for very long and, besides, he wanted to go exploring. He stood up again in as quiet and respectful a manner as he could. He took a few backward steps away, and with only the slightest squeeze of his hand she both acknowledged his departure and granted him permission to roam. He smiled for her, but she didn't open her eyes to see it.

He glanced briefly at his father's tombstone, but he had seen it often enough: a bulky cross with engraved ivy branches and the dates of his father's earthly life. The Von Koppersmith coat-of-arms held the four arms of the cross together like a shield-shaped buckle, impressed with all of the elements so familiar to Leopold: a medieval man playing a flute and followed closely by little children, atop the Latin words *Defensor Familia* upon a carved banner.

Leopold felt a strange nothing when he considered his father; he had never spent much time with him. He had a fog-filled antechamber in his memory that held a mental shoebox of ragtag shared experiences: together on a path, reading a comic book with him, drinking hot chocolate…they weren't much compared to the One Big Memory, the walking in and SEEING, but this of course was the memory he kept face down at the bottom of the shoebox almost all the time. Mostly, Theodore Von Koppersmith wasn't much more than the many photographs Leopold's mother had shown him: a sleepy smile and deep, kind eyes. Just an image in framed pictures. But if that image could have come to life, strode forth and wiped away the dark circles under his mother's eyes—Leopold would have liked that very much.

A sudden gust of wind rattled the spectral branches of the pecan trees that hovered over the old graves. Leopold stuffed his hands into his corduroy pockets and trudged towards the cemetery chapel.

The chapel had been unused and untended for many years. Around the front doors' black, wrought iron handles was a thick chain, but it had too much slack in it, and even now one of the doors swayed slightly with the pushing of winter air. Leopold squeezed his gangly nine-year old body through the opening, as he had done many times before.

Sunlight came through narrow stained glass windows in red, blue and yellow beams that were cloudy with restless dust. The artistry of the windows was not extraordinary: a lily was depicted on one, a lamb on another, and a crown of thorns on another. There were eight pews in all, with three of them pushed against the wall during some long forgotten renovation that was never completed.

Leo ambled down the center aisle towards the cobwebbed altar, taking in the familiar sights of the faded Sacred Heart of Jesus painting on the left, the Mary painting on the right. Mary always looked distraught to Leopold, sober and concerned about something.

Was someone here? It felt like it. Leopold turned, making a panoramic review of the old chapel.

He heard a noise. It came from behind the altar…behind the white altarpiece…from the sacristy. Leopold thought it was the wind, at first, but somehow he knew almost right away that it was not.

He stepped up into the little sanctuary and moved cautiously around the altar. Had a cat gotten in? A raccoon?

The thought intrigued him—he loved discovering roaming animals on the estate. He stepped around the corner and into the sacristy and heard the noise again. It seemed like breathing, but low, coarse, and feral.

Leopold saw that the door leading onto the back steps of the chapel was open. A weak, moaning wind swept in and out, and he thought that here was the source of the sound he had heard, though he knew really it wasn't. Overgrown branches blotted out sunlight and held the top of the door in a gray claw. Leopold slipped through.

More tombstones stood in the grass, hemmed in by low black wire fences. Oak branches and Spanish moss hung close to the ground. Leopold saw something move behind one of the stones. He thought it was an animal. He trotted forward quietly, hoping to spy on it before it noticed him.

···+··+··+··+··+··+··→

On the stone bench in front of her husband's tombstone, Mrs. Von Koppersmith felt a shadow fall across the back of her head.

"Anselm?" He must have finished his pipe, she thought.

"Ready to head back, Anselm?"

She opened her eyes and turned. It was not Anselm.

···+··+··+··+··+··+··→

When he heard his mother's scream, Leopold whirled towards the chapel. He stood frozen, waiting, listening.

She screamed again.

He was about to run to her, when he heard the feral breathing sound once more. It hissed and snarled among the tombstones under the oak branches behind him, drawing Leopold's attention like a hook in his ear.

As he watched, a head and an upper torso grew out of one of the graves like a perverse kind of plant. One thin arm was propped to the side. An old, tattered shirt clung to the gaunt figure. Its head was down, and strands of black hair hung upon his cheeks like a raggedy cowl.

Leopold stared. The thing wriggled laboriously out of the ground, freeing its other arm, slowly dragging its legs up. Despite its exertions, no dirt moved around it and no grass was disturbed. Its body was translucent, like a murky green hologram.

Leopold snapped out of his quiet shock. He turned to run back into the chapel, desperate with conflicting impulses to both escape the ghastly apparition and to rescue his mother from whatever had made her scream.

He pushed into the doorway to the sacristy. As wind blew through the trees and the clawed branches over the top of the door shivered, Leopold became stuck. He could only squeeze half of himself through.

He shot a look back in the direction from which he had come. The ghost was coming closer, in weather beaten brown boots and worm-eaten trousers. Its head still drooped, as if too heavy for the gangly neck.

Leopold let out a muffled cry and shoved himself farther in. A button on his coat ripped off.

But he still wasn't inside all the way.

The ghost drifted closer. It slowly raised its head, and its dark hair spread to reveal a pallid gray-green face with a long, thick nose. Its eyes were like wet, black snake eggs.

It reached for Leopold with one green, wiry hand. With the other hand it pointed to its throat. It opened its mouth, showing rotted teeth and a swollen gray tongue, and a rasping hiss slid out like a wooden bolt.

Leopold recoiled. The fabric of his coat tore loudly and he tumbled into the sacristy. He scrambled to his feet and tore madly through the chapel, sending the dust swirling into the stained glass light in little soundless cyclones. Bursting out of the front doors, he sprinted back down the path to his father's grave.

He found his mother. Hovering in the air several feet above her, without wires or wings, was a man.

Leopold was still too far away to see him clearly; he took in only the flash impression of short, gleaming blond hair and a white, toothy grin. In his right hand was Anselm. The driver's eyes were closed. His feet dangled and his chin was slumped against his chest. The material of his coat was gathered tightly in the man's fist.

"Stay out of the cemetery, woman."

He opened his fingers and Anselm tumbled to the ground like a two hundred pound bag of flesh.

Leopold cried out and ran to his mother. No sooner had he reached her, the flying man swiped at him. It was a small movement, just a tap, but the boy struck the ground so hard that it knocked all the air out of his little lungs. Mrs. Von Koppersmith howled and dove to him, cradling him in her arms as he struggled to breathe.

Anselm regained consciousness with a groan. Rubbing blood from the back of his head, he pulled himself to Mrs. Von Koppersmith's side. Leopold began at last to take in huge gulps of air, and his mother looked around desperately for their attacker. He was gone.

Leopold broke into tears now as he tried to explain what he had seen behind the chapel. His mother listened and her face drew up so tightly that Leopold thought she was going to scream again. She gained control of herself, pulling out her cell phone and tremulously dialing while urging the boy to his feet. "Come on, honey! Into the car, quickly! *Quickly!*"

She called back to Anselm, who was hastily recovering. Together they tore into the black limousine, and seconds later they were speeding across the estate, to the towering mansion that waited for them like a stern, sheltering giant.

Two

Approximately eight centuries ago…

Journal, A Thought-Provoking Anniversary

I watched the moon set early this morning, just before dawn. I call it "Mother," because Earth seems like her child; the star of day is "Father." My little Family. Mother Moon was round and beautiful when she slipped beneath the horizon, but I must admit that it made me feel sad. I did not know why at the time, but I think that now I understand: it was exactly one hundred ninety thousand years ago today that I first came to live here on the Island.

This is not a complaint. The Island is lovely, bursting with life and color. It is only that I feel so out of place, for I am the only rational creature here, the only kind who can know and understand and love. Yes, I always have my Oblates with me—good, faithful Oblates! But they cannot converse with me on any deep level at all (though I have no doubt they would gladly spend all the day doing that if only they could). Besides them, there are the insects and the birds that were here originally. There are the rich green forests and the steep, towering mountains, and the ocean, stretching off in white-capped waves in every direction as far as my eyes can see. But that is all.

If only there were other intelligent beings here; someone to share myself with and whose selves I could share in return! How I miss my humans, so far away!

Journal, A Troubling Conversation Today

How does he know? Kak seems to be able to sense when I am in a particular mood.

Not long after I finished my Journal entry yesterday, as the sun was beginning to sag heavily towards the sea and as the sharks began to patrol the northern coasts, Kak appeared, hovering in the air not far from the highest tower of my mountain palace. That was as close as he could come, of course—all the Throtrex power in the universe could not have gained him entry to a Protector's fortress. He just drifted there outside, grinning his ridiculous grin, the orange of his warty skin a strange match to the angry red clouds smearing the western horizon.

"What do you want?" I said, in no mood for the tiresome word-games the old Archthrotrex likes to play.

"What do you have to give?" he replied with a sneer.

"A Spear—through your gut."

Kak clapped his hands and giggled. "Not before I give you the slip, chump. As I always do."

"You are spoiling the sunset. You have a few seconds before I release the Oblates upon you. What do you want?"

Kak rested one long finger on his chin. "I want…a place to call home. There's nowhere for the Enemy of Man to lay his head! You wouldn't believe it, Zechariah, but the world has become infested with your nasty little human monkeys. They have spread like fungus."

He could see the obvious look of interest on my face.

"Oh, nobody's told you? My, my…do you ever think you're playing for the wrong team, Zekkie? They don't tell you *anything*! I don't think I've ever met a more ignorant, disavowed stooge than you! Yes, humans are the new sparkling link on the pleasant end of the food chain these days. All kinds of things have happened since you last saw them, in fact—they've gotten quite the boost, hierarchically speaking. But that really doesn't concern you and I, does it? Or does it? It doesn't concern *me*, anyway. I couldn't care less about whatever super big bonus destiny they're supposed to have—oh, but I guess you *do* care, don't you?"

I just stared at him, hating him, and hating myself for being so cut off from the ones I should be watching over.

"Well," he said, mocking me with a faux expression of sympathy, "There, there, old chum, there, there. Don't lose heart! I'm sure you've got some *really important* job that will be handed to you any day now. I mean, it's only been about two hundred thousand years, right? I'm sure you haven't been forgotten and left to rot on a miserable little island in the middle of nowhere!"

He vanished then, in a puff of grotesque-smelling blue-black gas. His squealing laugh lingered among the fading sunrays.

A troubling conversation. I don't feel much like writing anymore today.

Journal, Memories of humans…

The air today is filled with a fragrance of flowers and herbs, and gentle winds sweep the forests down by the River. I did not assign the Oblates any task at all in the palace, but let them roam freely around the Island.

The unwelcome visit from Kak last week still haunts me, I have to admit. It has stirred memories of my two humans, back when they were new. I remember when the first one emerged, filled with spirit and love; strong, sleek, elegant. Higher than the animals, yet below the spirits. I was eager to speak with him and learn about him, but my instructions for the time being were to only observe and guard. It wasn't long before he discovered a second human, much like him, yet different. It is difficult to describe…both of them human, yet in two distinct modes: a "man" and a "woman." Even more marvelous, was that their spirits and bodies fit together like a lock and key!

Eventually, I was allowed to introduce myself. Those were joyful days. The three of us—two humans and their Protector…what a time! Perhaps I was naïve for not wondering why I was there to protect them, since there seemed no danger present. It is my everlasting regret.

My humans were gathering wood for a fire one evening when the worst happened. No portent preceded it other than the darkening sky, which I saw only as a lovely turning from sun to rain. Then I spied Kak.

I was momentarily stunned. What was he doing there?! Of all the Throtrex I have ever encountered, he is the most odious: that fat, orange body and those maniacal eyes. I cannot imagine that the Throtrex king himself, the Corpse, could be much more revolting. Lurking behind a tree, Kak stared at my humans with all the murderous intent of a hunting snake. As I write this, with the benefit of hindsight, I realize that he was also casting occasional glances at me, with that one bulbous eye and it's smaller, blue-veined companion.

I shouted for my humans to take cover, and they promptly fled farther into the forest. I withdrew my Spear and prepared to do battle.

At the time I thought Kak was a fool. He knew perfectly well that I was superior to him in combat. He made efforts to slash at me, which I parried. He retreated, breathing billows of flame at me like a troll-shaped volcano—I couldn't understand why he kept making the attempt, since of course his fire cannot leave even the slightest mark on me. All the while I made every attempt to strike him down, never noticing that he was drawing me farther and farther away from my humans.

Kak was not the fool at all. I was. After nearly half an hour's worth of his vain clawing and craven dodging, he suddenly stopped. His mouth spread into that huge, awful, mirthless grin and he said: "I'm so bored! Time to go!" With a cackle, and a pop of stinking blue-black fumes, he disappeared.

I knew then that I had been deceived. I did not know how yet, but I travelled at top speed back in the direction of where I had last seen my humans.

By then, night had fallen. It was truly the first night of Earth that had ever contained fear. I could feel it poisoning the air; I could taste it in the wild winds raking the trees. I looked everywhere but I could not find my humans. Worse, I had the distinct feeling that they did not *want* to be found.

The next day I was sent away. I was told that everything had changed; the humans had done something terrible, something awful, on behalf of none other than the Corpse himself. I was bewildered, yet now at last Kak's feint made sense: he had been on a mission to distract me so that the Corpse, the "World King" as he is so fond of calling himself, could corrupt my poor humans! What had he done? What hollow promise had he made them? Whatever it was, it was clearly effective. As a result, I was no longer required to protect them, of course. A Protector can't protect someone who does not wish to be protected.

So, I was sent here, to this Island. A new assignment. It is not a punishment, I know this—so why does it feel like a punishment? I am not to blame for the choice the humans made, and yet I feel deeply responsible. If I had ignored Kak's lures, perhaps, and stayed beside my humans and fled with them…perhaps my self-assurance made me blind.

Then, when they needed me most, I was not there. I was away swiping at shadows.

And so the Island seems like banishment. I know that isn't true...at least I think I know. There is *something* to all of this—there always is. I just do not know what it is yet.

Journal, Joy!

Today has been, without question, the most exciting day I have ever experienced on the Island. My mind is like a churning star when it erupts with flares of plasma and lights up entire planets! How can I contain my joy long enough to write of this day's supremely marvelous events? I can only try, I suppose!

I and a few of my Oblates had wandered to the top of the old mountain next to mine—the one that looks like a giant's finger pointing up at the sun —and we were appreciating the view of the valley below and of all the little green foothills marching away to the north. The winds blew as strongly as they always do up there, and a few clouds swept by, but there was really very little for me to do or think about. I decided to pass the time with some idle composing; I sat and admired the colored auras that radiated softly from my Spear as the beginnings of a melody developed, but I couldn't shape it into anything specific and I began to lose interest.

Right then I heard a noise—a scream! Though filled with fear, it was the unmistakable sound of a rational creature. I whirled just in time to

17

watch a figure fall upon the ground right at my very feet! It was a small being, dressed in ragged brown and black clothes, but before I had a chance to take in any more details yet another little person fell to the ground next to the first one!

I bent and grabbed them both by their pale, lanky arms and turned them so that I could see their faces. Imagine my profound shock when I looked upon the faces of two humans! They were very small humans, and I realized they were young ones, not more than ten or eleven years old.

I was baffled. They had not climbed up the mountain to meet us. *They had fallen from the sky.* My eyes drifted upwards, and I beheld a third human child tumble down with a muffled shriek. He just *appeared*, as if through an invisible trap door in the air a few yards above us!

Three little humans! They were in a state of terrible fear, and were bruised and bloodied because of their fall. In a flash I put my Oblates on watch, and it was a good thing I did, for right then a fourth little child in torn clothes plummeted through the invisible passageway! This fourth one landed in the arms of a faithful Oblate instead of upon the rough surface of the mountaintop, thank goodness. Right behind him, though, there came another! And then another!

So began what was surely the strangest game ever invented, as my Oblates rushed to catch one falling human child after another and place them safely next to me. Nor did this game end quickly. Dozens upon dozens of little humans (all of them the boy kind) plopped out of whatever mysterious sky portal it was up there and kept right on coming.

When the event finally came to an end nearly the entire surface area of the mountaintop was bobbing with little human heads. And they were brave, too! There was a little crying, and the occasional wail, but besides that they all looked up at me with their big, wondering eyes waiting to see what I would do next.

I made a quick count: Four hundred fifty-one! I can hardly believe it even as I write it! Four hundred fifty-one little humans! It was not entirely appropriate, I suppose, but I could not help but throw my head back and laugh like I had not laughed in almost two hundred thousand years!

The Oblates and I brought them safely down into the valley, and I have only just completed making some hasty sleeping areas for them and gotten some good food into them (something which they had clearly not had for some time, by the looks of them). I have already learned a great deal about who they are and where they came from, but I do not presently have the time to chronicle it all, as I must continue to tend to them I will write more later!

Journal, Building new lives…

These past weeks have nearly been beyond words! My little humans are intoxicating to me. They are full of wonder about everything. Now that they have found out that my Island is populated by hardly anything besides the Oblates and myself, they ask me every day to make animals for them. I am thrilled to comply. As a Protector, I have been given the Life Power, but only in cooperation with humans. Being able to finally put my gifts to work is exhilarating. Using all the odds and ends and pets and insects and such, which they brought with them from their homeland, I have brought forth all manner of stupendous new creatures and flowers and trees. The ones I am proudest of are those we made using a tree frog that one of the boys had been carrying around. They are bright, entertaining little fellows now, almost as tall as the children, and great companions. Of course it is the humans' great right and privilege to name things, and it wasn't long before they began referring to our new frog-creatures as "Cheevilnids." Isn't that a clever name?

We also made the Waywobs, our version of what the children called 'sheep' where they came from, using a swatch of one of their sheep wool shirts. The Waywobs are perfectly round, and they move around by rolling—not very sheep-like, I know, but not bad for my first attempt, and everybody seems pleased with the result, all in all!

These meager recorded descriptions are just scratching the surface, though. We've populated the entire Island with charming creatures, new kinds of birds and trees, things to swim in the rivers that make you laugh to look at them. And how the humans love to build! The children come to me often and ask for twisting, towering structures to climb upon. My Oblates have never worked so much in their lives! We even created a huge living edifice made of trees that they call Tunneltrees that are hollow on the inside and which grow in huge tangled bundles. When it rains, water flows fast through the trunks, and the children spend hours sliding through them!

Journal, About Walwich Herstog

One of the children left today. It made me quite sad, but there was nothing I could do to convince him to stay. I think he had simply seen too much evil; too many adults had failed him and, to him, even though I am not human, I might as well have been just another grown-up who would betray him sooner or later. He gathered up supplies and moved into the forests to the southeast, farther down the big River that everyone now calls the "Fillwishing."

I will miss him. Walwich is his name, of a family called Herstog. I liked him immediately from the first day, perhaps because his humped back and his shriveled, twisted leg inspired pity in me. He seemed so lonely and confused, and yet responded so lovingly to my affections that I thought he would find here on the Island the happiness that I think must have eluded him all of his life. Alas, he is gone now. He left early this morning. I will continue to check up on him from time to time, and hopefully one day he will find peace and return to us here in the valley beneath my mountain.

Journal, Getting Ready for Sleep...

I made some more new trees for the children today—Tabletop trees, they call them, very tall and mighty, but with branches that grow flat at the top so they can climb up and play upon them.

I am starting to get weary. My yearly Sleep is almost upon me, and I must submit to the Washing soon. I hate to Sleep when I have protecting to do, but it cannot be helped—and, anyway, I won't be any good to my little wards if I am not washed and renewed.

One thing that gives me pleasure about it (and I see I haven't recorded this fact yet, so it is good that I am doing so now) is that I select one of the children to preside during the Sleep. The children have always been very interested in the whole process, and they find it amusing that they have to go to sleep every few hours but I only sleep once a year! They went wild with excitement when I began including them. This will be the third year that we do what has become this very fine tradition: one boy chosen by me will help lower me and my Spear into the waters of the Sleeping Pool and watch over me for the few hours that I sleep. When I awake, my Spear and I will be completely rejuvenated, and the chosen child always feels extra proud about it. It makes me glad to see them walking a little taller among their fellows, taking credit for how well rested I am afterwards! And I know that each of them will eventually get their turn —they do not age here, after all. This is my Island, and it does not fit into the flow of time the way the rest of the Earth does. Perhaps one day the children will be called off of the Island again and they will grow and mature then, but for now they will stay young, and I cannot say that this notion displeases me in the slightest!

Anyway, I will choose someone soon for the Washing ritual. My Sleep is still a few days off, but it will certainly feel good when it comes at last!

Journal, A Nice Surprise Today

A great thing has happened. My little Walwich Herstog has returned from the forests! I thought maybe I was delirious with the Sleep beginning to fall upon me, but even after I rubbed my bleary eyes there was Walwich, supporting his weight on his walking stick and smiling tenderly up at me. "Protector," he said, "I've been stupid and suspicious. I know you would never hurt me. I want to come back to the valley, to the village of Relm, where I belong."

I was overjoyed! I scooped him up and held him close. "Walwich, my boy," I said, "I want you to preside over my next Sleep!" The other children thought this was a very good idea and they cheered, and Walwich never looked happier in the few short years I've known him.

Tomorrow evening, when Mother Moon lies upon her side as a silver-white crescent, I will take Walwich with me up to the palace and prepare the Sleeping Pool for the Washing ritual and my much-needed Sleep. I will Sleep in bliss knowing that Walwich is back among us here!

Journal

     Zechariah is GONE. No more leaders. No more shepherds, or guardians. No more Protectors. My name is not Walwich Herstog anymore. I'm the Watchdog. The Island belongs to Kak now, and the Throtrex, because I, THE WATCHDOG, have given it to them. I'm going far away now, to the west, and I'll never need anyone or anything ever again. I am all I need.

Three

Present day...

The chiming of the doorbell was not a sound that Mrs. Von Koppersmith heard very often. It made her uncomfortable. She hurried down the dim, paneled hall to the top of the wide staircase, and the hem of her pale-gray-and-charcoal floral print dress flowed behind her like the wake of a gliding swan. "Anselm? What is it?"

The ringing of the bell was the only response.

She almost never left the mansion these days, and even going down to the first floor was unusual. She dipped her toe onto the first step and paused. Where was Anselm? Was something wrong?

She laughed softly at herself—she was in the habit of assuming the worst, and she knew it, and every so often she saw it for the ridiculous vice it was.

The doorbell rang again.

"Anselm!"

Finally her head of housekeeping appeared at the foot of the stairs. His face shone.

"Ma'am! He's back! He's come back!"

"Who, Anselm?"

The silvery knob on one of the huge front entrance doors turned with a small peal and the door swung open. White afternoon light spilled into the foyer, and was blotted out by a young man with brown eyes, dark, disheveled hair and an untrimmed beard.

Mrs. Von Koppersmith clutched at her black sweater with one hand, and with the other she cupped her face in disbelief. Her eyes began to water. "Leopold!"

She hastily flowed down the stairs and embraced her son tightly. "You're here? When did you get back? You should have called and told me, I would have gotten things ready…"

"I'm sorry. It was kind of unplanned, until a couple of days ago. Do you mind if I stay a little while?"

"Oh, honey, of course I don't mind…" Her voice caught and she turned away briefly to hide a new burst of tears, then turned back again suddenly, her face a mix of happiness and hurt. "I'm sorry! I'm not sad! It's been so long and I'm so glad you're here. Are you hungry? I bet you are. Anselm, take him to the kitchen and help him fix something to eat. I'm just going to clean myself up a little."

She pulled away, hiding her sobbing as she ascended the stairs. Leo gave an awkward glance to Anselm, who returned it with a subtle frown.

···✦··✦·✦·✦·✦·✦·✦

Anselm and Leo stood in the kitchen making sandwiches for dinner. Beneath hanging racks of copper pots and burnished ladles, they sorted slices of soft wheat bread and tomatoes and peeled the corners from packages of roast beef.

Leo secretly noted the changes that had taken place in his old housekeeper's face. Anselm had always had a large, long nose and a jutting chin, but age had made large larger, long longer, and jutting nearly telescopic. It was as if his chin and his nose were trying to connect and turn his smooth head into a big coffee cup.

"I should take a nutcracker to your nose, you know," he said in his soft, precise voice without looking at Leo. "You've been gone for five years. In all that time you called your mother…what? Ten times, maybe? Wrote three letters? In five years? Do you not know how much that hurts people?"

Leo sighed uncomfortably as he transported mayonnaise to bread slices. "She knows I was backpacking across Europe. It's not easy to send letters."

"For a little while you were, yes, but then you flew to South America. To Peru. You could have dropped in for a visit on your way."

Leo nodded stiffly. Anselm almost pressed him for more of a reaction, but then didn't.

"How was Peru?"

"Peruvian."

"Clever." Anselm said it with a bozo voice and faux amusement.

"Sorry. It was amazing. Beautiful. I met a girl. Then I decided to go back to Europe for a little while, and she went with me. She moved there.."

Anselm's eyebrows went up. "A girl from Peru moved to Europe—to be with you?"

"Yes. Maritza. That was her name."

27

"She *moved*. From Peru to Europe. For you…"

"Yep. She thought we were going to get married."

"And why did she think that?"

"Well, probably because I told her we would."

"But then you didn't get married…"

"I backed out."

"Interesting. And what happened to Maritza?"

"I heard she went back to Peru. Her parents flew her back."

Anselm grunted. His face grew flushed with anger, and he nearly spoke, but didn't.

"I know," said Leo. "It sounds bad. It *is* bad. But I couldn't go through with it."

They continued assembling sandwiches in silence for a few seconds before Anselm spoke again.

"Young, unsuspecting South American girls are one thing, Leo. But your *mother*…you cannot simply back out on her. She's alone. You were the only child she was able to have. She has no career…"

"She doesn't need one. We've been living on family inheritance and investments since…"

"She's *alone*. She's your mother. You're twenty-nine now, and I'm getting too old to take care of things here properly…"

"Anselm." Leo prepared to defend himself, but any words he thought he was going to say dissolved and rippled over his face as expressions of

28

frustration and resentment. Finally: "I have a lot on my mind, Anselm. I came back to try and work some things out, O.K.?"

"I can appreciate that," Anselm said as he inserted long toothpicks through the center of each sandwich. "But remember: everyone is trying to work things out. Not just you."

···+·+·+·+·+·+·+→

Leo was simply going to use the cutting board to carry dinner upstairs to the den, but Anselm shook his head grimly. He insisted on using the silver-plated serving tray, and on carrying it all himself, with Leo walking behind him—to do less would have been an insult to tradition and memory. Leo marveled at how active Anselm still was: there was still power in those shoulders that had once carried rifles and packs through the harsh cold of the Korean War.

The den had always been a favorite area of the mansion for Leo and his mother. Many times she had read him stories or watched him play with his Legos or draw pictures with pencils and crayons here in the light of the huge fireplace. She was waiting for them now, and she couldn't resist rising up from the leather couch like a black and white fountain to give her son another fragile hug. It was Advent season and she had been listening to *O Come, O Come Emmanuel* on a CD player, but now she turned it off.

As Anselm arranged dinner on an enormous oak coffee table, Leo fondly took in the sight of his old den. The fireplace glowed brightly the way he had always remembered; over there was the towering grandfather clock with the engraved brass face that reminded him of a church when it tolled; there was the bookstand where he stored toys—was that his old box of Legos? There, proudly mounted on the wall to the right of the fireplace, was the shiny, silver-tipped shovel that was used to break the ground on this wing of the mansion when it was built back in 1912. Leo recalled having seen, somewhere else in the house, a dog-eared photograph of his great-grandfather and a group of anonymous bland men staring straight ahead, gathered around a patch of dirt with that very shovel poised to dig.

So much history here, he thought. *And so much of it bad.*

Anselm unobtrusively retreated from the room, mumbling a promise of coffee and tea soon to come.

In between bites, Mrs. Von Koppersmith patted her son's arm. "I'm so glad you're here, sweetheart."

Leo's face twisted up with embarrassment, but with a teasing tone he soberly declared, "I'm a bad son."

She grinned against the back of her hand as she chewed. "You've been talking to Anselm."

Leo nodded heavily, and they smiled affectionately at each other.

"Well, you're here, and that makes me happy."

He swallowed the last of his sandwich and took a long drink of iced tea until the ice cubes rattled down the glass and landed on his upper lip. He set the glass down and positioned himself on the edge of the big leather couch.

"Mama." The way he spoke sounded as if he had nothing else to say, or as if the word "mama" was a thesis, and everything to follow would only serve to prove it. Staring down at the red swirls in the rug, he took a small breath and continued.

"Is it true that dad was wandering around repeating himself before he died?"

His mother looked at him sympathetically. "Who told you that?"

"Grandma. A long time ago. She said he kept saying the same number over and over: 1212."

His mother gave a small sigh of mild resolution. "Yes, that is true."

"Why? What does 'twelve-twelve' mean?"

"Oh, it doesn't mean anything, honey. Not anything at all. It was just something his poor, tired mind became fixed on. Just a symptom; your grandmother and I noticed he was doing it a lot the day of..." She paused to gather power to say the word she never liked to say: "...his suicide. We got him to lie down and rest, which he did. He wasn't a stubborn kind of man, you know...he lay right down and went to sleep. At least I thought he was sleeping. I called Dr. Westford about it—do you remember Dr. Westford? He was a good man. I called him, and he said to see how your father was after he woke back up. It was when I went back to

31

check on him later that I found he had already…
died."

Without meaning to, Leo winced, almost incospicuously. In that one fog-filled antechamber of his memory, he'd put his hand into the mental shoebox where he kept images of his father and had turned over the One Big Memory, the one he almost always kept face down.

"Mom…I *know*, remember? I was there. I walked in three seconds after you did. I saw him hanging there."

She shuddered slightly and closed her eyes, taking a sip of iced tea. "That poor man."

Poor man. The two words stung Leo. "Poor man," he muttered. "Right. He hanged himself, mom. And he left everybody else to clean up his mess."

His mother started to plunge into an apologia, but Leo cut her off. "And what about Grandad? Was he a 'poor man,' too?"

She looked at him with confusion. "Granddad? My dad…?

"No, I mean *my* dad's dad."

"What are you getting at, sweetheart? What's on your mind?"

Leo made an effort to stifle the bitter tone that had begun to mark his words. "Granddad was so depressed all the time. Then he *left*."

An embarrassed half-smile crept over his mother's face. "I didn't know you knew about that. Yes…he moved to Canada when your dad was…oh, about ten or eleven, I think."

"His diaries are in our library. I used to read them when I was younger. Have you ever looked at them? They're all sad. They're all about how much he hated the mansion, and how regretful he was for getting married and having kids. And there are all these disturbing drawings in the margins, of little children's faces with dark eyes. Along with that same number. 1212."

She rested her palm on his knuckles. He looked down and saw how lovely her hand still was, how pale and elegant, with only the barest stippling of brown and some wrinkling around the knuckles. "You know, your great *great* grandfather had a similar constitution. He had to be put into a sanitarium."

"What?! No one told me that!"

"They had to give him an emergency blood transfusion, because they caught him one night… he'd cut his hand open and was using his blood to draw pictures of faces on the walls…children's faces, kind of like the ones in that diary, now that you mention it."

She shuddered again.

"And his brother went on a sailing expedition across the Pacific—by himself. No one ever heard from him again. His other brother joined a traveling carnival and disappeared, too. And their father— your great, great, great grandfather—jumped off the top of Stone Mountain in Georgia. While his wife and kids watched."

At first Leo could only stare in stupefaction, his mouth hanging open like an empty birdhouse.

"*That,* right there, is what I'm getting at, Mom. There was something wrong with all of them.

Something psychologically wrong, or medically, I don't know. And I'm next."

She nodded and said flatly: "I see." Outside, the sun had set, and a drowsy rainfall had begun. "I think there's a curse on this family."

Leo looked at his mother as if she had just passed a death sentence, but then he laughed in spite of it. "My gosh, Mom, I came back here to settle some questions, but you're only making things worse."

"I'm sorry, sugar. I don't mean to be gloomy. I only know what I see. Your dad saw doctors—they never found anything physically wrong. He was diagnosed with depression, but therapy never achieved anything. God knows I don't have any answers for you. Then again, life doesn't really give anybody a lot of answers. Do you really need them, honey? I know your father let you down, and I know this house wasn't the most inspiring place to grow up in. But you don't have to agree to the same things your ancestors did. Can't you just be free? Be happy?"

Leo stood. "No, mom, I can't! I need to know if one day I'm going to just suddenly lose my shit and jump off a mountain, or..."

He choked up, wiping tears away. "*Hang* myself."

He closed his eyes for a moment and took a deep, calming breath. "You know, Mom, I saw a ghost in our cemetery that day when I was nine years old, that same day you and Anselm were attacked by that weird guy. I told you, but I don't think you believed me."

His mother stood, wanting to hold him again. "Leo, please, sometimes things don't..."

"I saw a ghost. We talked a little about it after it happened, but then the whole thing just got swept away into that same damn compartment where our family sweeps everything, so that it never gets talked about again or dealt with or resolved. But what if me seeing that ghost was the beginning of me starting to lose *my* mind and slowly morph into whatever this is that happens to the men in our family? I can't just sit back and wait to see if that's going to happen or not, and in the meantime just be *free* and *happy*. I have to protect myself. I need to look for answers, and the best place I can think of to look is here."

She could summon no words. Her eyes had become damp. Leo looked at her, and loved her, but when she reached out to take his hand he pulled away and trudged out of the room.

Four

The morning was cold. Leo stared at a flock of brown birds that spewed out of the bright green grass of the fields as he jogged down the road that led to the cemetery. He listened to the pad of his running shoes and the measured breath flowing in and out of his lungs. There were no other sounds. The cemetery grew closer.

Nothing had changed. The Von Koppersmith family cemetery was an outdoor museum, of sorts. A lawn care company kept it neat, but nothing was ever altered—nor would it be, Leo realized, until his own mother was added. And then he himself, sometime after that.

He found his way to his father's grave. The stone was a little more weathered than it used to be. His eyes wandered over the coat-of-arms. *Defensor Familia.*

This was not why he was here. He knew that. He knew it even before he had started his run. Even the run itself had been just a charade.

His feet found their own way down the old, familiar path to the chapel. The chain still hung limply around the black wrought iron handles, but Leo was now too big to fit through that slim opening between the doors.

He made his way around the side, pushing through tall, thick bushes that stood like leafy sentinels. A gust of cold wind met him behind the chapel and shook the arching branches above him.

He stopped and let his eyes find the grave. His stomach clenched up with nausea as old memories pumped like blood through his mind.

The wind blew again. No grayish green figure seeped out of the ground now, no raspy breathing sounds chafed the air.

He walked towards the grave.

The tombstone was ancient. There was evidence that attempts to restore it had taken place: the cracks in the hoary gray stone were filled in with a cleaner, white material. The inscriptions had been meticulously cleaned, as well: *Nicholas of Hamelin, 1218. Requiescat in Pace.*

Leo blinked. "1218..." Definitely one of the graves that had been exhumed in the seventeenth century by the Von Koppersmiths and brought here to the family cemetery.

He crouched down and examined the headstone. It was rectangular, with no cross upon it.

1218...pretty close to 1212, the number his father had repeated deliriously before his death.

A dry yellow leaf drifted down and landed on the "H." Leo brushed it off.

He stood back up. He was surprised to note that he suddenly felt...good? 'Good' was not quite right, but a certain lightness played in his chest. The trees looked beautiful again and the chilly air was refreshing.

It seems like everybody's seen a ghost at one point or another in their life, he mused. *It doesn't have to be such a big deal.* He slipped his hands into the soft, cotton pockets of his warm-up pants and he began walking back to the entrance of the cemetery, passive thoughts drifting behind his brown eyes.

All at once his fingers went cold. The hairs on the back of his head rose. There was something here; an invisible presence…

He glanced at the chapel, where a tree branch was brushing a rear window. When he turned back to Nicholas' gravestone, the same pale green specter he had seen when he was a child was now reaching for him as it slunk from its burial place.

Its rotting mouth hung open, and its black snake egg eyes dully reflected the morning light. The spindly fingers of one hand reached out to him. The other hand pointed to its throat. A ghastly hiss slid off of its tongue, a hoarse, muffled rasp that sounded as if the ghost was choking on rust.

···+·+·+·+·+·+·+

Leo burst through the bushes on the side of the chapel, tearing off some of the skin from his hands and from the right side of his face. He sprinted past his father's grave and down the paved road without a single glance back.

He avoided his mother and Anselm for the rest of the day. He wandered up the stairs to the third floor and looked out of random windows, then drifted down to the second floor. He wafted through the library, thinking he might distract himself with an entry in an encyclopedia or an old issue of National Geographic, but he only ended up pulling down one of his grandfather's diaries—just another relic of one more Von Koppersmith man who had abandoned his wife and child.

The scent of it was of mold, and slow atrophy, and regret; every few pages those mysterious charcoal scribbles of children, which he had described to his mother the day before, stared up at him with dark hollow eyes in simple, round heads, standing motionless in a dusky paper prison.

He clamped the diary shut. He left the library, hurried downstairs and out the front door, as if escaping.

He knew his mother was worried about him, and that she regularly peered at him from around corners or from high verandas. He knew how unfair it was to her to allow himself to descend into this self-involved brooding, how it must look, how it must resemble his own father.

But how else was he supposed to act? All he could feel was a relentless pressure to explore the murky depths of—and how ridiculous he felt for allowing himself to categorize it in this way—this *curse*. His thoughts twisted frantically in dark waters, but he couldn't rope them together into anything sensible, and in time the day drug itself, like a dying elephant, to an end.

He retreated to the den, and sat beside the fire. After so many hours sealed in the deprivation chamber of his own mind, he now found himself burdened not only by supernatural dread but also by the most mundane hunger pangs, so he was startled yet grateful when Anselm suddenly appeared at the doorway, holding his silver-plated serving tray.

Anselm set the tray on the coffee table. The vapors of hot chicken soup and freshly baked bread rose like liquid glass.

"Are you alright?"

Leo shrugged. "Do you think there's such a thing as curses?"

"Is this about your father?"

"Some, I guess."

"This is about you? Do you believe you're cursed?"

"It doesn't matter if I believe it or not. I just want to know if I am."

"How does one ascertain that? Do you base it on an experience of evil? Of hardship? Because if you do, then, yes, you and all of us are cursed."

"Maybe some more than others. Remember that ghost I saw in the cemetery, when I was a kid?"

"I remember you thought you saw a ghost."

"Like I 'thought' I saw a flying man on the same day, holding you in midair?"

"Leo, I have to maintain some objectivity here. All I know is that a trespasser approached me from behind and knocked me unconscious."

"Mom saw him, too, remember?"

"Your mother has had a difficult time since your father's death…"

"I have, as well! That doesn't mean I just make up things that aren't there. That ghost was real, and I saw him again today, in the cemetery."

Anselm opened his mouth to respond, but Leo cut him off.

"This morning! Same spot; same tombstone: Nicholas of Hamelin. Who is that, Anselm?"

40

The old man crossed his arms at the wrists and resigned himself to Leo's scrutiny. "The oldest known forebear of your family from Germany."

"Hamelin, Germany...I <u>knew</u> that name rung a bell..."

"That's why the Von Koppersmith coat-of-arms has an engraving of the Pied Piper on it."

"So why is his ghost roaming around? What does it want?" His eyes wandered to the coat-of-arms hanging over the fireplace, and a low-grade disgust scratched at him. "I never liked that creepy orange guy with the flute..."

"That's the Pied Piper of Hamelin. He's there because Nicholas was from the same time and place as the original story."

This quirk of family lore was well-known to Leo, but whatever charm it once might have had was gone. "To tell you the truth, if it was up to me, I'd take a chisel to every coat-of-arms in the mansion and get rid of that Piper. He's weird."

Anselm's eyebrows rose. "Did your mother ever tell you about Ernst, your great grandfather, who went throughout the entire mansion, gathered up all of the coats-of-arms into one big pile, and then tried to set them on fire? The servants had to restrain him. He would have burnt the whole place down..."

"I don't want to hear any more wacko stories about my deranged family. Mom told me enough."

"But that may explain why you think you're seeing ghosts."

The 'you-*think*-you're-seeing-ghosts,' like an ice arrow, found a raw spot in Leo's pride. His

41

expression chilled. "Thanks for the soup. I just want to sit here and think."

As lightly as goose down, regret passed over Anselm's face, but the head of house keeping nodded and left.

Alone again, Leo sat hunched over on the brown leather couch, tugging idly at his short, dark, scraggly beard. His face was a flickering mask in the mix of twilight coming in through the tall windows and the wagging glow from the fireplace.

1212, his dad had kept repeating. What if he'd meant the <u>year</u> 1212? That's the same time frame when Nicholas died. And when the Pied Piper story got started.

Upon the coat-of-arms, the sinister orange piper stared at his bewitched little followers: little *children*, kind of like the ones from the diary...did all this have something to do with his family's problems?

He began eating his soup, with the mindless repetition of a prison inmate. When he was done, he let the metal spoon clatter into the oily film that was left at the bottom of the bowl. He lay back, resting his hands on his stomach, feeling warmth and weariness overtake him.

It would be so easy to fall asleep. Twilight had faded to black. The logs in the fire softly crumbled around the edges. The flames hissed.

And hissed again.

But it wasn't the fire.

Leo jumped to his feet as the ghost of Nicholas melted out of one dark corner of the den, its hair hanging in front of its face like black fingers.

It moved towards Leo on brown shoes that, though vaporous, seemed heavy. It lifted its head and hissed.

Leo lurched and his shins scraped painfully against the edge of the coffee table, rattling the empty soup bowl and its silver tray. He stumbled back, instinctively putting one hand in front of his face, wanting to block out the phantasm, to somehow will it away.

When he looked between his outstretched fingers again, he saw that the ghost had stopped. It now only stared at him. There was not even a tremor of movement in its coal-black eyes. Its scrawny arms hung at its sides.

Wild words forced their way out of Leo's mouth: *"What do you want?!"*

There was a tiny but arresting squeal from somewhere in the room. It sounded like a rat.

His heart still pounding, Leo searched for the source of the sound. The squeal alternately raised and lowered in pitch—like metal twisting. What was it? Leo's ears led him to the side of the room, to the right of the fireplace. Bolts in shadow turned upon the wall, and before Leo's eyes the old groundbreaking shovel pitched forward and clattered upon the floor.

Leo looked at Nicholas' hideous spirit. Its inscrutable dark eyes stared back at him, and one grisly arm slowly pointed across the room, towards the window, towards the faraway cemetery where its gravestone lay fixed in the hard earth.

"O.K.," said Leo heavily, wiping cold sweat out of one eye. "But in the *morning*. If you think I'm going out there in the middle of the night then you're out of your *mind*."

Like a spent votive candle, the apparition shuddered and disappeared.

Five

A thin rain fell on the cemetery. The night bleached itself to a wet, chalky glow as Leo moved digging tools from the trunk of his car. His breathing came in gauzy curls of steam. A single bird from some hidden perch made an inquisitive caw, but it had no fellows willing to respond at such a dismal hour in such a cold, abandoned place.

Leo took a drink of hot, black coffee from a dark blue thermos, listening to the raindrops lightly pummeling the hood of his green North Face coat. The silver-bladed centenarian shovel taken from the den, along with spades and crowbars from the tool house, grew dark and damp beside the gravestone of Nicholas of Hamelin. Leo turned to his right and left, half-expecting to see the gray-green phantom watching him with its black eyes. He saw nothing, but he knew with a nauseous feeling that he was not alone.

He pulled on thick brown gloves, grabbed the shovel, and began digging.

Before three hours had passed he was clearing dirt from the top of a coffin. There were wood straps across it stamped with the date "1642," the year that the coffin had been relocated to America from its original spot outside of Rome. The crowbar split the wood straps easily. The coffin itself was Roman marble, its once polished surface now an ugly gray and black. The lid was fixed with stone pegs.

The rain had stopped. Leo pulled his hood back and the heat that rose from his sweaty scalp became a faint vapor in the icy air. Black dirt was smeared down one side of his face.

He suddenly wanted to stop everything he was doing. He wanted to go home, take a hot shower, put on fresh clothes, and drive away, far away from his home and from his past and go to a secluded beach somewhere. The notion lasted only a few seconds before he made a scoffing sound at it and shook his head. *Right…a magic beach that exists inside a curse-proof bio-dome somewhere, where dads don't commit suicide or lose their minds or abandon their kids to go join the circus or whatever.* There was no running away anymore. If there was any path to a normal life, it was down here in the dirt, where the rot was, where the lost memory of some rupture with peace and sanity was waiting. He fit the edge of the crowbar under the coffin lid beside one stone peg and began to push it loose.

The lid submitted to Leo's crowbar with a muted crunch, breaking like dry bread into three long pieces. As they were shoved back, the gray light of the drizzly morning penetrated the stale darkness underneath. Right away Leo saw the bones: the ribs pointing like long, brittle fingers; the thicker segments of leg; the leering, brown rows of teeth. Leo's heart seemed to hang inside his chest by an executioner's noose at the sight of death's awful consequence sprawled before him, naked in its marble cell.

But it was a dull-edged fear he experienced, a featureless revulsion not much different than the emotions caused by a foul smell or a badly told joke. It was not until he pushed the lid completely away and he saw the entire contents of the coffin that he felt a true jolt.

A man lay next to the skeleton. He was wrapped in some kind of white robe. There was no sign of decomposition to the body; in fact, he might have died less than an hour ago, for all Leo could tell.

Leo leaned in close. The interior of the coffin did not stink, as he would have imagined. On the contrary, he could smell something like cedar and rosemary, scents that seemed to come from the body of the dead man. Leo leaned in closer. A big guy…olive skin…black hair cut almost to the scalp…a spear's point nose…something strange about the face, couldn't really place him or guess his age when he died…

The man's eyes opened.

Leo fell back with arms flapping and curses flying out of his mouth.

Pulling himself into a sitting position, the man stood, rising with ease, and gazed at the cemetery around him. Leo lay sprawled against the soft wall of the grave, too stunned to move or speak.

The man suddenly stared at him. The whites of his eyes were expansive and bright; the irises were deep and dark. A few seconds passed, and Leo knew beyond all doubt that he was about to be strangled to death or beaten with his own shovel. Finally, his conscious mind reconnected with the body that housed it and he scurried out of the grave.

He began to run, and in the same moment remembered that his car keys were still lying with the rest of the tools. He twisted backwards and violently snatched the key ring, certain he could almost feel the undead man's long, heavy arm on his wrist.

He ran. He was safe for now...no one had grabbed him.

No one had grabbed him.

He stopped just before the thick bushes on the side of the chapel. He turned. He could see the man still standing in the coffin. From this perspective only his head was visible, like a living bust, peering across the gray grass of the cemetery with an expression that Leo was finally forced to admit was—undeniably—confusion.

Leo took a step towards the grave. It *was* confusion; not a stupor, but the mild puzzlement of a lucid foreigner studying bus routes on a city map.

"Are you..." Leo had begun speaking without knowing what he was saying. "...O.K.?"

The man remained where he was, but his face dipped below ground level as he stared down at himself. He looked back up at Leo. He said nothing.

Leo's primal instincts began to subside and he felt stupid for automatically thinking of the man as "undead." This was a living person, and clearly in need of some kind of assistance.

"Are you hurt?" He approached the grave. The man abruptly climbed out, with the grace and precision of a swimmer mounting the ladder onto a diving board. He was tall—well over six feet.

"I'm Leo. What's your name?"

The man stared at him, and then his eyelids suddenly grew heavy as a wave of fatigue crossed his face. He seemed almost about to pass out. Leo reached out to steady him, but the man recovered and then became vaguely interested in the trees and in the random droplets of water that tumbled from their wet branches.

Leo slipped out his cell phone, but was instantly struck with the thought: *Who would I call? An ambulance? The man isn't visibly hurt. The police? How would I explain any of this? 'Well, sir, I was just out digging up my dead ancestors when all of a sudden...'*

"You seem like you're in shock," he said to the man in a voice that was slow and deliberate and a little too loud. "Can you walk?"

The man looked down at his legs, and then confidently took three steps forward. He smiled. It was a simple, pleasant smile. Leo was comforted by it, even as he felt a fresh tide of irrational anxiety.

He quickly gathered up most of his tools, ignoring the smaller ones and the gloves that toppled out of his grip. He led the man to his car. He opened the trunk and let everything tumble in noisily.

"I'm just going to bring you to the house, O.K.?" Leo realized he sounded like he was talking to a stray puppy. He opened the passenger door and encouraged the man to enter, but the man stared down the length of the car and inside at its dashboard like a child from a jungle nation seeing an automobile for the first time.

"Um...just...get in..."

Leo guided the man into the seat, and had to push his legs in to make him understand how to sit properly in a car. He gently closed the door, but then scrambled around to the back to make sure the trunk was fully closed, not knowing why he was scrambling.

He started to open the driver's side door, stooping over to look through the glass at his mysterious passenger. He gave him a reassuring smile, which seemed pointless since the man looked in no way in need of reassurance. He simply looked back at him with a serenely inquisitive stare. Until something else outside of the car caught his eye.

Following his gaze, Leo fell back against the car with an almost womanly shriek.

The gray green specter was there, shambling soundlessly towards him. Its blank, snake egg eyes held him in place. It pointed at him with one hand, and with the other it pointed to its throat. The dreadful scrape of hissing air made Leo's skin crawl.

Some interior wall finally collapsed. He was physically spent, and emotionally exhausted from a nearly eleven-hour crush of fear and uncertainty. His body steeled and he found himself shouting with rage at the ghost.

"What?! What is it now?! I just found a *living man* sealed inside your coffin! If that isn't what you wanted me to find, WHAT IS?!?"

The ghost slowly advanced, horrifying and inconsolable. Now the pointing arm drifted back in the direction of the grave. Waves of panic filled Leo and he staggered backwards, but he felt incapable of running from that green face with its stringy black

50

hair and its rotting teeth. The rasp and hiss filled Leo's ears. The open, festering mouth came at him, opening wide to engulf him. Leo cried out and fell.

His eyes had instinctively shut. Now they opened, having been told by some sixth sense that the ghost was gone again. Leo stood and rested his arm against the car. He remembered the man inside, but when he looked he was met by the same gentle, perplexed expression, as if nothing had happened, as if nothing ever happened.

The ghost of his forebear had pointed to the grave; there was no disputing that. Then, for the first time, as Leo pondered the history of Nicholas' visitations, he considered what the other hand always pointed at. The one hand pointed to Leo or towards the grave…*but the other hand always pointed at its own throat.*

With the car still running, Leo tramped back to the grave. He stepped down into it, bringing little chunks of dirt down with him. He crouched and took another look at the ugly, yellow skeleton of Nicholas.

The skull's jaw hung halfway open. Something past it caught his eye, something back within the recesses of the mouth cavity. Leo peered in, unable to decide what he was looking at. It was brownish-white and roughly cylindrical. Half of it lay along the upper spine, and half pointed up like a bone-colored tongue.

When he understood at last, he scowled and made a sound of mild disgust. The object inside the skull was a rolled up piece of paper.

Immediately he thought of the ghost, pointing with one hand towards its throat and making that awful rasping sound.

He began to reach toward the paper, but his hand drew back on its own. He tried again, and his fingers slid slowly between the ancient, dead jaws until his knuckles brushed against the top teeth, sending an icy chill through him and making him recoil again. He reached under the jaw and tapped against the paper, but it did not budge easily, as if the saliva that had once been present in the mouth had left enough of a residue to paste it down.

Leo grew quickly frustrated with himself for being so timid. He picked up one of the arm bones and used the knobby end to push against the paper. There was a light crack as the paper finally broke free from the spine and jutted out from the mouth cavity.

Leo gingerly closed his fingers around it and pulled it free; it made a dry scrape against the bone of the skull. He was careful not to unfold it quickly —surely, he thought, paper from an old tomb would be brittle. Yet his fingertips told him this was not quite like paper. It was slightly thicker and almost pliable, and he could unroll it without much trouble.

He decided he wanted to get it back home and on to a flat table where he could work with it more easily, but he now had it unfurled enough to see writing. The letters were unmistakably medieval, with all of the swirls and stylizations that most anyone recognizes right away.

He slid it delicately into the inside pocket of his coat. Returning to his car, he found the man still waiting patiently inside, gazing at him as he approached the vehicle. Leo opened the door, but paused, ready for another appearance from Nicholas. Only the cold winds that had been pushing that morning's rain showers came through the trees to meet him, and instead of the hiss of ghosts there was just the placid knell of the car warning him that the door was now open.

Six

Later that night. Downtown Chicago, Illinois…

The winter clouds covering the night sky reflected Chicago's light back in dismal tones, like phosphorous in an upside down bay. People bound in coats and flapping scarves scurried along sidewalks and thronged the entrances to restaurants and clubs to a clattering, pulsing soundtrack of cabs and cars and rushing wheels.

"Fat Thumbs" Mike stepped gracelessly from the elevator onto the twenty-sixth floor above *The Watchdog Lounge*. The door waiting across the landing had a translucent smoked glass window, like a newsroom from old black and white movies. A name in black ink and an elegantly professional font was printed on the glass:

THE WATCHDOG

"It's me, boss," said Mike through the glass, giving a coded rap on the door: two shorts, one long, three shorts.

A deadbolt unlocked, and a tall, goateed man in green and black with a baseball bat over one shoulder opened the door and grunted: "Fat Thumbs."

Mike grunted back: "Carl. Where's WD?" In his thick Chicago accent the "w" came out as "dubba-ya".

"Potty break."

No sooner had Carl closed the door and twisted the deadbolt back in, the bathroom door swung open. The Watchdog emerged, and the lamplight cast a sheen over his gelled blond hair as he adjusted the elastic waistband of his glossy white warm up pants.

"There's somebody downstairs looking for you, WD."

The Watchdog had office furniture positioned in such a way that it almost formed a kind of partition between his space and the rest of the room, so that he had to lean slightly forward around a potted ficus tree and duck his head into the glow of a lamp in order to look into Mike's eyes.

"Is it the Ballard brothers? They're too early…our meeting isn't for another hour. Tell them I said to get out, and remind them that if they don't have my product for me this time I will bend them into small, edible shapes…"

"No, boss, it ain't them," said Mike. "I never seen this guy."

The Watchdog blinked. "Oh. Well who is it?"

Mike's very small brain trembled as it tried to process what he guessed must be a kind of trick question. "I never seen this guy."

Carl thumped the back of Mike's head. "You doofus. Go tell him WD's busy. Get his name and have him make an appointment, if he's serious."

After the door closed behind Mike, the Watchdog exchanged a brief look of mild irritation with Carl before sitting down at his clean, polished desk. He poured himself a short glass of scotch and pulled a file marked "Ballards" from the top drawer.

"Get the boys, Carl. We need to go over some things."

Carl thrust his head through a pair of glass doors that led onto a wide veranda and gave a whistle. Three men who had been idly smoking and watching the ebb and flow of Chicagoans down on the streets now straightened up and shuffled back inside.

"Put that out," the Watchdog grumbled to one who still had a smoldering cigar between his teeth. "You know I don't like that smell." The man hastily did as he was told.

"Gentlemen," he said imperially after another swallow of scotch, "We have a meeting with the Ballard brothers tonight, as you know. And, as you also know, before key appointments like these I like to go over the principles upon which our little organization is founded. So, I put it to you: why am I so successful?"

His gathered men looked at each other with faint discomfort.

The Watchdog flashed a bright white smile. "Relax. This is not a test. I'm just asking you: why am I so successful in this city? Why am I so... unstoppable? Think about it: I've been here no more than nine months. No one knew the name 'Watchdog' before that. Now it's the name that keeps our competitors up at night, wondering what I'll do next, wondering how they can stop me."

Carl smiled, and the other three seemed to be infected by it and began snorting and grinning. "They can't stop you, boss," declared Carl.

The Watchdog smiled up at Carl. "Is it that I'm too smart for them, do you think? Is it my courage? My personal charisma, maybe…or something else? A destiny to rule…?"

Again Carl spoke for the group. "Yep, all of those—and the fact that you've personally put all the bigwigs and their bodyguards in the morgue using nothing but your bare hands." All four of them nodded and made grunting sounds of approval.

"It's like Julius Caesar, boss," Carl continued like a kind of statesman for hired thugs, "You came, you saw, you conquered!"

The Watchdog shined with pleasure and made a long, enthusiastic "ahhhhhhhh" sound towards Carl for remembering so well what he had forced him to memorize, upon pain of losing a pinky.

"*Veni, vidi, vici,* right, boys?"

"Right, boss!" They all chortled. "That! What you said!"

A sudden strangled cry from the stairwell made them all stop and stare at the door. A silhouette fell across the translucent glass followed by a pounding of fists upon the wood. "Boss, lemme in, quick!"

"It's Mike!" Carl started towards the door, but the Watchdog froze him with a snapped command. He called to the silhouette at the door in a voice that was almost tender. "Mike? You know the knock."

57

The reply was frantic, and shadowy limbs gesticulated crazily behind the glass. The knocks upon the door came with so much force that the doorknob rattled: two shorts, one long, one short, and then the hand that made them dragged wildly over the glass with a squeal. "Boss, please, help!"

"WD," said Carl, his baseball bat in one hand and a .22 caliber pistol now in the other, and all of his limbs taut with anxiety, "We gotta do somethin'. Mike's in trouble!"

The Watchdog stood. "No one gets in if they don't do the knock, Carl. No one."

"Boss...!" This time the cry was so muffled as to be nearly unintelligible. Shadow hands squashed against the glass and then dragged down the length of the door, followed by the dull thudding of a body on the floor.

The Watchdog waited. The others, like Carl, all had guns drawn. Every pair of eyes was on the door.

A new shadow began to take shape behind the glass as a figure approached it. The silhouette sharpened: a tall, narrow rectangle on top of a thin, black line. A top hat.

They heard the sound of a cork coming out of a bottle, followed by the hiss of steam.

The Watchdog groaned and sat back in his chair. "Stand down, boys..."

But they were already so vibratile with adrenaline that they found it physically impossible to obey. They shrieked like baboons when the door instantaneously shrunk to the size of a dollar bill. It was now indistinguishable from a little girl's toy dollhouse door and, as they watched, it tipped over and landed with a tiny clack.

Mike, whose unconscious body had been pressed against it when it was still normal-sized, now rolled slightly in to the room. He was almost completely covered in fat, squirming blue ants.

Standing above Mike in the newly exposed doorway was a short, stumpy man in a tall, black, crumpled top hat. He wore a long, dark coat that was sewn with multitudinous pockets over the chest and around the sides and on the sleeves. Below the hem of the coat his two flat, black boots jutted out like oar blades. The collar was pulled up high so that, between it and the brim of the hat, the head was just a cantaloupe-sized orb hidden in darkness. The only facial features visible were two orange eyes, glowing like miniscule stovetops.

Carl was the kind of man who had always found it best to respond to anything unusual with an overwhelming display of violence. Bellowing like a Viking in a monastery he charged the uninvited guest with his baseball bat poised to crush.

With a green, scaly hand the visitor plucked a pouch from one of the many pockets of his long coat and spattered Carl with a hundred tiny globules of something like wet sand. They stuck to his limbs and rapidly spread like melting, gray butter before hardening into a stone shell. Carl's still-exposed nostrils whistled and puffed and one eyeball vacillated anxiously, but most of the rest of him stood immobile. His bat hovered in mid-strike.

"*Concretis*," announced the Watchdog in a bored voice, but before the word was done leaving his mouth the stumpy man in the top hat hurled a small terra cotta sphere into the midst of the other three henchmen. Yellow smoke instantly drowned the floor and spat a six-foot by six-foot jungle up at them. Like a nature documentary on fast-forward, a gnarled jumble of green growth punched into the ceiling and engulfed them. The only evidence left of their presence in the room now was a single white wriggling hand protruding from the pillar of wet vines and narrow winding tree limbs.

"*Instant Jungle,*" Watchdog called out, still sounding bored as he topped off his scotch. "And *Slumberants…*" He gestured vaguely towards the fat blue ants that were now marching into a wide reed tube that the intruder held for them at floor level and which he clicked with one sharp nail as a rhythmic command. They left Mike with hundreds of puffy red bites and a loud snore. The Watchdog shook his head in disgust. "Do you have any ideas that you *didn't* steal from us, Bentpin?"

The voice that responded from the shade between the top hat and the coat collar was reptilian and sedate: "*I _deserve_ those ideas, because I use them better.*" He snapped a cap over the Slumberants' reed house and slipped it into a pocket that ran the length of one sleeve.

The Watchdog looked dubiously at the cylindrical Congo next to his desk as it quivered frantically and issued muffled groans of terror. "Tell that to *them.* What are you doing here, anyway? This is going to bring me all kinds of unwanted attention. I'll have to find a new city; I'll have to abandon months of hard work and carefully planned homicides."

"*He is free.*"

The Watchdog's body went rigid. "What?"

"*Someone dug him up. He be awakened.*"

The Watchdog stood up and his chair fell over. He glared at Bentpin, whose only response was the faintest mocking squint of his orange eyes.

The Watchdog ran to the glass doors of his twenty-seven story high veranda and flung them open. The colossal towers of the city rose around him and formed a glowing crossword puzzle of electric auras above glimmering rivers of trolling headlights. A freezing wind pressed against the Watchdog's shirt, showing a hard chest and the outlines of solid abdominal muscles.

He ran to the rail of his veranda and jumped off. The night swallowed him.

Seven

Earlier, Leo and his recently disinterred new acquaintance had managed to sneak into the mansion without encountering anyone. Leo was eager to examine the scroll he had discovered in the skeleton's mouth, but there were two problems that needed solving first.

"You're wearing white robes," he said to the man. "We need to get some normal clothes for you; from my dad's closet, I guess, though they'll be small on you. Also, my bladder feels like I swallowed a waterbed. What about you? Do you need to go? Or clean up or something?"

The man stared calmly at him with his deep, dark eyes. He bent his head slightly, and then gently frowned as if he was trying to remember something unimportant. Then he stared at Leo again.

"Right," said Leo. "You know, I really can't tell if you speak English or not. Never mind, just come with me…"

The man did not object to being hastened throughout the labyrinthine old house; he didn't object to anything, in fact. It wasn't because he was mindless—Leo was sure of that. His eyes were filled with the glow of intelligence, to an almost disconcerting degree, and his face was warm and patient. Whoever he was, he was lost and confused, and yet he seemed imperturbable.

Leo, on the other hand, continued to feel unexplainably jittery. Leading the way down a dim hall and up a short flight of steps towards a secluded bathroom, he flinched dramatically when he nearly collided with Anselm. The head of housekeeping had a basket of cleaning supplies in one hand and a dingy rag over his shoulder, and yet was dressed in his usual dapper brown-and-green checkered jacket and neatly pressed trousers.

"Good afternoon, Leopold! You were out early today. And I see we have a guest..." Politely but unswervingly, his stare fixed itself upon Leo's white-robed companion.

Leo looked back and forth from Anselm to the 'guest', and for long, awkward seconds he could not think of a single intelligible phrase with which to respond. At last he stammered, "This is Mister... Man."

Anselm exhaled loudly in a way that expressed both genteel pleasure and a sophisticated caution. "Mister...'Man', is it...?"

Leo wrinkled his nose with dissatisfaction. "'*Grave*', I mean."

Anselm nodded courteously. "Mr. Grave..."

"'Grave*s*.' Mr. 'Gravely'. 'Gravestone', actually. Mr..." Leo abruptly winced at the direction things had taken. "Mr. Man."

Anselm gave Leo a look of careful regard. "Mr...Man...?"

Leo frowned impatiently. "Yes...Mr. *Man*. Didn't you hear me the first time?" He hurried past, making wooden apologies, adding, "don't tell mom we're here..." and giving a few slapdash instructions regarding the delivery of food and drink to the library. Perplexed, Anselm stood in place for a few seconds, watching them go, before rolling his eyes and returning to his duties.

Clothes were eventually located for the freshly-christened Mr. Man: dark trousers that stopped much too high above white socks; a shirt, a vest, a jacket, a frayed belt, and a clunky pair of old shoes, all of them a hodge-podge of black and gray, some from Leo's dad and some from a big cedar trunk that belonged to Leo's granddad. "Well," said Leo, assessing the result, "You look a little like Edgar Allen Poe. But it's an improvement. Now let's go downstairs to the library—that'll be the perfect room to take a closer look at this scroll."

Though it was no older than any other part of the mansion, the many thousands of venerable tomes that filled its stretching rows of wood shelves and the rich scent of leather bindings made the library seem quite ancient. Past tables displaying thick, musty incunabula and illuminated manuscripts that radiated vividly under soft track lighting, Leo led the way to a particular corner of the library that had always been a favorite spot of his. It looked out upon the back lawns of the estate through an eighteen-foot high bay window trimmed with red and gold curtains. A blue and silver telescope on a heavy black tripod faced the sky. A long octagonal table here had always been ideal for reading and writing, and it was on this table that Leo carefully spread out the scroll from Nicholas' grave, weighing it down at the corners with various glass paperweights or miniature globes from around the room.

Leo decided that it must be made of 'vellum' (after googling the term on his smartphone), which would account for its distinctive thickness and durability. A privileged man's writing material from an age long past.

Like a pseudo-Sherlock, Leo scrutinized the writing through a massive magnifying glass. "It has to be Middle English—or Early English? Is there such a thing? Some kind of medieval version of English...or maybe German? I don't know..." Leo went to a shelf and referenced a big reddish book on the English language, postulating amateur theories as he went. The book didn't end up helping much, and he returned to the table muttering about the origins of the document.

He paused when he realized how one-sided his conversation was. For the entire day his enigmatic guest's only participation in dialogue had been facial expressions that were sometimes quizzical, sometimes blank, and always unaccompanied by words.

"You know, I used to have a dog when I was a little kid here. A Siberian Husky. I named it Dinkle. That's a pretty stupid name. But it's still a lot better than 'Mr. Man'. My point is: I wish you could just tell me your *name*."

Mr. Man met this entreaty with the silence of a congenital mute. Leo shrugged and continued his investigations. Through the bay window the afternoon sky changed to evening with a slow melting of Persian blues and copper and gray.

Anselm brought coffee in a silver pot, along with a tray of fruit and sandwiches. Leo devoured the food while hunting up and down the bookshelves or searching the internet and thinking out loud. Mr. Man, no longer in any direct engagement with Leo, wandered casually with arms clasped behind his back, following the mosaic of tan and brown tiles that covered the floor around the table. Sometimes he sat in a leather chair staring out of the enormous bay window, casually scratching his black, grizzled hair. Occasionally he stood and gave a curious but deadpan look at the mysterious vellum manuscript in a way that reminded Leo of Buster Keaton, but then would go back to sitting or wandering.

He never ate a bite of the sandwiches. He smelled them once with his long, sharp nose, and he peered inquisitively between the slices of bread like a scientist examining a short stack of research papers, but then he lost interest.

After the sun set, there was a small knock on the library door.

"Leo?"

"Mom…" Leo hurried to the door as it slowly opened.

Mrs. Von Koppersmith timidly leaned her moon-colored face into the library, as if she had no right to be there. "I was just checking on you, sweetheart. Anselm tells me we have company…?"

Leo cleared his throat and clumsily introduced his guest from across the room, using gestures that did not invite his mother any farther into the room. "We're just…working on something…pretty important…"

Mrs. Von Koppersmith waved bashfully, but Mr. Man did not respond in kind. He stood beside the table, with white socks peeking out from the spaces between the legs of his trousers and his black shoes, either staring at her or stealing more Buster Keaton-style glances at the old vellum scroll.

Leo's mother wrung her soft hands. "Shall we have dinner together…?"

Leo cleared his throat and declined the invitation, ushering his mom back out of the library with a kiss on the cheek and a nudge. He walked back to the table, where Mr. Man was now gazing intently at the swirling letters of the ancient parchment.

"I can read that."

Leo stared at him, and neither quite realized what had just happened.

"You spoke!"

"I…" Mr. Man hesitated, feeling the movements of his mouth like the Tin Man after Dorothy oiled his lips. "I *can* speak." He smiled at himself. His voice was deep and resonant, with no trace of an accent.

Leo searched his face. "Who *are* you? What's your name?"

"I do not know," replied the man, with only a faint shadow of bewilderment in his eyes. "And…I do not know."

For some reason Leo found himself unable to ask the most painfully obvious question, which was "what in the world were you doing inside someone else's grave?" He stood mutely rolling the words around in the back of his mouth.

The man turned his head slightly and looked with curiosity at the unrolled parchment. "But I *can* read this."

In awkward deference, Leo stepped to the side.

Mr. Man, folding his hands casually behind his back, thoughtfully inspected the swirling glyphs. A vague self-satisfied smile played along his mouth as he read the first sentence:

"To all who have suffered because of me..."

He paused, again pleased with himself.

"To all who have suffered because of me, and, above all, to our Almighty Judge and Ruler:

Alas, I die now in sin, a sin for which I can find no forgiveness! And yet what is now more urgent to me than my salvation is the well being of those betrayed by me. To whosoever will undertake what I failed to accomplish, I here relate my dismal tale:

Not long ago I found myself the leader of an army. Twas no ordinary army, but one unlike any the world had ever seen, for it was an army of children! It had come to be believed by my people that in a war against enemies of Christ, the innocence of children was a greater weapon than a thousand ships, or a thousand siege engines. As the innocence of our Lord overthrew the devil, we became convinced that the innocence of children could overthrow the servants of the devil. Consumed with surety, I gathered to this cause children from across the countryside that well resolved we might march forth and drive the enemies of Christ, those Mohammedans, from the Holy Land.

Years later, sunk down in the luxuries of my estate, I see now the foolishness of it. And, indeed, it did fail. We never came within a thousand miles of the Holy Land, nor did we ever face even a single Mohammedan.

Truly, the end of the thing came during our audience with Innocent, our Holy Father in Rome. I still remember his kind and thoughtful face even as his words stung my ears, for although he praised our courage he nonetheless instructed us to cease our quest and go back home.

I went away from him feeling mocked and slighted. Never could I bear the thought of returning to Hamelin in shame, or of telling the children that, perhaps, I had been wrong to lead them on such a journey, for had I not pridefully assured everyone that the mission could not fail, that even the sea itself would part for me and allow us passage?

Forsooth, I didst not know what course to take! We had all but exhausted what provisions and gold Providence had seen fit to supply, and aching hunger had scratched beneath the glister of the name "army" to reveal only the hundreds of helpless orphans I had gathered to my mad-bred foray. Many had already died since our departure. Were they all so ill-fated? Marry, twas a wretched plight, for I could see no good way forward, while the notion of return sickened me. It was then, in my hour of darkness, that I was visited.

Late that very night after my audience with Innocent, the one who calls himself Kak bid me follow him hence to a house in an old, ruinous corner of the city. Therein, up a flight of rickety

stairs, was a strongly locked door, to which Kak
carried the keys. After gaining entrance, I beheld
in the light of my trembling lamp a room filled
with a measureless wealth. There were chests full
of gold, more gold than I had ever seen or longed
for. 'Why go to all the trouble fighting for the
Holy Land,' quoth Kak, 'When you could simply
buy the Holy Land? Or better yet: forget that
fiend-ridden blotch of sod and establish a
kingdom for yourself right here!'

Reader, my stomach clenches even as I
write of this, for the treasure Kak offered me was
in exchange for the children. 'Be free!' quoth Kak.
'Be a man of riches and power! You have brought
the little ones so far already. Lay down your
burden. Let Uncle Kak take care of them now.'

I did not even ask what would happen to
them. I did not want to know. I remember
shaking my head violently as if it was
inconceivable that I would make such a bargain,
but I was just pretending, just fooling myself. I
began to reason that this was better for the

children. I told myself that Kak, having so much gold at his disposal, would surely provide well for them. For hours I deliberated in my own mind, but at last, before dawn, Kak was putting into my hands the keys to the house and its room filled with gold.

I took him to the place where the children were all sleeping. There we made the bargain with solemn formality: I declared that the children who had been put into my care were now his.

No sooner did I abdicate, Kak produced a peculiar flute. He started to play it, and right away the children began to follow him. (The flute had no magic of itself, I think; I believe that whatever power it had didst come from my betrayal. As I had given my wards to him, they were now bound to go along with him.) With the sun rising, Kak led them all by the song of his flute, and they followed him helplessly through the streets. People everywhere stopped to watch, looking out from windows and doorways.

Perhaps I can earn some good will with my assurance that at last I tried to stop him. In the light of morning, seeing all those orphans who had followed me faithfully across the land now mindlessly marching after that filthy creature, I could not help but cry out for them to stop. They did not obey me, for they could not, and Kak kept playing and leading them farther along towards the city gates. I cried out again, and now the townspeople began to draw closer to see what was the matter. I lied and told them Kak had stolen the children!

We gathered quickly and began to run after them. By the time we organized ourselves, Kak had led the children outside the city to a small, ugly stone hill. I ran as fast as I could to catch up, only to watch in horror as a dark, mysterious doorway appeared in the hillside. Into this strange portal Kak led the children, playing his evil flute, and not a single child so much as hesitated but marched right inside and down some black passage. No sooner had the last child gone through did the doorway disappear. I clawed at the side of the hill until my fingers bled, but ne'er again wouldst I find that ghostly artery by which my hexed innocents drifted away from me forever.

I compelled myself to forget what could ne'er be forgotten. I married, though I made a sullen husband. I cultivated my newfound wealth and built a tremendous household outside of Rome, though it brought me only little pleasure at first, and overwhelming disgust as the months went by. My one and only comfort has been my newborn son, even though I cannot but see it as a cruelty that a child should be brought hither to me by the God who knows well what evil I am to children. But so it is, and so I mean for all of my treasure to be passed on to my boy, if only so that he may never know what it is to be an orphan trapped by the rule of false cajoling rogues. As for me, my subjugation is complete, and my twin masters Dejection and Self-Reproach will never unlock my chains, and neither the softest most expensive bed nor the sweetest wines in all the world can make it less so.

My body fails. My end approaches. My goodly wife, though I have given her little cause for fealty, will see to it that, after my flesh has given up its ghost, this confession of my guilt will be stuffed into my mouth. In this way I and my sins will never be separated, and perchance (only perchance) there may come a day when another will unearth my corpse and read my words and be moved to search for Kak's purchase! Mercy be granted, may all who are lost be found, and may all evil deeds be set aright!

-Nicholas , anno Domini 1218"

Eight

The front door rang, and the sound of the bell echoed eerily among the hallways and corners of the house. It made Anselm grimace, because he had been in the kitchen on the cusp of loosening his top buttons and spreading butter on to freshly toasted bread.

The bell tolled again before he made it to the door. Through the peephole he saw a man made absurdly wide by the fisheye glass: a Caucasian in his thirties, wearing a white jumpsuit with dark stripes down the legs and white and gray Ecco BIOM running shoes, the highly expensive kind made from genuine yak leather.

"How did you get through the gate at this hour?" Anselm's voice came through a tinny speaker on an intercom box on the porch. "May I help you?"

The man eyed the box with mild chagrin, pushing a tan button on it to respond.

"Yes, I'm looking for someone. A tall man with dark hair. He doesn't live here, I know, but have you, perhaps, seen someone like that wandering the premises?"

Anselm considered the words for a few moments, then pushed the button on his side of the door. "What business do you have with this person?"

"Business? Oh…no business! He's a very old friend, and I was hoping we could catch up. So, you have seen him then?"

76

Anselm regretted having revealed so much. "He was here earlier. He is gone now."

Through the peephole he could see the man listening carefully with an expression like flint.

"Do you know where he went?"

Anselm resented the way the conversation was going. "Sir, it is late. No one you are looking for is here. You should be on your way now."

The man frowned and leaned close to the intercom, squashing the tan button. He almost spoke, but instead let his finger fall heavily off the button again, causing a tiny, ugly squeal. He squinted with one eye into the peephole, which from Anselm's point of view made his face huge and stretched. The next moment the man stepped off the porch, out of the light and into shadow.

"I do not like that," Anselm muttered to himself. "I do not like that one bit." He walked to the landline phone down the hall and called the police.

···+··+·+··+·+··+·+

Leo walked slowly away from the table, absorbed in thought. He followed the bookshelves, scanning the titles.

He had once been a student at Finbar College near Charleston. He never graduated, and now he wished he had taken more History of Western Civilization classes. Even so, he had managed to absorb a little of that subject, and he found himself mentally referencing it now. In fact, it didn't take a scholar to see that Nicholas' letter was referring generally to the Crusades, but it reminded Leo of something even more specific, a historical episode that he vaguely recalled from one of his classes.

He continued deliberately down an aisle between shelves, his fingers brushing the spines, his eyes searching.

When he returned to the table he set a thick, dark brown book upon it. Mr. Man watched with a keen expression as Leo opened the cover to a title page that read, in florid letters:

American Council of Learned Societies'
Dictionary of the Middle Ages, Volume 4

Leo flipped some pages until he found what he wanted, and he began to read aloud:

"CRUSADE, CHILDREN'S. The usual view of the Children's Crusade of 1212 depicts the departure of thousands of children from France and Germany to follow a boy prophet who would lead them to Jerusalem and convert the Muslims. Armed only with the conviction that God would part the waters and allow them to cross to the Holy Land without wetting their feet, the children streamed south to the Mediterranean amid great suffering..."

Leo glanced at Mr. Man, even as his mind hummed with the reverberations of the date he had read: *1212*. The number his father had been unable to stop mumbling on the day of his suicide.

His eyes darted back to the page. He scanned ahead a few sentences and began reading again:

"There seems to have been in 1212 at least two popular movements, one in Germany and one in France. Their similarities allowed later chroniclers to lump them together as the Children's Crusade.

The German movement began first, in the early spring, led by a boy named Nicholas from around Cologne. Wearing the sign of the cross and carrying banners, the growing throng wended its way amid great tumult up the Rhine and crossed the Alps into Lombardy. Some 7,000 arrived in Genoa in late August. The waters did not part as promised by Nicholas, and the band seems to have broken up. Some left for home, while others may have gone to Rome or Brindisi. Still others may have traveled down the Rhône to Marseilles, where they were probably sold into slavery. Few returned home, and none reached the Holy Land."

Leo's mouth opened slightly as he stared past the fringe of the page, past the floorboards and into a distant place where all the misshapen pieces of his life and his entire family tree came together in a sad mosaic.

"It says this Nicholas was from 'around Cologne'…"

Leo looked at Mr. Man. "My family's patriarch, Nicholas, was from Hamelin—that's close to Cologne. Less than three hours by car…"

His thoughts were moving quickly now, as if a cerebral vent had been unblocked. He tapped a brightly colored picture book he'd pulled from a shelf and opened it. "The 'Pied Piper of Hamelin'… do you know that poem, by Robert Browning? About the town overrun with thousands of rats? '*You should have heard the Hamelin people, ringing the bells till they rocked the steeple, 'Go,' cried the Mayor, 'and get long poles, poke out the nests and block up the holes!*' But they couldn't make the rats go away. Then this mysterious guy shows up, and he has this magic flute, and he says he can get rid of the rats with it, but the people of Hamelin will have to pay him a thousand guilders. Hamelin's desperate, so they agree, but after the Piper takes away the rats the people decide not to pay him for it. So, to get his revenge, the Piper plays his flute again, and this time he leads away all their children. '*When, lo, as they reached the mountain-side, a wondrous portal opened wide…*' Just like the letter described. 'A mysterious doorway'. The Pied Piper took them in and that was the last anyone ever saw of them."

Leo pointed to the coat-of-arms over the fireplace. "*That* Pied Piper."

He began to pace, his arms swatting the air with agitation. "The whole Pied Piper of Hamelin story is *real!* Some of the facts have been mixed up, that's all. It didn't happen in Hamelin—the story only says that because Nicholas was *from* Hamelin. It happened outside *Rome*, after Nicholas' audience with the pope, just like in the letter. Either way, that's why the Pied Piper is on our stupid family crest! Nicholas, my own forefather, is the very same Nicholas the Religious Nut who led the Children's Crusade in 1212, and he betrayed all the kids he was supposed to be leading. He sold them out to…who? 'Kak'? This is *crazy*—the Pied Piper's real name is 'Kak', if you can believe it! And then Nicholas died a few years later, in 1218, like in the letter, with all THAT on his head."

Leo clasped his fingers behind his neck and made a breathy sound of exasperation and mock amusement. "So, I'm the inheritor of a fortune made from selling off little children. That's what's wrong with all the Von Koppersmith men. We have betrayal in our blood! *That's the curse!* Somehow all the guilt, all the pain, all the…*evil*…that came out of what Nicholas did was passed on to his kid and his kid's kids and their kids like a…a *birth defect*…ruining their minds, never letting them rest! The only difference is: I know why. They didn't. For them, it was just like a bad dream, a sense that things weren't right, eating away at their subconscious. They all slowly went insane. My own dad killed himself!"

81

There was silence for a few moments before Mr. Man cautiously announced, "I am sorry."

Leo turned and stared at him with a subtle contempt. "So who are *you*? You aren't Nicholas. The letter was in the skeleton's throat, not yours. How did you end up in Nicholas' grave?"

Leo buried his face in his hands and rubbed his eyes as if he were tempted to gouge them out. "Maybe *I'm* going insane…"

All of a sudden the two of them realized that there was a third person in the room.

Leo's spine went cold from the bottom up, like a beaker quickly filling with icy water. The specter from the grave, Nicholas of Hamelin, watched them with his black snake egg eyes from beside the long red curtains of the bay window.

He did not point; both of his arms hung by his side. There was no scraping sound of labored breath, since the letter had been removed and read.

Leo trembled, but he shook his head in disgust at the ancient spirit. "The money…all the money in our family, passed down from generation to generation…*my* money. It all came from the deal you made that day?"

The ghost only stared at him.

Leo wanted to run out of the library and out the front door, but he forced himself to stay in place, and with a scowl he continued his unlikely jeremiad. "Why are you even here? What am I supposed to do about any of this? What…'find what was lost'? 'Set evil deeds aright'? Forget it! You know something? You don't even frighten me anymore. You're nothing more than a pathetic ghost of a man. You had your chance, and you blew it. It's *your* fault my entire family tree is so screwed up! It's your fault my dad is dead! *Now leave me alone!*"

Nicholas drifted towards him with soundless steps.

His arms spread wide, with green, cadaverous fingers splayed imploringly. His sickening mouth opened, and out coiled aching words heavy with centuries:

"*Save us...*"

As the ghost came closer, its face began to twist and warp until it showed the features of another man, someone Leo did not recognize. The eyes remained black. Before another step was taken the face melted and changed again; a different man, but with eyes just as dark and empty.

"*Save us…!*"

Leo's legs wouldn't move. He stared, horrified. The ghost came closer and its face, as if made of gray-green clay, stretched into the visages of dozens of more men one after the other, with eyes always black and lifeless. When the phantom was within a few feet Leo began to recognize the different people: ghastly duplications of old photographs from albums or dusty frames in the corners of the mansion. His great-great grandfather; then his great grandfather, then his grandfather…

…At last his own father, Theodore, staring at Leo with stygian eyes, a deep purple rope burn on his neck, shriveled arms reaching desperately for Leo…

"*SAVE US!*"

A cold wind shook the curtains and the edges of the ancient letter on the table, and for a second the ghost was Nicholas again, blankly watching Leo. Then, he disappeared, as if an invisible fist had crushed him into nothing.

Leo crumpled to the floor and sat beneath the table, sobbing.

Nine

The Watchdog cautiously, quietly circumnavigated the entire Von Koppersmith house. There were a number of ways he might enter, but he was determined to proceed with at least some prudence. He felt fairly sure that the Protector was here somewhere, but he had no idea who else lived here, how many, or if there were alarm systems or armed guards.

Finally he settled on a window facing east, glowing warmly on the third floor. He craned his neck and spotted the flicker of shadows in the room. Time for a closer look.

All at once he found himself squinching his eyes in bright light. An amplified voice said, "What are you doing there?"

The Watchdog made a small groan of irritation. He tried to block the spotlight with one hand but the voice sternly instructed him to put both arms in the air. He did.

Blue and red lights began flashing from the police car that had softly rolled up to the curb, and two officers steadily approached him.

"Just keep your hands up," said the one closest. Both men had their hands on the grips of their still-holstered service revolvers.

"You want to tell us what you're doing sneaking around the Von Koppersmith house at night like this?"

"No, I don't."

The cops glanced at each other. "You don't, huh? What's your name?"

The Watchdog smiled, and his white teeth softly reflected the array of police lights. With his arms held high, he said, "You don't need to know that."

The second cop had had enough. "Sir, I want to see your license right now…"

The first drew close to the Watchdog, hand still hovering around his revolver. "You're about to go to jail for unlawful trespassing, so I suggest you stop playing games and show us your driver's license…"

The Watchdog smirked. "I don't have a driver's license. But if I did, I would use it to peel the skin off the side of your face."

The policemen stared at him, not quite believing what they had just heard. With an arrogant sniff he suddenly reached out, but only to nonchalantly straighten his sleeves.

The movement snapped the cops to attention; the first one loudly reminded him that both hands should be in the air. He stepped around behind him, reaching for his handcuffs.

The Watchdog spun. In one fluid motion he grabbed the cop's wrist and a fistful of shirt and threw him at his partner, sending both officers slamming against the side of their car.

The Watchdog rushed upon them. He snatched up the first policeman again, lifting him as easily as if he were a bed pillow. He twirled three times like a discus thrower, holding the man at arm's length. On the third spin he let go.

As the second officer stared in shock, his partner careened over the car, across the street, and into the dark tree line with a series of snapping branches and tearing leaves that sounded like distant firecrackers on the Fourth of July.

The second officer crawled backwards wildly like some kind of crustacean, shouting for immediate assistance into his radio. That conversation ended prematurely when the Watchdog crushed the black plastic in one hand. He then set about crushing other things.

····+·+·+·+·+·+·+

Mrs. Von Koppersmith twisted the bathtub valves closed and the bathroom became very quiet. She ran her hand through the water, feeling the invisible fumes of steam upon her forearm, and decided that it needed a minute to cool down.

She took her glass of white wine and strolled back into her bedroom, reflecting on the troubling change in Leo's behavior today and on the tall stranger he had brought into her house. Should she tell Leo that the stranger ought to leave? That seemed unnecessarily harsh...

Red and blue lights flashing outside caught her attention.

She walked to the window.

Rising up, close enough to touch the window glass, a man suddenly hovered against the backdrop of the night. His blond hair was carefully combed, and his white jump suit dimly glowed in the lamplight of Mrs. Von Koppersmith's room.

She froze, but didn't scream. He wasn't on a ladder. He was suspended in the air. *He was flying.*

His eyes stared rapaciously, like a wolf that had suddenly been given a damned human soul. She had seen those eyes before, long ago in the cemetery when Leopold was still a boy. "Stay out of the cemetery," he had told her then, while effortlessly holding the two hundred pound Anselm in one hand.

Now she screamed.

Ten

Leo leapt to his feet when he heard his mother's scream. Mr. Man followed him as he ran out of the library and to a balcony that looked out over the foyer. Above them they heard Mrs. Von Koppersmith's bedroom door fling open, followed by the sound of her padding feet.

"Mama!" Leo shouted. "What's wrong?"

She appeared at a third floor balcony and stared down at Leo with terrified eyes. "He's here! Run, Leo! You run *now!*"

Before Leo could ask "who" they all heard a shattering of window glass. Mrs. Von Koppersmith fled towards a stairwell.

The Watchdog appeared at the balcony, hovering a few feet above it, glossy Ecco BIOMS shifting lightly in mid-air. Leo looked up at him and, like his mother, he remembered. He remembered vividly. The man's eyes gazed down upon him only for a moment before settling with wolfish triumph on Mr. Man.

"There you are!"

He glided towards them across the empty space far above the foyer.

The explosion of Anselm's hunting rifle was exaggerated to a factor of ten by the hard, polished floors and the towering space between the balconies. The bullet raked past the Watchdog's head, shearing off the very top of his right ear. He snarled and slapped his hand to the side of his face.

Anselm ducked under the stairs to reload. Leo and Mr. Man turned and ran, but the Watchdog's eyes stayed fixed on them as his ears recovered from the gun blast.

They sprinted back to the library. "What did he mean, 'there you are'?" Leo shouted. "Why is he looking for you?" They reached the library and slammed the door behind them.

"I do not know!"

Leo locked the deadbolt. "What?! He knows you! How do you not know him?"

"He is familiar to me, yes! But there are many things that are familiar to me. I do not remember anything with certainty!"

The door handle rattled. A thump followed. A second later, the brass hinges tore off their frame and the door crashed upon the red Persian rug. After hovering in its place for a moment, the Watchdog drifted into the room and landed, his shoes crunching splinters of wood.

Leo stood alone, with his back to the bookshelves.

The Watchdog strode towards him, taking in the room as he went. "Where is he?"

Leo wanted to come up with some clever lie, or with anything at all that might convince this bizarre intruder to go far away, but it was as if any capacity for speech was canceled out by the pounding of his heart.

The Watchdog gathered the front of Leo's shirt in a crushing grip and pinned him decisively against the thick bookshelves.

He was stunned at the force in the arms that held him. Leo may as well have been a housefly caught by a pair of steel pliers. The man leaned in close, and his breath smelled like single-malt scotch and Altoids peppermints. A spicy cologne had been applied so liberally that it was nearly emetic. His frosted blond hair was slick with gel, and his chin was smooth-shaven and glossy, flawless except where blood had trickled down from his wounded ear.

"Where is Zechariah?"

"Wh..who?"

The Watchdog abruptly drew Leo forward a few inches and then smacked him firmly against the bookshelves again, knocking the air out of his lungs and sending books tumbling.

"*Zech-a-riah.*"

As Leo desperately tried to suck air back in to his chest, the Watchdog suddenly smiled at him with soap-white teeth. "You didn't know his name? Of course. He probably can't remember it."

As the two of them stood with their noses nearly pressed together, Leo noticed details about his attacker that he had not before. The man was exceedingly handsome, for one thing, in a way that was exactly like European models in fashion magazines: an annoying combination of swollen lips and arching eyebrows and misty gray eyes. He also had a tattoo—three pairs of tiny black characters on the lower center of his forehead, just above the level of his eyebrows, stacked in a vertical column:

mɛ
mɛ
mɛ

Mentally Leo read it to himself: *Me me me.*

The man's prom king smile melted, and Leo felt himself lifted like a stuffed animal.

"I really don't mind killing you."

Leo responded with an uncontrollable mix of fear and anger, spilling out in a hoarse whisper: "*Killing* me?!? What are you talking about?!? *Who are you?*"

"I can understand your frustration, but he belongs to me. He's my responsibility. I watch him. That's what I do—I'm the Watchdog. I keep tabs on him and make sure that he stays out of the picture indefinitely. In return…" He took one hand away and let the other slide up and take hold of Leo's neck. "…in return, I stay this age, in this perfect shape, and I get to be just about unstoppable. Like he used to be. But now he's nothing. He's not in control of anything anymore. *I* am…" As if to prove a point, he used his free hand to casually sweep away fragments of glass and wood particles from the front of his satiny jump suit. He sniffed arrogantly and looked up at Leo with gray, lupine eyes burning coldly beneath the tiny, black *ME* triad.

"…And I always do what I have to do."

Leo felt his trachea begin to slowly contract. The gray eyes watched, waiting for either confession or strangulation.

Into that silence there came a distinct click. Both men glanced down to see one of the lower bookshelves float open on hinges. The book spines were a façade, concealing a long cabinet that Leo used to hide in as a boy.

Leo groaned. "No, you were supposed to stay in there!"

Mr. Man crawled out and stood, his face grim and uncertain. "I do not know what you want from me. But please do not hurt him, and I will obey you as far as I am able."

The Watchdog released his grip and Leo dropped to the floor, coughing and gasping for air.

"Eight centuries, old man. I bury you in Nicholas' coffin, and you stay there for only eight centuries. What are you doing out of your grave? Never mind—you don't know anything! From what I hear, you don't even know your own name, do you?" He gave Mr. Man a gimlet stare. "You don't, do you?"

Mr. Man could only stare back mutely with a look of frustration and dread.

The Watchdog laughed low and maliciously. "Kak said you would be impaired, but there was no way to know how much. Now, I see! You're completely broken, aren't you? The village idiot! Well, even so, I prefer you in the Sleep, and buried in a hole somewhere. It just puts my mind at ease, you know?"

He grinned, and then acknowledged Leo's stunned expression.

"How about you? Do you know *your* name?"

"Leo."

"Leo what?"

"Von Koppersmith."

"O.K. Von Koppersmith, you can wipe that terrified-slash-dimwit look off of your face, because in a couple of seconds I'm going far away and you'll never see me again. I'll set up shop somewhere else in the world and stick the village idiot here in another hole. And after I'm gone, you should go down to your kitchen and make a big, fat juicy hot dog to celebrate, because there are a lot of people who would have liked to have been able to say what *you* will be able to say to all of your friends for the rest of your otherwise very boring life, which is: 'the Watchdog didn't kill me! He allowed me to keep breathing!'"

From the cargo pocket of his right pants leg the Watchdog pulled a wooden medieval-looking flute. It was an ugly greenish-brown thing, its surface uneven with warty knots and notches. He breathed into its oval-shaped mouth-hole.

A melody began. The Watchdog did not play it; it seemed to play itself. Somber notes slithered out of its flaring bell, weaving what to Leo sounded like a requiem for a suicidal princess or a theme to a murder mystery.

The bookshelf tore open.

Leo stared in disbelief. It was not that the wood of the bookshelf broke and splintered, or that the books were cast aside; rather, the area in which the entire bookshelf existed tore in two like a canvas ripped by a saw. Inside was darkness. A low moaning wind spilled into the breach, and tattered shreds of reality flapped around the edges.

The Watchdog shoved Zechariah through.

"Freeze! Put your hands in the air now!" The Watchdog turned to see policemen entering the library with revolvers and riot shotguns pointed at his chest. He sneered and raised his arms.

As focused on the Watchdog as they tried to remain, none of the policemen could resist casting glimpses at the black, windswept hole gaping at them from the bookshelf. It was a thing that should not exist: a fissure punched through reality as if the world we all see is only foil. The edges of it shivered and rippled.

The policemen slowly advanced upon the Watchdog, some of them muttering into their radios. A lieutenant with thick forearms growled instructions: "Now put your hands behind your head, fingers interlocking, and slowly—*slowly*—get down on your knees…"

The Watchdog crisscrossed his fingers behind his head as commanded, but instead of sinking to his knees he gently fell backwards into the dark portal, which instantly contracted with a sound like the last swirl of water down a huge drain. A shouting swarm of bullets eagerly pursued him, but found only wood and book spines to bite into.

Eleven

A minute before, when Leo first scrambled through the aperture and into the uncanny space in which he now found himself, darkness had seemed absolute. Lamplight came in from the library, but something about the portal muted and distorted it, and even the Watchdog, still facing the policemen, seemed like a reflection in a rippling pond. As Leo's eyes had adjusted he became aware of a weak haze of bluish-whiteness with no clear origin filling the area. The air was warm and fragrant, like a greenhouse.

Mr. Man—Zechariah—sat upright next to him. "Leo! Are you alright?"

"What's wrong with the ground?" Leo stared down at his legs, which were sunk nearly to the calves. He took an awkward step forward, and another, and nearly fell over. "It's like walking on pizza dough! Where are we?"

Zechariah stood, and his legs wobbled. "I don't know. But we cannot go back."

Leo knew it was true, and as he gaped at the bluish-black around them he mentally scolded himself. He could have just stayed in the library and kept his head down and let the police handle things. At the same time he knew that was never truly an option. The wailing plea of Nicholas and of his other ancestors still hung in his mind but, more than that, he had felt almost *pushed* through the Watchdog's portal by his own desperate need to reach the depths of the curse that haunted his future, in the hope of finding some way to bend it off course.

He had found a wall, and though it was made of the same blubbery substance as the floor it at least helped him get a better sense of the place. There was a kind of passage, down which air currents rushed towards a faint but certain brightening of the blue-white light. They had begun making their way forward, but they were like babies learning to walk on a waterbed.

"So, your name is Zechariah?" Leo whispered when he spoke.

"Yes—I suppose so."

Their arms waved to keep balance as they slowly rounded a corner and left the shuddering, glowing aperture behind them. "What did he mean?" Leo panted. "He said eight centuries ago he put you in Nicholas' grave! How is that possible? Is he just crazy? You and he can't really be that old, right?"

In the dark behind them they heard the rushing sound of the fissure closing, and a brief muffled drumroll of the policemen's bullets. An oppressive silence followed.

Zechariah started to turn around. "Should we…?"

Leo pressed on his shoulder to keep him moving forward, whispering sharply, "Just go!"

They tried to speed up, but it was nearly impossible. As soon as they raised one leg to take a step forward the other sunk a little deeper into the squashy floor, costing precious seconds for every advance. Worse, the passageway was beginning to narrow. The dim light was not enough to see very far forward, and Leo had the sinking feeling that they were headed down a dead end.

"Zechariah?"

The Watchdog's voice rolled down the passage at them. There was no insistence in his tone; just a warning.

"Are you hiding from me?"

The passage had now grown so narrow that they had to turn sideways to continue. The rubbery wall pressed against Leo's beard and cheek—it felt warm, like a fat belly. Somewhere inside him the question "what is this place?" still pulsed, but there was currently no room for it in his conscious mind.

The walls came together more closely. He pushed Zechariah farther in with one arm, certain that at any moment he would feel that iron plier grip of the Watchdog on his neck again...

...all at once it seemed like Zechariah had lurched ahead out of reach, and Leo could feel cold air. His left leg was at such an angle that it was sunk in to the floor and wedged between the walls at the same time.

"Zechariah!" The Watchdog's voice was close. It seemed only feet away. Leo heaved his leg through the fatty, compressed walls with so much frantic force that he overdid it and fell.

He rolled into an area where the bluish-white light became much brighter. Leo could now easily see Zechariah, who had continued down a slope towards the source of the light: a huge, round disc the size of a swimming pool. The floor bent steeply around it on all sides, giving the impression of a giant well. The air here was freezing cold, and some kind of white steam or mist swirled around the surface of the disc.

Leo stomped clumsily down the slope until he was by Zechariah's side. His eyes stinging in the light, he suddenly realized that the blue disc was actually a wide opening, leading like a round mouth into another area.

Leo crouched and stared down through the opening, and as his eyes adjusted to the blaze of cold light he felt his heart squeeze tightly. It took long seconds of stunned, bewildered staring for Leo to understand what he was seeing.

It was the *sky*—a daytime sky, in fact. How had an entire night gone by since they left the library? There was more, though: the sky was not *up*. It was down. No, not down…it <u>was</u> up. But so was Leo. He was at the top of the sky, looking down thousands of feet.

Bone-numbingly cold wind eddied around Leo and Zechariah, making a deep, oscillating moan like the ghost of a whale. Through the opening, off to one side, Leo could see a green countryside stretching away, obscured by a thin veil of haze that hung in the mile of air between it and him. Clouds flowed past the portal, sending moist white fingers up the sides. It was as if Leo had found a secret trap door that proved the entire Von Koppersmith mansion was just hanging up in the air like a Christmas tree ornament.

"VON KOPPERSMITH!"

The scream shocked Leo's nerves. Up the slope of the floor, squeezing in between the fleshy walls, was the Watchdog's rancorous face. Leo's guts turned to jelly.

"Jump, Leo!" Zechariah shouted, and he stepped off into the void.

"WAIT!" Leo howled. Incredulous, he watched Zechariah plunge like a skydiver.

The Watchdog shoved past the doughy doorway and into the room, and the smell of his spicy, vomitous cologne swirled through the cold air. "Welcome to the Wayover," he declared matter-of-factly. "That's what we always called it, anyway. Strange, isn't it?"

As if to demonstrate, he took a couple of deliberate steps across the elastic floor. "The whole universe is honeycombed with Wayovers—it's just made that way. Kak found out how to use them, and then he showed me. He gave me the flute to open them," he patted the cargo pocket of his warm-up pants, where the thaumaturgic instrument was enclosed. "Music is at the heart of everything, you know. It's the language of God."

The Watchdog's voice went from conversational to malicious and he rose slowly into the air, leaving the floor wobbling beneath him.

"I hate music."

He flew across the room with hands outstretched. Leo ducked, but in the same instant felt himself teetering on the edge of the windswept opening in the sky, and his hands instinctively grabbed the Watchdog's ankle. He ended up sprawled with one leg hanging over the edge, trying to crawl up his attacker to keep from falling.

The Watchdog scoffed. Reaching over, he grabbed Leo's leg and lifted him, dangling him upside down above the opening in the sky. Leo's smartphone slipped out and plummeted.

"I told you, Von Koppersmith. I always do what I have to do..."

"NO!" Leo screamed. "Please don't!"

His assailant snorted and began to loosen his grip. "Or what?"

"Or...or I'll break this thing in half!"

Clutched close to Leo's upside-down face was the green flute, plucked a few seconds before from the Watchdog's cargo pocket almost by accident.

The Watchdog's face became a mask of rage. "Give me that...!"

Somehow, between the Watchdog's already loosened grip and his twisting reach for the stolen flute, Leo jerked free.

And he fell into the sky.

Twelve

Falling out of the sky gives one a fresh perspective.

Looking down from the edge of the opening Leo had only caught a glimpse of land far below, but now he saw that ten yards directly down was the small, flat top of a narrow mountain; Leo was seeing it literally from a bird's eye view. And he was sure that he would miss it, that he would just fall right past it.

A breathless three seconds later he hit solid ground on all fours. His palms met snow and loose rock and he slid forward, towards the edges of the flat peak. He hung above the world, about to plunge into it, about to live out every broken-rollercoaster nightmare he had ever had.

His limbs turned to spaghetti noodles and his intestines went cold. He sunk to the scrap of rock that formed the peak and he lay prostrate, refusing to move.

He could hear Zechariah shouting his name, but everything seemed to have slowed down and become surreal.

There was a shape to his left: a small building. On his right the Watchdog's flute lay on the snow-dusted ground.

"Zechariah!"

The Watchdog's voice pierced the cold air and the tumbling clouds, and it was so filled with hatred and murder that Leo instantly overcame his paralysis. His right hand smacked down on the flute, and he rolled with it against the building. It was some kind of small, round house, made of stones and mortar and mounted on columns, but leaning to one side like it might fall over at any moment. Scrambling like a desperate animal, Leo instinctively sought the shaded refuge beneath the structure.

He peered out, looking for Zechariah. A coil of thick rope blocked his view. It curled around several times and then snaked up into the center of the house through a small hole in the wooden floorboards.

Shoving the rope to one side with his forearm, Leo spied Zechariah standing on the opposite end of the mountain peak, but right away his view was blocked again by the Watchdog's white Ecco BIOMS landing with a hard smack of rubber against rock.

The Watchdog and Zechariah were now facing each other. If the Watchdog knew Leo was beneath the stone-and-mortar house, he wasn't indicating it.

"Trapping you inside Nicholas' grave seemed so right, Zechariah. At least at the time. You two *belonged* together. If it were up to me, I would like to take every man who has ever claimed to be in authority over me and stuff them all into one big grave. Besides, I figured that was safe—an old, forgotten thirteenth century grave from outside of Rome…who would ever look in there? I didn't even mind too much when I discovered that Nicholas' family transplanted the coffin to America centuries later. As long as no one looked inside. But wouldn't you know it? Of all the improbable things, some kid goes and digs it up and looks inside…"

As Leo listened, he could tell that Zechariah and the Watchdog were exchanging a look, that something surprising had been thought and then expressed upon the face and subsequently read by the other.

"No," Leo heard Zechariah say. "Leave him alone. He's done nothing to you…"

"Von Koppersmith is Nicholas' spawn! His great-great-whatever!" The Watchdog loudly guffawed. "I can't believe it! And you know what? I'm getting a very good idea here. I don't know why I didn't think of it a long time ago. As soon as we get back, I think I'll set about putting an end to that family once and for all. That mother of his could certainly use some loving attention. Hey, where did that kid go, anyway?"

The expensive white Eccos shifted as the Watchdog scanned the peak for Leo.

"Where are you, boy? I'm a fool—I should have just squashed you back in that library when I had the chance! If only I'd known…"

"I'm here!" Leo had meant to sound more confident when he said it, but his voice was weak. Regardless, he stood as upright as he could on the other side of the stone house.

"Leo, what are you doing?" Zechariah stood with knees slightly bent, ready to spring, not sure what to do next.

In his raised hand Leo held the greenish-brown flute, brandishing it like a stick for a foxhound.

The Watchdog's eyes pinched and his voice was deadly. "Von Koppersmith, I'm about to push your head against the rocks and grind your face into *butter...*"

Leo hurled the warty green flute off the side of the mountain and into the cloud-swept void.

The Watchdog had only an instant to scowl at Leo before speeding after his flute. It had already fallen fifty yards, twirling like a dislodged rotor from a toy helicopter, but the Watchdog knew he would have it back in his hands in mere seconds, and then he could finish what he...

The rope Leo had secretly tied around the Watchdog's ankle went as tight as a ripcord. The other end snapped off a huge weakened section of the stone-and-mortar house's eastward facing wall.

The sudden halt jounced the Watchdog's body, even as the wall rolled ponderously down the shoulder of the mountain. The Watchdog's eyes went wild and he snatched at the knot that held him, but before he could free himself the wall found a sheer ledge and collapsed into open air.

With arms flapping hysterically, the Watchdog gave a shriek that steadily shrunk to a distant mewl that finally evaporated in the clouds and the plummeting distance below.

Leo and Zechariah stared down the side of the mountain until they realized that a strange new sound was filling the air. They both turned to see the little stone building vibrating, and its thatched roof growing like a bristling toadstool, shedding snow and all of its pieces as a bizarre shape steadily grew out of it.

Part 2 – Downward. An Old Foe Becomes a
New Foe. The Children, a Coat and a
Maelstrom.

Thirteen

The chunk of wall that had torn away partially revealed an interior made of wooden gears of different sizes, all spinning and making painful squeaks as a result of the rope having been pulled. Bundled tubes of wood vibrated and groaned, and Leo could see water dribbling from the joints. The entire structure shook and its walls coughed up pieces of itself.

"Leo," cried Zechariah, "Stand away from it!"

Leo wanted to, but the edges of the mountaintop were unbearably close. He shuffled back from the rumbling building as far as his legs would let him.

A wooden tube cracked and a geyser of water blasted over Leo's shoulder with the force of a fire hose. The mesh of sticks on the roof crumbled as the figure inside fully emerged, squealing and twisting.

A pair of wooden staffs extended like arms. Other staffs reached up from between them, connected by a network of cords and pulleys. Water rushing through more wooden tubes filled the figure so that it grew and unfolded, rising up like a gigantic centipede.

All at once, in a flurry of collapsing panels and creaking interlocking pieces, a new shape emerged out of the center and stood on quivering, spindly poles. It was as wide as a car, but it looked like an enormous crown. Covering it was a mosaic of thin, flat, irregularly shaped pieces of colored glass.

An array of gears inside it came to life. The crown began to spin horizontally, vertically, and diagonally, thanks to an ingeniously designed axis. A tremendous fountain of water flared from the center, but it was clearly not the accidental result of a cracked tube. Sunlight breaking through the wispy clouds fell upon the structure, refracting through the glass and the fountain, and all at once the mountaintop was a shimmery blaze of rainbow light.

Leo and Zechariah stood squinting up at the whirling crown, using their hands to shield their faces from the flashing pennants of colored light and the cold misty water falling in random sheets.

Leo slowly shook his head. "What…what is that?"

They watched and waited. For half a minute there was only the sound of the huge, glass-covered wooden crown twirling like an alien windmill, and of the spraying fountain, and of the dull, haunting moans of wind meandering around the mountain.

Nothing happened. The crown just spun and glittered. Leo glanced nervously at Zechariah. "It's… pointless!" *Like a decoration at a carnival,* he thought, *or a centerpiece at a rich kid's birthday party.*

Zechariah continued staring at it, and a pleasant expression lit up his face. "I like it…"

Leo snorted impatiently. Satisfied that the crown represented no immediate threat, he turned away and began searching the sky.

"I don't see it!" Leo shifted his position, straining his eyes. "The hole in the sky! Where did it go?"

He had only a vague idea of just how high up they were. His best estimates were based entirely on aerial photographs he had seen on the internet: five thousand feet, maybe?

He tried to catch a glimpse of a city or a suburb somewhere below. He could see the gray-blue ocean off in the distance, though he couldn't judge for sure how far away it was. Another mountain rose beside them, reaching up even higher than theirs, its pinnacle obscured by mist. Other than that there were only sprawling forests and hills.

"We're stuck on top of a mountain! How do we get home?"

Zechariah said nothing, but only watched Leo or admired the enormous rainbow whirligig.

"I hate heights!" Leo found himself instinctively stooping, suddenly afraid that the groaning winds would flip him off the mountain as easily as a person flips the red plastic top off of a gallon of milk. "I mean I really hate heights! We're stuck up here! What do we do?"

Zechariah did not respond. His expression showed that he was mildly perplexed, and yet he retained a sense of calm that Leo suddenly found intolerable.

"WHERE ARE WE?"

His exclamation tumbled uselessly off the side of the mountain and disappeared in the high-altitude winds.

"Leo." Something about Zechariah's voice was arresting. "It's alright. Did you see the steps?"

Leo followed Zechariah's pointing finger to the beginning of a staircase cut into the stone of the mountain. Timidly, Leo shambled closer, and his guts clenched up. The steps followed the craggy shoulder of the peak, winding steadily down along the outside.

Leo looked at Zechariah angrily. "Come *on*! We can't go down those. There isn't even a guardrail! What about the hole in the sky? Maybe it's there but we just can't see it, you know? We need to get back up—that's the way home! How do we get back up?"

Zechariah stared up at the bright blue sky and the gray white clouds that sailed past. "Even if it is there, and we cannot see it, we still have no way to get up to it. It is too high. We need to go down and see if we can find someone to help us."

Leo frowned. "Who?"

"Whoever built this fantastic machine! Whoever carved these marvelous steps!" He began descending the staircase as if there was no difference between it and the average flight of steps in a suburban home. He occasionally adjusted his walk to keep the winds from blowing him off-balance, but even then it did not seem to especially concern him.

Leo tried to place his foot on the first step, and the movement unloosed small chunks of rock that clattered off the edge and into the vast abyss.

"Wait!"

"What's wrong?" Zechariah had to shout to be heard above the sound of the wind. His clunky black shoes shifted restlessly.

With each second that he considered the staircase, Leo's knees bent a little more. "I can't do this…" He tried to laugh it off but he couldn't sustain the effort, and instead found himself sinking flat against the cold, hard stones of the mountain. "I don't want to move!"

He was not being stubborn; he meant it as a self-diagnosis, and it was as matter-of-fact as a plumber declaring that a rusted faucet did not want to turn. "I just want to go home…"

Zechariah called out Leo's name. "We cannot stay here! We have to go down and look for some help!" With an encouraging half-smile he added: "We must go down before we can go up!"

Leo tried extending his right leg, stretching the tip of his shoe to the next step. He was at war with himself, though, and the opposing force in him would not allow his torso to follow his leg. His white-knuckled fingers clung to the corners of the steps.

Then Leo remembered some advice Anselm had given him a long time ago when he was still a child and had gotten himself stuck in a pine tree. Climbing up had been fun, but when he was ready to come down he became paralyzed with fear. "Don't look down," Anselm told him, "Just concentrate on one small spot and let your arms and legs feel their way down."

Leo turned onto his stomach and focused on that first stair, nearly pressing his face against it, and quickly became intimately familiar with every pore of its surface and every grain of sand that vibrated in the unceasing winds.

He stretched his leg again, but this time he forced his torso to follow. It felt like the greatest act of will of his life so far. He continued to move only by dragging his body over the rough stone, a slow process that gathered his shirt up and left his stomach red and raw. At last he was fully on the staircase, completely exposed like a bug on a skyscraper.

Zechariah patiently waited for him. They were an odd pair: one standing confidently upright, the other in a frantic prostrate position and not even facing the right way.

The steps made one spiral. Leo scraped himself over them, stopping completely whenever a wet, rushing cloud engulfed him. When at long last the rubber of his shoe met the solid rock of a landing, he twisted up into a squatting position, still not daring to look out into the open air.

Here the mountainside formed the right side of the stairs. The left side was still just blue space and a screaming fall. By huddling against the wall he was sheltered from the brunt of the winds, and Zechariah waited for him to collect himself before continuing their descent.

The sunlight waxed and waned depending on the density of the clouds rolling by. The stairs led around the peak in a slow descent, so after they circled back to the other side they were blasted with winds again. Leo was getting used to it, however (though not comfortable), and he began to proceed with a little more confidence.

The stairs wound around again, although it took longer because the peak was widening as they descended. On the third time around, on the sheltered side, the stairs passed under a kind of natural rock awning and came to an end.

Beneath the awning the shadow was very dark, and it took their eyes a few moments to adjust. Finally they could see that before them stood a painted green door with a smooth, round wooden handle.

The door made a painful creak as they opened it. Inside was a passageway that at first seemed so utterly devoid of light that there would certainly be no way to continue, but once again their vision adapted and they realized there was, in fact, a faint gleam coming from somewhere within.

They inched inside, feeling along the walls and in front of them. They soon found themselves at the top of another long flight of cobblestone stairs winding down into the mountain like a jagged throat. The light they had seen was coming in from outside through bell-shaped window-holes cut through the rock along the way.

"Just a minute," Leo muttered, leaning against the wall. He needed to rest and just *think* for a few seconds. He rubbed his eyes; he felt tired and sore from the exposure to the wind. "Zechariah, what's *happening*? How did we just leave the house like that, at night, and end up on top of a mountain in the middle of the day?"

Zechariah sighed and nodded. "Yes, that is a good question. It reminds one of the Pied Piper story, does it not?"

Leo nodded back at him. "'*A wondrous portal opened wide'*. The Watchdog got his flute from the original Pied Piper, this guy named Kak (whoever he is), and used it to open that tunnel-thing—the 'Wayover'…the same as the one the Children's Crusade went through."

They both stood in silent contemplation for a second or two.

"My gosh, Zechariah. Did we go where they went?"

Zechariah breathed in profoundly through his nostrils. "When I look into my mind for answers to any questions, whether they be profound or prosaic, I see only a nebulous patchwork. I hear music, melted. Past experiences curled 'round by fog, like those clouds outside. My own name is lost to me. We should just keep moving, Leo. It is the only way we will understand, I think."

It was quiet. After enduring the low rushing and roaring of winds there was a particular uncanny intensity to the quietness. Each cobblestone step down that they took made little reverberations, and they wondered if anyone was listening somewhere in the depths.

Fourteen

By the time the staircase reached the end the two men were almost completely in darkness. They could look up and see high above them shafts of sun spilling through the bell-shaped windows, but very little of that light found its way down to the bottom of the stairwell.

When their eyes finally adjusted they found another door. It was not painted like the first one, and the top was rounded. Clinging to the wall around the doorjambs and the lintel were mats of green vines dotted liberally with long, white, cigar-shaped flowers.

Leo looked over his shoulder at Zechariah. "Do you think we should…"

Before he could finish his sentence the space at the bottom of the stairwell lit up.

A dozen of the white, cigar-shaped flowers nearest him had swollen to the size of grapefruits and now emitted a soft, white glow.

"Look at that!"

At the sound of Leo's exclamation a dozen more of the flowers quivered and inflated, casting more light.

Zechariah stared in wonder. "Are they responding to our voices…?" The question prompted the last of the flowers to awaken.

It was now almost too bright. Squinting, they opened the door and went through.

There was more darkness beyond, but they knew instantly that there was a dramatic increase in the amount of space around them. They could feel that they were walking on a wooden platform, perhaps a bridge. Cool air moved gently around them, and somewhere below was the distant but distinctive sound of rushing water.

Leo made a bland comment about being careful where they walked. His words trailed away in wonder as more of the white flowers inflated around them. He reacted with words of surprise, which woke up even more of the shining blooms.

The mountain was hollow. The platform they stood upon reached to the far wall, its edges blocked by thin railing. Another similar platform ran perpendicular to the first, so that together they formed a huge wood cross suspended above the massive pit of the mountain's interior.

The green vines seemed to be covering every square inch of the walls, from top to bottom, acres of it, somehow thriving in this subterranean environment. Beyond the few flowers that had come to round, glowing life at the sound of Leo's voice, there were countless more waiting in dormancy among the sprawling fields of climbing vines.

Leo smiled at them as he and Zechariah crossed the platform. "Convenient…"

More flowers lit up. He spoke again, but raised his voice: "Very convenient!"

The entire platform became bathed in light.

They could now easily see that there was a massive pair of royal blue double doors off to the right, where the perpendicular platform met the cavern wall. Far to their left was a vast system of wooden tubes and gears. It was from this conduit, stretching up from the depths, that the weird rainbow crown structure on the mountain's peak received its water.

In the central area, where the two platforms intersected, was a small wooden house. Large pulleys were built into the top, and thick ropes dangled from the bottom.

Leo frowned curiously. "Is that an elevator?" His words caused more of the white flowers to light up. "This mountain is so weird. It's like a big shell. It's practically hollow."

Zechariah hesitated. "Hollowchest. That's its name."

"You know that? How?"

The tall man stared in fascination up at the high walls and at the crossed platforms. "This place...Hollowchest...it is a very good place, isn't it?"

Leo stopped and looked at him. "Well, it's amazing—but we don't know yet if it's a good place, right? Maybe the Watchdog has friends here..."

Zechariah seemed nearly delirious, as if he was feeling waves of intense emotions. He ignored Leo's cautions, and softly repeated the word "amazing."

"Zechariah? Are you O.K.?"

The tall, strange man seemed lost in some vision he was experiencing. "I know this place..."

He surveyed the glowing flowers and the intricate clicking, churning, wooden hydraulic system and the elevator at the center of the cross, and a boyish smile dawned across his face. He leaned over a section of railing and peered down. He gathered up as much air as his lungs could hold and then shouted, "I KNOW THIS PLACE!"

Everywhere the white blooms swelled in response and began to shine like thousands of Chinese lanterns, travelling in a cascade down the walls of the mountain's interior in soundless waterfalls of light nearly to the very bottom, where a clean, cold river swept by with endless vigor.

···+·+·+·+·+·+·→

Although neither one realized it, the royal blue double doors they had seen on the far side of the platform led outside to a broad, flat section of rock. It jutted out like a natural terrace, overhung with craggy stones and a grove of small, scrubby trees. A body lay sprawled upon it.

The Watchdog regained consciousness with a cry of pain. Cursing, he stood up fast, and in the act of doing so he pulled loose from the branch upon which he unknowingly had been impaled. Blood spurted from the hole it left in his stomach. He clutched at it, moaning miserably. His face was a horror-movie mask of dirt and blood and hanging flesh.

He stood for a moment blinking up at the sun, scowling at it as if it was somehow the cause of all his woes. All of a sudden the sunlight was put out. A shadow covered the Watchdog's face.

"Gosh, Watchdog," said a silky, perverse voice, "You look like a big doo-doo ball. I don't know whether to laugh or cry. Probably laugh."

The Watchdog froze, his eyes wide with emotion. "Kak!" He sunk to his knees, and felt a surge of agony through his bleeding side. "Help me!"

From the dark silhouette blocking the sun came a snort. "Help you?" The right hand held a long spear, and the opaque face turned towards it. "You know, I have to keep this Thing close at hand all the time in case anyone tries to steal it, and you know what I've discovered? When I'm holding it, I can...*feel* where Zechariah is. His essence radiates through it. *That's* how I knew, Watchdog. That's how I knew you had bungled the easiest job anyone had ever been given: to watch a brainless vegetable man and make sure he doesn't go anywhere. I even did you the courtesy of sending Bentpin to alert you that he'd been dug up, so that you could take care of things. Now Zechariah is not only up and moving around, he's on the one island in the world where he is least welcome: *my* island. And what are you doing about it? You're rolling down the side of a mountain like a doo-doo ball!"

The Watchdog shifted painfully on his knees. His shoulders sagged.

"That's what I thought," came the oily voice. "I'll have to take care of things myself. Bye-bye, Watchdog..." From the center of the silhouette's face the color orange began to burn, and the sound of fire rising from a pit grew steadily louder.

"Wait, Kak, please!" The Watchdog's bloody hands were stretched up, imploring. "I can still get him back! I can stop him! I just need more power!"

The orange glow swirled and the sound of fire grew to a low roar.

"*Give me more power!*"

The churning maw of flame suddenly subsided, and from the silhouette came a laugh, a little-girl cackle. "More power? I made you Hell's Captain Marvel! How much more power do you need?"

The Watchdog's eyes stared wildly through trickles of blood and sweat. "I just want...*more*. More strength. I need to be *bigger*. I need to be *unstoppable*."

The silhouette hovered in silence. Wind fled past the rocky overhang as the Watchdog waited, not even breathing.

At last a response: "I'm going to need a name, please."

The Watchdog gasped, stunned at first that his request was going to be granted. He recovered himself quickly, firmly stating, "Walwich Herstog."

Kak snorted. "Oh come on, you know better. That *was* your name, a long, long, long, *long* irretrievable time ago. What's your *name*?"

The Watchdog cleared his throat and glanced at the ground in embarrassment. "Watchdog."

"There it is. Say it again?"

"Watchdog."

"What wazzat?"

The Watchdog felt he was being mocked, and he grimaced. "Watchdog!"

As the name left his mouth he doubled over in pain. He clutched at his guts.

"Louder, please," Kak said calmly. "You have to mean it. You give me your name and I'll give you a new one in return…"

The Watchdog staggered, and his face was blood red as he tried to speak. The inside of his stomach felt like it was filled with sharp tearing claws. He opened his mouth, and this time when his name came out it was deeper and more guttural. His forearms swelled up to twice their normal size and pushed out thick strands of hair.

Kak clapped his hands and squealed. "That's it! Say it again!"

The Watchdog's legs tore through his trousers with sharp sounds of ripping fabric and his neck bulged and grew thick mats of fur. His mouth was widening and the lower jaw beginning to jut, pushing out its little square teeth so they sprinkled upon the ground like spilled candy. In their place sharp teeth, as thick as tusks, were beginning to sprout.

It all hurt like nothing he could have imagined, but he forced himself to say his name: "Wa…chh…d…og!" It came out even deeper and louder than before, but he could no longer make his widening mouth form syllables properly.

Kak howled with degenerate glee. "Again!"

"Ahhcchhh…og!!"

Kak spun flamboyantly on his spindly legs. The thing that now swayed before him was twenty feet tall, over three times taller than a man. Umber-colored shag hung from nearly every inch of it, hirsute thatch shivering with every move that it made. Its head was enormously wide and flat, and it was directly connected to its colossal chest with no neck in between, as if it had been squashed on. The two misty gray eyes that had once been so captivating were now tiny and close set and burning orange-red.

Kak stared up at him and his bulging eyes glinted with demonic triumph. "What's your name?"

"*Ch...og!*"

" 'Chog' it is," Kak said with a giggle. "See? In the end, I don't really give names. You give them to yourself. I just facilitate."

The beast that was once the Watchdog, and who long before that was Walwich Herstog from the quiet village of Hamelin, now stared down at his enormous hands with three fingers and a thumb on each, and felt the staggering power running through them. He turned his shoulders—the only way he could look to either side now—and observed his surroundings from his towering new perspective. He inhaled and felt air fill his massive lungs, and when it came back out it made a noise like coal and old foghorns being slowly crunched together. He raised his shaggy arms and roared, "*Chog!*" The sound shook the tree branches and sent birds fleeing in panic.

Kak covered his ears and scowled. "Alright, Stupid, don't get carried away. And pay attention! Zechariah is right through those two doors."

Fifteen

"What was that?"

Leo and Zechariah had gotten the elevator working. A lever inside released the brake, allowing them to sluggishly descend, and Leo wondered if the faint, distant roar that had just reverberated through the mountain was a sound of some part of the elevator's machinery.

"We should go back up, Leo." Zechariah was staring into the uppermost reaches of the cavern, listening.

"What? Really?"

"*Now*, Leo." His voice was soft but stern. He pulled the lever and brought them to a jarring stop.

Leo fumbled for a few seconds, investigating how to make them go the other way. They had only just begun to ascend when the blue double doors were demolished with a sharp, deafening explosion that filled the hollow interior of the mountain. Sunlight tumbled in like a firebomb, and in response the glowing flowers on the walls snapped back into their cigar shapes.

Leo was stunned and confused. "What is it...?"

"I do not know." Zechariah grabbed the ropes and helped Leo get the elevator to its original position flush with the platforms. "But we do not want to be inside here, suspended thousands of feet above a pit!"

The double doors' threshold filled with a towering silhouette.

Leo and Zechariah scrambled to get out of the elevator as a rhythmic pounding told them that something huge was charging at them.

A giant arm swept through the elevator, tearing it into wood shreds. The force shoved Leo forward and he landed on his chest. He rolled over quickly and saw two close-set orange-red eyes glaring down at the elevator's wreckage from beneath a big, dark chunk of a brow. There was enough sunlight and flower-light to show a long mouth with a jutting lower jaw where irregular tusk-like teeth grew like gray stalagmites.

"Back to the stairs, Leo!" Zechariah dragged him to his feet and they sprinted down the platform towards the vine-covered doorway, which suddenly seemed very far away.

The rhythmic pounding began again.

A noise like coal and old foghorns being slowly crunched together filled the cavern, rising in intensity. Leo felt the shaking of the platform and heard a desperate breathing behind him, right behind him…

When he and Zechariah shot through the doorway and into the stairwell an arm followed them, a gigantic furry arm that was the same diameter from shoulder to wrist, ending in an immense hand with stout, thick digits—three fingers and a thumb—that strained for them. The momentum of the pursuer was too much for the doorway, and its bricks and vines heaved into the bottom of the stairwell.

Leo ended up sprawled across the first steps with lumps of rubble covering him. He looked back at the doorway to see that terrible hand grasping for him, the two orange eyes staring at him, and the long, jagged mouth opening to make a guttural sound:

"*Kopp'smith...!*"

Leo's breath caught in his throat. "Watchdog?"

Zechariah's hand came down hard on Leo's shoulder and pulled him up. They ran for the top of the stairs, and the rest of the doorway collapsed as the hairy, prodigious beast forced its way in to the stairwell.

Leo looked down at the thing as he climbed, and the full sight of it made him think for a second that he might pass out and fall. The creature was not just massive—it was not simply like seeing an elephant and being amazed at its size. Though thick with dark brown fur and horrifying, it moved and acted with the intentionality of a human being, a *person* blown up to gargantuan size but still unmistakably intelligent.

"The Watchdog..." Leo whispered the name as he stared down from the top of the stairs in disbelief. The creature could not have heard him, yet it seemed to respond, to *object*:

"*Chog!*" The roar shook the walls and loosened rocks.

Zechariah and Leo fled back out onto the cold face of the mountain. Chog hoisted himself up the stairwell, grunting and snarling.

Leo waddled up the winding stairs of the mountainside—*waddled*, not ran, because he feared and hated every step, yet he compelled himself because he knew he had no other choice.

He kept his left hand on the wall as he went, as if that would help at all if he tripped and plunged over the edge. He tried to keep his eyes focused on the backs of Zechariah's black shoes, but the man wearing them moved quickly and confidently and was soon many steps ahead.

The crunch of stone somewhere behind and beneath told Leo that the thing that used to be the Watchdog was shoving its way out of the mountain and onto the precarious stairs. It was coming after them…it was coming and there was no where to run but up to the top of the mountain, where there was nothing to help them and nowhere to go…

Leo wound his way one slow step at a time around the spindly mountain, growling with the effort of overcoming his paralyzing fear of heights. His eyes snatched views of the world: misty gray clouds…sunlight filtering through them as a gleaming whiteness…

And a circle…

Leo looked down to watch his step, and then realized what he had just spotted. He glanced up again.

It was not merely a circle, but a sphere of some kind. It was colored the same as the clouds and, except for its thin dark perimeter, it blended into the sky. It looked like an enormous bubble hovering hundreds of yards away and about on the same level as the mountain peak.

"Leo, *hurry!*" Zechariah had stopped many steps up and was pointing over Leo's shoulder.

Chog had rounded the bend in the mountain and was clutching at its stony sides with its hairy forearms, shimmying up the stairs at twice the speed that Leo was moving. It rumbled and snapped its jaws.

Leo sprang forward. Another part of his mind tried to stop him cold, but he forced that impulse down. He was now doing a fast walk up the stairs, crunching over patches of snow. He almost froze again when Chog let out a roar, but he kept pushing himself along…*cannot stop*, he told himself repeatedly. *Cannot stop…*

The staircase curved back around to the other side as the peak narrowed. Smaller aggregates of clouds drifted by in constant intervals here, preventing him from seeing anything. The stairs disappeared, and the sounds of Chog's rumbling and barking grew closer.

Leo shouted uncontrollably when an arm reached out at him.

"Leo!" Zechariah held the fabric of his shirt and hustled him along.

Leo shook his head violently. "No, Zechariah! Don't wait for me! You go!"

"I will not." His voice was solid and simple. "If it takes you, then it takes me, as well—and we will take it down with us."

They circled the mountain for the last time. A gap opened unexpectedly in the clouds, and the sky was visible again in all its vastness. The cloud-colored sphere Leo had seen before was much closer now, maybe a hundred yards out.

"I don't believe it!" Leo shouted. "A hot air balloon!"

A gondola was suspended underneath it, with a tongue of flame pointing up from the center. Passengers waved at them: just stick people from this distance.

The stairs wound up to the spiny tip of the peak. As Leo's shoes met the short, flat stretch of the top, he glanced back to see Chog climbing slowly but steadily out of the flowing clouds like a kraken from the deep, his burning orange-red eyes searching for them.

Leo's rational mind temporarily evaporated. There was nothing left to do and no back-up plan. He jumped and caught hold of the structure that bore the whirling, glittering crown, and water from its spraying fountain rained over his face and shoulders. His feet pushed up on the sides of the stone building that formed its base and he climbed instinctively like a monkey fleeing a tiger. All he had left to put hope in was a series of pathetic *maybes*: *maybe* the passage back home is still above them, *maybe* he could climb to the top of the spinning crown and *maybe* he could leap up and somehow his hands would find the invisible opening and he could pull himself up…

…but the little stone building was already weak and unstable. Leo only got a few feet before the rest of the walls cracked, and the wooden tubes and staffs and the ropes holding them together tumbled over in a fit of violent seizures. The crown collapsed, and the multicolored sheets of glass shattered in a sharp, screaming spray. The tattered remains of the wondrous, mysterious structure spilled down the side of the cliff.

Leo fell flat on his back on the rough ground. Chog's dark shadow covered him.

The balloon filled the air where the crown had been. Long wooden propeller blades were whirling at the back of the gondola, driving the balloon to the peak. Someone stood at the rails, motioning wildly.

"*Zechariah!*" It was a child's voice. More children's voices repeated the name.

Leo then knew only a frantic rush. The hot air balloon that had seemed from a distance to be trolling leisurely was now speeding past them, even as Chog rose like a fur-covered nightmare upon the last steps. His huge, leathery fingers reached for Zechariah.

The tall, dark-eyed man snatched Leo's arm and together the two of them broke into a dead sprint. The balloon sailed past the peak, rushing away.

Chog bore down upon his prey like a tidal wave; Leo and Zechariah leapt out into the open air, experiencing the electric shock of their shoes leaving the solid surface of the peak and of seeing the countryside waiting thousands of feet below, even as Chog swiped at them.

The gondola of the balloon pitched and shook when the two men's hands caught the edges, but the whirling rotor blades steadied the balloon's flight and shot it farther out into the sky.

Chog stood at the spire of the craggy mountain and roared with miserable rage, watching as Leo and Zechariah tumbled into the safety of the gondola and sailed away under the cloud-colored balloon.

···+·+·+·+·+·+·+

"So stupid."

Kak stood staring up the side of the mountain from the stone terrace where the Watchdog had first been transformed into Chog. He could see the wooly monstrosity reaching out in vain from the peak; he could see the balloon gliding away; his orange fingers felt the pulse in the Spear that told him Zechariah was escaping. Again.

"I know you're there, Bentpin."

A short, stumpy shape melted out from the shadow of the mountain's insides on oar-blade-sized boots. Using one green, scaly hand to keep his crumpled black top hat from blowing away in the wind, Crawlsome Bentpin stepped awkwardly over the ragged blue pieces of the double doors that Chog had knocked in.

*"Why do you bother sending him at all? **You** catchest Zechariah."*

Kak didn't turn around, but stared out over the forests to the distant sea. "Me? I'm so busy. I have volunteers working day and night to get my palace ready. I mean, *he* had a palace. I should get one, too! I deserve a place where I can enjoy the fruits of my labors and get my toes sucked."

"Besides, this Spear isn't something I can just leave lying around. Every Throtrex on the Island would try to get its claws on it. Or eat it. But I also don't want to come too close to Zechariah with it—what if he touched it? I'm sure you can appreciate my dilemma. That's why I need low-ranking paeans to do this. AND IT ISN'T VERY DIFFICULT, AFTER ALL. He's an *imbecile* without his Spear…a blabbering booby…a harmless pack of bumps! All anybody has to do is just take him back through the Wayover and make sure he stays over there, which he should, since he would need a MAGIC FLUTE to open the Wayover back up again. Is this hard? This isn't hard. What's hard is keeping five hundred easily distracted Throtrex focused on building a palace for me to enjoy the fruits of my labors and get my toes sucked! Now *that's* hard. In fact, I've got to get back *right now* or they will accidentally throw all the bricks in the ocean or go running after a flock of birds and fall in a hole."

Kak leaned back dramatically and put the back of one hand to his forehead. "Ahhh, woe is me, woe is me! Is there no one in all my kingdom who will rid me of Zechariah? No one at all?"

Kak stepped off the terrace and walked upon the open air as if it was just as solid as the mountainside. "*Au revoir*, Crawlsome Bentpin!"

Sixteen

For five minutes Leo lay in a fetal position on the floor of the gondola, trying to get his breath back.

When at last he looked up, he saw several children. Some were clinging to Zechariah's waist and legs, hugging him with all of their strength. Others were doing ridiculous dances around the warm, flickering burner of the gondola and giving high-pitched hoots as if their elementary school had just won a regional basketball tournament. One of them stood on the opposite side of the gondola and, although he was responsible for manning the balloon's wide pirate-ship steering wheel, he could hardly take his eyes off of Zechariah and kept beaming big grins at him.

"We saw the old Rainbow Crown!" Leo heard them saying gleefully. "We saw it, even though we were far away! Aren't you proud of us, Protector? We saw it and we knew we had to come quick! Who would have guessed the Rainbow Crown would end up being so useful?"

One of the boys (they were all boys, Leo now realized, none more than ten years old) suddenly saw that Leo was at last recovering from his brush with death. He marched over to him with a smile. He had tousled brown hair and was scarecrow skinny.

"You must be new to the Island! My name is Oddo."

Leo blinked at him.

The boy peered closely at him with big green eyes and frowned. " 'Odd-o,' I said." Still not getting a response from Leo, he yelled deliberately: "WHAT...IS...YOUR...NAME?"

Leo sunk back. "Don't shout..." He carefully stood, gripping the sides of the gondola with white knuckles and refusing to look over the edge. "My name is Leo. Leo Von Koppersmith." He looked back over at Zechariah, who was resting his hands on the heads of the children who clung to him, staring down at them solemnly. "Who are they, Zechariah?"

The tall man responded with a sudden, sharp expression. Tears had welled up in his eyes. He said nothing, but his anguished face and a small, fretful movement of his shoulders gave Leo a clear, painful answer: *I do not know.*

Oddo cupped one hand near his mouth and turned toward the balloon's driver, who was a little taller and not as thin. "Wilwell, you know what to do!"

The driver looked over his shoulder, beaming another smile, and his blue eyes flashed in the sun. "I'm already doing it!" He was spinning the big steering wheel and adjusting some small levers by his side, which Leo now saw were connected to the balloon's central burner by smooth wooden tubes like the ones that were part of the machinery back on the hollow mountain. The flames of the burner lowered and ligneous parts that were connected to the gondola's aft section began to gyrate or pivot.

With an amphoric rushing of wind the gray balloon swung around the hollow mountain and sailed in the direction of the other, taller mountain whose top stayed hidden above the clouds. Between the two peaks lay a forested valley, and the balloon began to slowly descend into it.

Leo realized another boy had moved close and was giving him a drowsy, good-natured smile. Of all the children he was the tallest and probably the oldest. His clothes were of thin brown and reddish wool and held together with fat rows of yellow stitching. All of the boys were dressed this way, and none of the clothes fit too well or were especially clean.

"Hello," said the boy in a slow voice that reminded Leo of a cartoon turtle. "My name is Benjamus. I am the strongest boy here."

"And I'm the smartest," Oddo interjected. "Well...the second smartest, I guess. Probably Wilwell is the smartest, but I'm the best at inventing and coming up with good plans. Benjamus is the oldest, but he isn't really...*comfortable* being the leader."

Benjamus smiled sleepily.

Oddo began listing the other boys' names, but Leo had no chance to attach them to their owners before Wilwell suddenly spun the steering wheel and sent the balloon lurching to the right, shouting with a controlled insistence, "Billodriffs! Heads down!"

The boys bent over and covered their heads, but Leo and Zechariah did not understand what was happening and saw no reason to behave similarly.

All of sudden Leo's ears were stunned by a piercing scream and he felt something brush his face. He recoiled, catching a glimpse of what seemed like a large bird, and felt a savage burn in his shoulder. He shrieked in pain and surprise and dove to the floor of the gondola.

Wilwell called out again, straightforward and reliable like an airplane pilot. "We're past 'em now! Heads up!"

The boys helped Leo up, and Benjamus could see him rubbing his shoulder and hissing. "Did a Billodriff get you?"

Leo looked back the way they had come. A flock of white and sapphire falcon-headed creatures filled the air. They were feathered, but they weren't flying. They traveled the air currents the way that jellyfish swim through the ocean, with malleable bodies that filled with air and discharged it in a series of hypnotic ripples. They *undulated*. Beneath them hung sharp, writhing tentacles.

Benjamus patted Leo's arm sympathetically, making Leo wince. "The stingers really hurt, don't they?"

Oddo grimaced. "Sorry about that! We told Zechariah to make 'em that way, but we shouldn't have!"

"Zechariah said it was best to just leave them as is." Wilwell called back. "He said it would help them to survive."

Leo stared after the bizarre animals as they moved like feathered ghosts into the distance. From here their cries sounded plaintive. He shook his head in bewilderment and edged his way over to Zechariah. "Where are we? What is going *on*?"

Seeing Zechariah's pale, tightly drawn face, he temporarily forgot his own disorientation. The tall man stared into Leo's eyes with a look that was desperate and pitiful. "I know these children…but I do not remember them! I do not remember what I am to them!"

Little Wilwell hopped in place and cried, "I can see home!"

The other boys crowded the edges of the gondola, staring below and pointing excitedly.

Leo looked and saw a blue river running through the middle of the valley. A little town of some kind was nestled up and down the banks.

One of the boys, a sturdy fellow with copper-blond hair and a toothy, goofy grin, raised his little arms in triumph and cheered. "Almost time, right Zechariah?"

This inspired a fresh wave of paroxysmal victory dancing and hollering. Various enthusiastic exhortations continued to be lobbed in Zechariah's general direction:

"You're going to really smash 'em, aren't you, Zechariah?"

"Squash 'em!"

"Throw 'em all right into the ocean, Zechariah!"

"Let the fish eat their guts up!"

"No, even fish don't want 'em!" "Even sharks don't want 'em!" "Even octopuses don't want 'em!"

Leo could see the buildings of the town more clearly now. Most of them were small and looked like the houses of an archaic village. There were two millwheels, but they were hanging off of

136

their axes and lying limply in the gliding waters. The entire town, Leo could now see, was in a state of disrepair and seemed deserted. One section looked like it had been struck by fire, judging from the black walls and charred, exposed rafters.

Something moved inside one of the houses.

They were still a long distance from the ground, so Leo thought at first that his eyes had deceived him. Then there was another movement among the houses in one of the un-burnt sections of the town. And then another. Dark black figures were darting everywhere, out of doorways or scuttling between houses.

"What are those?"

The copper-blond-haired boy with the goofy grin put his hands defiantly on his hips. "Those are dead Throtrex! They just don't know it yet!"

"Zechariah, are you feeling alright?" Oddo was holding Zechariah's wrist and staring up at him with tender concern. "And, incidentally, as long as we're on the subject, where were you trapped? In a dungeon?"

Wilwell steadied the wheel and let the balloon slowly sink straight downward into the valley, which allowed him to stop piloting the vessel and come give Zechariah a hug. "I'm sorry Walwich did that to you. I'm so glad you're back…"

Zechariah embraced him in return and then crouched before him, staring deeply into his blue eyes. "Please forgive me…but I do not remember your name."

Wilwell and Oddo laughed.

Leo bent down beside them. "Boys, he isn't kidding. Now, tell me what those things are down there. What are we doing?"

"In the valley below is Relm, our village. The Throtrex took it from us, but the Protector is about to take it back!"

The air turned warmer as they steadily neared the valley floor.

"It's almost time, Zechariah!" Benjamus was leaning over the rail as he said it.

A boy beside him with black hair and freckles jeered and shook his small fist at the dark black creatures below. "Bye-bye, you ugly stupid-balls! Zechariah's about to turn you inside out and squash you like flies!"

Benjamus hooted, and in his turtle voice he shouted, "Like flies! Like stupid-ball flies!"

Leo could now distinctly hear the sounds that the creatures made: a cacophony of shrieks and snarls that grew steadily louder as the balloon descended.

Leo glanced over the side.

Wiry humanoids with oily black skin were gathered in a riotous mob of hundreds upon hundreds directly below, their numbers constantly being added to as more and more swarmed from houses and from the surrounding forests. They were variously five, six, or seven feet tall. They all faintly resembled Chog in the way that they were neck-less and their mouths were long and fanged and almost in the center of their chests, with beady orange eyes staring like evil round coals. They leapt in place, squealing and jabbering. They swept their hands barbarously at the descending balloon, and Leo could see that their fingers ended in hard, black tapered claws.

Albert, the boy with the copper-blond hair, rested one robust arm on the rails and winked. "Get started anytime you like, Zechariah!"

Oddo pressed Zechariah's arm eagerly. "Yes! Get 'em! We want our village back!"

Wilwell fizzed with anticipation. "I can't wait!"

As the furious din of the massing humanoids grew louder, Zechariah slowly stood and gazed over the rails with profound bafflement. He looked around at the children, who were now beginning to notice his reluctance, and then at Leo.

"Can I do something? What can I do? How do I fight them?"

Leo scrambled over to Wilwell. "We have to go back up! Stop lowering us!"

Wilwell looked at him blankly.

"He's not who you think he is!"

Oddo chortled. "But he's the Protector…"

Leo gave the boy's skinny arm an emphatic throttle. "No! What I mean is: whatever you think he can do, *he can't do right now*! We're all going to be slaughtered if this thing lands! Get us back up!" Leo ran to the steering wheel and began frantically trying to work the controls.

Something struck the gondola.

Albert's toothy grin dissolved and a hyperbolic frown darkened his entire forehead. "Hey, that one nearly made it on board. Come on, Zechariah, we're just about to land. Get 'em!"

Benjamus and the black-haired boy began cheering in agreement, but Oddo quietly stood close to Zechariah, looking up at him with an expression of somber assessment.

Wilwell charged over to Leo's side. "Here, let me do it!"

With a pulling of levers and a rotation of the smaller wheels, flames burst out of the burner with a roar and the propeller angled downward at forty-five degrees.

The ground slowly stopped rising as the balloon painfully reversed its course, but the demonic clamor now filled everyone's ears. Rocks and debris from the village were being hurled at the swollen gray sides of the balloon.

Leo watched as Wilwell turned more levers and put his small pale hands firmly upon the steering wheel. "That's it! It's working! We're starting to go back up!"

The gondola lurched and tossed as the black humanoids jumped and struck its sides. Leo instinctively crouched.

Spiders wriggled on the edges of the gondola.

Leo looked closer and realized they weren't spiders—they were Throtrex hands. The long, tapered fingers were composed of reversible joints. They could bend in almost any direction, and were adjusting themselves along the rails of the gondola to find a better grip.

The creatures were hanging from the sides, and the balloon had stopped rising.

Suddenly one of the creatures lunged up and over and grabbed Oddo by the front of his shirt. Oddo howled.

From the long, chomping, gaping mouth came a voice unlike any Leo had ever heard, in tones that were like creaking metal and out-of-tune keys from the lowest part of a piano:

"Lit-tle boy bones and chew-y meat!"

Leo seized the creature's black claw to pull it loose, but as the fingers let go they bent completely backwards and enveloped Leo's hand like a trap.

The boys were now shrieking and running wildly with arms over their heads, except for Wilwell, who stood frantically adjusting the balloon's controls to overcome the weight of the creatures cleaving to the gondola.

Zechariah broke out of his mental paralysis and leapt to Leo's rescue. He put his full weight on the creature's arm to break its grip and then battered at the thing's facial area until it toppled off of the gondola.

Together Leo and Zechariah scrambled around the railing, pummeling at the screeching, wiry, ink-skinned stowaways until they had all tumbled back into the fulminating hordes now boiling among the houses of the village.

Seventeen

All the boys except Wilwell had decided that Zechariah was officially Sick, as a result of the time he spent in the Watchdog's "dungeon".

They all gathered around him and gave him reassuring hugs. Oddo promised him they would find a cure. "I don't know anything about medicine. But I'll learn!"

Albert tried to wipe away his tears of concern before anyone noticed. "You'll be back to yourself in no time, Zechariah!"

Leo was breathing normally again, now that what the boys called Relm was safely far below them again. They were nearing the altitude where the hollow mountain's peak sat like a snow-covered thumb, but were now on a course that was taking them around to the other side of the second, taller mountain.

"So, Zechariah is from here?"

"Of course," said Albert.

Benjamus snorted. "This is *his* island."

"So, what was *that*?" Leo gestured violently over the side of the rails towards the town in the valley.

"Those are the Throtrex," said Wilwell. "They're not supposed to be here."

Leo laughed humorlessly. "They're not supposed to be *anywhere*."

Wilwell's face did not register Leo's sarcasm, and his eyes stayed clear and sweet. "We all live on

Zechariah's Island. He protects us. He built our village. Everything was wonderful…"

Benjamus grabbed Leo's forearm and stared at him with wide eyes. "…Until Walwich betrayed him!"

"He changed his name to the Watchdog," said Oddo gloomily. "He was one of us, until he decided to help Kak. Kak made him a grown-up with special powers."

"He always wanted to be as strong as Zechariah." Wilwell frowned as he spoke. "He could never just be *happy*."

Oddo sighed. "He had a hump."

"A hump?"

"On his back. A big one. We always told him: 'nobody cares about the hump'! But he hated it, and he could never walk very well because he had a bad leg, and he always thought everybody was laughing at him."

Benjamus looked at Leo again with big, earnest eyes. "But we weren't!"

Zechariah, who had been quietly taking the conversation in, spread his arms in a gentle display of vexation. "I do not understand any of this. I have no memory, little ones. I'm afraid that I just don't know what you are all talking about."

Leo turned to Wilwell. "What do you mean 'Kak made the Watchdog a grownup?'"

Oddo interrupted before Wilwell could answer. "You don't get any older on Zechariah's island. You might as well get used to it."

"Huh? How old are you?"

"I'm nine years old. But I've been that way for a really long time."

"How long?"

Oddo shrugged. "I don't know. I don't really care. But Walwich did, and he asked Kak to make him older and handsome and with mighty powers and all that. So, Kak did it."

The boy with black hair and freckles pointed ahead excitedly. "I can see our tree!"

The sun fell radiantly on this side of the tall mountain and across the green, spreading forests. Leo could see, rising higher than the trees, what he thought at first were odd-looking buildings, shaped like huge mushrooms or shorter, theme-park versions of the Seattle Space Needle. There were nearly twenty of them, all of equal height (though some with slightly smaller tops than others) and all at equal distance from one another. Leo realized that those were what the boy was pointing towards.

"Those aren't trees. Are those trees?"

Oddo couldn't help but laugh at Leo's confusion. "They're Tabletop trees! I thought of them! I'm a great inventor."

Wilwell shook his head. "Zechariah made them. We just think up ideas, and, if he can, he makes them."

Zechariah stared blankly at Leo, so overwhelmed was he by what was happening and so exhausted with not being able to recall anything about his alleged life on the Island.

Another flock of white and blue Billodriffs drifted by, giving their mournful calls, but they were not close enough to be a threat. The Tabletop trees grew closer, until finally Leo could clearly see that one had a building on it: a big, square structure laced with ladders and narrow circular stairways. Each corner had a huge hot-air balloon made of painted fabric keeping it aloft and a thick mooring tying it to the tree.

There were people visible, as well; Leo was worried that they might be Throtrex, but it quickly became obvious that they were, in fact, more children. They had spotted the gray balloon and were climbing down from the floating house by rope ladders and gathering around the treetop's perimeter, waving exuberantly.

Albert breathed a sigh of relief as they sailed close enough for lines to be thrown and secured. "Whew! Home at last!"

The gondola settled with a light thump, and the gate was opened. The small crowd of waiting children, all of whom were boys, thronged about Zechariah, cheering and crying and hugging him. They ignored Leo for the moment, leaving him free to scrutinize the tree upon which he had landed.

It was far taller and wider than even an Oregon redwood, and the only branches were the ones Leo was standing on—clustered at the very top and spread out for almost two thousand feet in every direction. The individual leaves were smaller than Leo's hand, but packed so densely together that they made the top of the tree a vast light-green table, a huge, flat surface perfect for walking on and even building on.

Some parts of the tree's surface had ankle-high grass growing on it in small green and lavender-colored fields. From out of one field in the distance Leo saw a herd of domesticated animals being guided over to the balloon landing site by a couple of boys with shepherd's crooks.

Wilwell had wandered over from the ebullient crowd to stand next to Leo, with Oddo trailing behind. "Here come our Waywobs. You've never seen creatures like *these* back in the Rest-of-the-World!"

The boys watched Leo's face eagerly, waiting to see his reaction. At first the animals seemed to Leo to be very fat sheep, with typically thick brown or piebald wool and making the monotone bleats that any sheep makes. Leo made an involuntary grunting sound once he realized that they had no legs. They were completely round. They moved by rolling.

"Poor Waywobs," said Oddo. "They miss the big fields next to the village in the valley, I think. But this is nice, too."

The animals were of various sizes, young and old, and they rolled gently past like a pack of wooly, sheep-sized marbles. Below the facial areas were little retractable paws that could jut out and propel the bodies as needed. A brow of hard leather helped protect their eyes.

"Weird," Leo breathed, but he smiled. "And you *made* these? Like those Billo-jellyfish birds?"

Oddo stuck his hands into his pockets and puffed out his chest. "Yes!"

"*Zechariah* made them," said Wilwell with a disapproving frown at Oddo, who pulled his hands out of his pockets and held his hands up defensively.

146

"Of course! I just meant that I invented them…"

Wilwell continued frowning. "Actually, *I* thought them up. But you probably need more explanation since you just came from the Rest-of-the-World, Leo. See, Zechariah can't create things on his own; only with humans. If we give him ideas and some elements to work with, he can make living creatures!"

"Elements?"

"Correct," said Oddo professorially. "You have to give him something."

"I gave him some wool from the clothes I came to the Island in. Then I told him we really wanted some sheep. But they should be round."

Oddo nodded. "So they could roll. We thought it would be easier for them, so that they wouldn't have to walk around all the time."

Leo laughed ironically, but the sound suddenly caught in his throat. "Wait…what did you mean 'he can only create things with humans'? He *is* human."

Wilwell and Oddo both gave a firm "no" at the same time.

"He is a Protector. He's *our* Protector."

Leo disregarded this paradox, choosing to focus on what he could understand. "But then the Watchdog kidnapped him, and the Throtrex overran the Island."

"Yes, and we lost many of us when it happened. The rest of us moved from place to place, and finally made our home here on the Tabletops."

"Actually we started out on *that* one." Oddo pointed towards a Tabletop four away from the one on which they stood, cluttered with the remains of toppled structures. "We used to live there."

"What happened? Why did you leave?"

"The Throtrex. They got to us. They slowly climbed until they finally reached the top. We found out in time, and ballooned over here."

Leo scowled. "Then they could climb *this* one, too. They could be on their way up *now*..."

"No," said Wilwell hastily. "We climb halfway down every couple of days and smear the trunk with Waywob poop. Whenever they try to climb up they just slip and fall!"

Oddo began imitating the sounds of Throtrex falling to their deaths, and he and Wilwell broke into giggles.

Leo stared out across the other Tabletops receding into a gray-blue haze like a dream and wondered how he had ever gotten into this *Through-the-Looking-Glass* mess. Faraway to his left he could see a white beach haunted by gray-capped waves and he thought, *I don't even know what ocean that is.*

It wasn't until after he turned to rejoin the squawking, chattering gang of boys and their long-lost Protector that Crawlsome Bentpin appeared from a hiding place among the grasses on a neighboring Tabletop tree. His face remained hidden, as always, between his crumpled black top hat and the high collar of his long black coat with the multitudinous pockets, but his orange eyes simmered like two buttons of molten lead. Around

him shadows were slowly lengthening as the sun
began to set.

Eighteen

Bentpin was thinking about baseball.

Forty Throtrex were gathered by his side, silent except for occasional grunts or the passing of gas. They watched in the dusk, as little flames flickered to life in the lanterns strung upon the children's Balloon House, and waited to see how Bentpin planned to cross the more than five hundred feet of open air between the children's Tabletop tree and their own.

"*Baseball*," said Bentpin.

A whispery shudder ran through the ring of Throtrex in response. *"A what-what?" "A Base-Ball?" "What be a Base-Ball?" "Eat Base-Ball?" "Yes, eat Base-Ball!" "Into my mouth, Base-Ball!"*

"I saw it once, during one of my forays into human society. It's a game they play in Japan."

"A ja-what?" "Japan Base-Ball?" "Into my mouth, Japan!"

Bentpin hissed. *"Be quiet!"* He looked around judiciously at the Throtrex, settling on one with particularly enlarged shoulders and a broader back than the others. *"You. You're the Pitcher. And you,"* he pointed with his green forefinger to a second Throtrex. *"You're the Baseball."*

As the last light of the setting sun melted away and the first stars were firing in the east, they gathered at the perimeter of the tree, where one more step led straight downwards thousands of feet. Bentpin reached into a pocket on the lower right

150

sleeve of his long black coat and pulled out a four-inch long green bottle. There was a low popping sound as he pulled its cork.

The Baseball Throtrex stood with hands upon his side and full of conceit as Bentpin sprinkled some of the liquid from the bottle upon his black, taloned feet. Greenish steam wafted up with a hiss, and the next second the Throtrex was the size of a mere toy. He looked up at the others and gave an arrogant battle cry that came out as only a peep.

The Pitcher picked him up in one hand, so that his tiny orange eyes and fanged mouth were peeking out above the knuckles.

"Remember," Bentpin said to him, *"Once you're on the other side, drink the Anti-Smallsteam Bigifier and <u>wait there</u>."*

The Baseball peeped in acknowledgement.

The Pitcher reared back his arm and with a growl he hurled the Baseball. It squealed victoriously as it sailed over the expanse between the two huge Tabletop trees.

It struck the edge of the children's tree with a dry smack, but the orientation of the dense branches was such that it ricocheted backwards and plunged into the black pit between the trees with a tiny scream of terror that quickly diminished until there was nothing left to hear.

The remaining Throtrex were silent for a few seconds. Then they burst into giddy, maniacal laughter.

Bentpin began repeatedly smacking them. "*Be silent, you idiots!*" He turned to the Pitcher. "*Whatest be wrong with you? Can you not throw any better than that?*"

He reached into his right sleeve for another green bottle of *Smallsteam*; he was secretly vexed because he knew he was almost out. He had already used one bottle on the door back at the Watchdog's office in Chicago; the other one on the failed Baseball; now he only had two more left. Regardless, he had no intention of revealing that fact to the Throtrex, for it was important to him that everyone think of him as a genius of alchemy with endless supplies of all manner of potions. If the Throtrex suspected otherwise they might fear him less and see him only as a harmless runt to persecute, perhaps even to devour.

"*We need a new Baseball*," he hissed.

There were no volunteers, so Bentpin chose one. He gave him a wood flask containing more of the *Anti-Smallsteam Bigifier* (he had an excess of that), and then sprinkled *Smallsteam* on the volunteer's feet. A moment later the Throtrex was figurine-sized.

This time the Pitcher added extra force to his throw, and the Baseball rolled a full yard into the perimeter of the children's tree. After he came to a stop, he stood shakily on his tiny little legs, holding his mouth closed to keep from throwing up.

At last, he opened the top to the wooden flask Bentpin had given him, and in a few seconds was back to normal size. He gave the others a wave, which they, having better night vision than owls, could see easily.

Next came a long, thick rope taken from the children's abandoned village back in the valley; the Throtrex wrestled with it clumsily, finally got it spinning and tossed it over to the Baseball. Each end was tied down tightly.

"*I shall now reveal a secret to you,*" Bentpin hissed to the Throtrex before letting them cross over. "*Kak bethinks I am doing this for him, but he is wrong. Indeed will I encapture the Protector and then I will presentest him to the World King myself. He will see how complacent and lazy Kak has become, and then will I be given the authority that Kak has squandered! This will not be the island of Zechariah…it will not be the island of Kak, no, no, no…it will be the island of Crawlsome Bentpin! You will be a part of this glorious revolution! So, leave Zechariah to mine own…but the children are yours, meat for the Dark Feast!*"

···+·+·+·+·+·+

Wilwell stood confidently and quieted everyone down with hushing sounds and a wave of his arms. "It's the Spear! That's what's wrong with Zechariah!"

The other boys—there were nearly fifty of them living at the top of the tree, by Leo's count, not including a few outside on guard duty—all looked at one another and at Wilwell and most began nodding and murmuring enthusiastically. Their heavy shadows, cast by lanterns hung around one big corner room of the Balloon House, wobbled along with them, making their small, dirty, wondering faces and their pale forearms seem almost disembodied.

153

One boy with chestnut hair was unimpressed by Wilwell's assertion. "But he's the Protector! He doesn't need his Spear to be him!" He stopped to shovel down a spoonful of some kind of stew that was making the rounds throughout the room, and another boy took the opportunity to opine: "Besides, Kak has it! How would we get it back?"

Leo glanced across the room at the subject of the whole debate. Children surrounded Zechariah; they swung from beams above him or sat against his legs or in his lap. He sat in a large, stately chair padded with red pillows, a chair they had been saving in the corner for his eventual return—they even referred to the entire room as the Chair Room.

Zechariah's face was unreadable. He seemed content to just sit and listen, as if he was waiting for something to be said or for something to happen that would suddenly clear the clouds from his mind and reestablish his self-recognition.

"Can I have some of that?" Leo had spoken almost without realizing it, and the boys all stopped and looked at him. "That stew, or whatever it is. I'm starving." His face was stern.

"Of course!" Oddo hopped down from a ledge and grabbed the wood bowl out of the chestnut-haired boy's hands and trotted with it over to Leo. "Sorry about that. Here you go!"

Leo drove the spoon into the contents of the bowl and began stuffing himself. It didn't taste like any stew he had ever had, and was filled with unrecognizable lumps and objects, but it was good enough.

"Want some Waywob milk to wash it down?" Oddo grabbed one of many wooden goblets from which the children were drinking, and Leo accepted it suspiciously. It was creamier than the milk he was used to but, like the stew, it wasn't bad.

Albert, the tough-built boy with copper-blond hair, gave Leo a good-natured pat on the shoulder. "Sorry! Zechariah doesn't ever have to eat, so we just thought you were like him, since you're the Assistant Protector."

Leo stopped chewing, with the spoon still half in his mouth. "Assistant Protector?"

The boys all smiled or chuckled. "That's what we decided to call you," chirped Oddo. "We've been waiting a long time for the Protector to come back, and even though he's Sick we know you will protect us until he is all the way better…"

Leo blanched. He cleared his throat and looked at everyone stoically. "I'm here by accident, kids. I…*found* Zechariah, and then the Watchdog showed up and chased us here. I have no idea what's going on or who you all are, and I don't c…"

Leo almost said "I don't care" but, as desperate as he was feeling, it seemed too cruel. "I need to leave. I'm not from here. I need to go back home. You understand that, right? You have your Protector, and he can stay here with you—in fact, this is probably what Nicholas wanted to happen: Zechariah is back with you, everybody's happy, Nicholas is happy."

Leo handed the bowl to someone else, and his voice unintentionally became pedantic. "Now, I know it's after dark, so I'm going to spend the night here. But in the morning, I will need you to get that hot-air balloon going and take me back to the top of the mountain so I can see if the Wayover is still even there…"

Oddo's eyebrows lifted. "The Wayover? Oh, of course it's there! It's always there!"

Leo stood quickly. "What? It is? That's great!"

"But once you leave, you would need a flute to get back. If you have one of those you can open a door anywhere and come here…"

"That's fine. That's perfect. I have no plans to return, though, just so you know."

Wilwell walked slowly to Leo's side. "Did you say 'Nicholas'?"

Leo nodded gravely, unsure of Wilwell's reaction to the mention of his ghostly forebear's name.

"You *met* him?"

The other boys began to gather close to Leo, as well, and their faces had become as somber as Wilwell's. One of them muttered, "Where is Nicholas?"

"Well…" Leo wrung his hands. "He's dead." The boys nodded, or looked down and shifted their feet, or murmured unintelligibly.

"Why? How did you know about Nicholas?"

"He was our leader," said Wilwell. His upper lip was trembling slightly. "He was supposed to take care of us."

"He gave us away," said Benjamus gloomily.

A fat boy, with the stew bowl tipped over his mouth, finished the dregs and sighed heavily. "He

156

gave us to Kak. He sold us for millions of gold coins."

Leo stared in astonishment. "Are you telling me that all of you are…" He paused, struggling to say the impossible truth. "The Children's Crusade?"

The boys looked at him obtusely. Albert lazily scratched the side of his face. "The what?"

Leo looked at Zechariah, who continued to have nothing to say and very little reaction. Then he turned away from everybody in the room and laughed scornfully. "You must be their descendants or something, right? You can't be the *same children*."

The boys watched Leo quietly.

"The children who left Germany to liberate the Holy Land? Led by Nicholas of Hamelin? Met the pope? Disappeared somewhere around the Mediterranean, never to be heard from again?"

Benjamus looked at Leo with his wide, innocent eyes. "We never made it! There was a big ocean in the way."

"So Nicholas sold us." The words caught in Albert's throat as he said them.

Leo blinked doltishly. "But that was over eight hundred years ago…" *You don't get any older on Zechariah's island*, Oddo had said back in the hot-air balloon.

At that moment a panting boy in a wool cap charged into the room from outside. "*Throtrex!*"

Nineteen

Wilwell tensed up like a bowstring. "Throtrex? Where?"

"Here!" gasped the boy in the wool cap. "They are on the tree!"

Through the walls they all heard an inhuman shriek, and then another, followed by the cries of the boys who had been keeping guard outside.

The room erupted in a volcano of activity. Many of the boys gathered close to Zechariah, and one of the youngest, not more than six years old, stared up at him and asked:

"Is it time, Zechariah? Are you going to make them go away at last?"

Zechariah cupped the boy's face and stared into his eyes with a look of anguish. The other boys huddled closer, asking the same kinds of questions, or confidently cheering him on: "Break them Throtrex to bits, Zechariah! Go get 'em!"

Zechariah looked at each of them until he couldn't bear it anymore. He stood straight, clenching his fists, shutting his eyes tightly. He opened them again when he felt Wilwell's small hand on his wrist.

"If you aren't ready yet, Zechariah, that's alright. Shall I have us release the moorings and move the Balloon House to a new tree?"

Tears filled the corners of Zechariah's eyes. "I'm sorry, little one. Yes, I think you had better do that."

Wilwell smiled up at him reassuringly and then whirled to face the other boys, who were in various modes of panic. "We're releasing the moorings and moving to a new tree, everybody! Quickly—you know what to do!"

The children assembled loosely into three groups and exited the room in a rush. Zechariah, Wilwell, Oddo and Benjamus stayed behind.

Leo stood where he was, braced for he-knew-not-what. "Wait—*I* don't know what to do! What are we doing?"

"This!" Wilwell scampered up a ladder to a loft where a long, thick lever protruded. He pulled it down sharply.

A clatter and rumble of gears and shifting weights followed, traveling down the length of the cable hanging underneath their section of the house, causing the mechanical claw at the end to release its grip on the tightly wound branches of the Tabletop and retract. The entire room tilted like a raft on an ocean wave and everyone stumbled as that corner of the Balloon House drifted free in the wind.

"Now," Wilwell shouted, "Just three more to go! This is how we escaped the Throtrex the last time. As soon as the levers are pulled at the other three corners of the house, we'll be safe in the sky in no time at all!"

Leo shook his head. "But they're already here! They're probably in the house by now!"

"Leo is right," said Zechariah, "Wilwell, we must help the others."

"Right!" Wilwell scrambled down from the loft and everyone jogged along after him out of the room and down a long hall.

The Balloon House was a haphazard creation, with passages that took them up ladders lashed to the wall or over thin, wriggling rope bridges, opening suddenly to the outside and then back inside again. The outside parts revealed radically opposed images: above, a glorious, sweeping night sky glimmering like an upside-down ocean of stars, but below, Throtex moving like wraiths back and forth beneath the floating house, carrying struggling, shouting children on their shoulders or chasing bleating, rolling Waywobs. A fire had broken out at the furthermost corner of the house. None of the other three moorings had yet been released.

"Zechariah!" A boy stood on a torch-lit platform on another section, stretching his arms out. "Protect us!"

Zechariah raised one hand reassuringly. "Stay where you are…"

A Throtrex galloped over the roof from out of the dark and tackled the boy on the platform. Squealing victoriously, he threw the writhing boy across his shoulder and leapt off the house.

"Zechariah, we have to keep moving!" Leo tried to pull him along, but he wouldn't budge. His eyes were clenched tightly again, and Leo saw that it was more than frustration; he was in some kind of physical pain.

"Leo," he said, his voice strained and heavy with emotion, "Help me. I do not understand what is happening to me."

Leo faced him, holding him tightly by the shoulders. "What is it, Zechariah? Tell me what's wrong!"

"I must protect them, Leo! I must…but I am unable!" He held his stomach and tried to take a step, but whatever mysterious agony he was experiencing overwhelmed him.

Leo helped him stand upright. "Wilwell and the others have already reached the next corner of the house, Zechariah. We need to make sure that lever gets pulled…Throtrex are already on board…"

The low, rumbling vibrations of turning gears ran through the floorboards. The Balloon House lurched as a second corner was released from its mooring. There were now only two more corners of the house still tied to the tree.

Wilwell, Oddo and Benjamus sped out of a doorway. "Zechariah! Leo! We pulled the lever, but we can't go that way anymore. There are Throtrex everywhere!"

They all turned and ran back the way they had come, towards the Chair Room. The fire Leo had seen lapping at the Balloon House's farthest corner had spread rapidly in the brisk winds. Children were leaping from flame-filled windows to the tree's surface below.

"Zechariah!" Everyone turned to see Benjamus recoiling from a Throtrex clambering over the side of a rail like a black insect.

Zechariah fell to one knee under another wave of pain.

Leo jumped over him. He charged like a linebacker, colliding with the Throtrex, his forehead squashing against its damp, rubbery skin. The creature was driven off of the house, screeching and furiously flailing its arms.

Benjamus was wide-eyed and breathing heavily. "Thank you, Leo," he said in his turtle-voice.

At Leo's urging, the boys continued on hastily to the Chair Room. After they disappeared down a ladder leading inside the house he felt a mild relief, but it only transformed into horror the moment he turned back around.

The section of the house that had caught fire at last collapsed to the Tabletop surface in a roar of flames and twisting wood, dragging its huge, deflated balloon with it. Although they were now held to the tree by only one last mooring, the lever to release it was in a section that had caught fire, as well, and the hot flames were already beginning to eat their way up to the Chair Room. If the Balloon House took flight now, it would only be a flying inferno with Leo, Zechariah and the boys trapped inside.

Demonic snarling and the cries of children filled the night air. Throtrex were everywhere, scuttling furiously along the roofs and down walls, their claws clicking against the surfaces and leaving trails of gouge marks. Leo shifted in place uselessly as Throtrex steadily closed in.

Zechariah had finally stumbled to his feet. His face was a sweating mask of despair. Nothing

Leo said or did could make him move. The Throtrex, gibbering and chomping their enormous jaws, were getting nearer.

"Zechariah!" Leo looked imploringly at the tall, mysterious man whose home, until recently, had been an ancient grave. "I'm prepared to accept that you are more than what you appear to be. So, if you are, then *please*—you have to do something! We are all about to die!"

Zechariah gasped. His body trembled.

Something changed in the man's eyes. They caught the reflection of flame and starlight, deepening like a sudden plunge into the ocean.

"Leo...I remember! I know who I am!"

The scurrying Throtrex stopped their advance; some of them drew back cautiously. It was the same Zechariah that Leo had met less than ten hours before, but now radiating an invisible, unearthly power that all those near him sensed.

The phenomenon passed like new paint melting in the rain. Swaying unsteadily, he became seized with panic and his chest began to palpitate.

"The children! They need my help!"

Suddenly he clasped his hands to his face, bent backwards and let out a guttural cry, a primitive explosion of fury and fear and resolve. It seemed to carry every last molecule of air out of him, and he fell to the ground in an unconscious heap.

Seeing this, the Throtrex slowly but surely began to reassert themselves.

Leo seized Zechariah and dragged his body to the ladder leading back down inside the Balloon House. They fell down the chute, but Leo was too frightened to feel the pain. Reaching up, he closed a trap door at the top of the ladder and bolted it shut.

The bedlam outside was now muffled. Into that relative silence came the small sound of a cork being pulled from a bottle.

Leo turned to see a squat, darksome person in a long, black coat with an excess of pockets of different shapes and sizes. He wore a black top hat, and his collar was pulled up high, so that all Leo could see of his head were two orange eyes peering out. He stood close beside Zechariah's unconscious body with a green bottle in his scaly hand.

"*Crawlsome Bentpin me is,*" he announced with a slithery voice. "*You be him who rolled the Watchdog down the mountain. Who are you?*"

Leo told him.

"*Leave this island, for its king shall be me after I deliverest my prize. Then will I hunt down anyone unloyal and be-hand them over for the Dark Feast.*"

Around Zechariah's body he poured a liquid from the bottle. As it splashed upon the floor it turned to hissing, writhing steam.

And Zechariah shrunk to the size of a mouse.

Deftly, almost gracefully, Bentpin took out a small wooden box, reached and put Zechariah's tiny body into it with a rude swat. He snapped the lid closed and tucked the box under his right arm.

There was a crash as Throtrex, at that moment, broke in part of the trap door at the top of the ladder. While Leo was distracted, Bentpin turned on his ungainly black shoes and padded quickly down the hallway.

164

"No!" Leo ran after him, feeling more alone and desperate than he had ever felt in his life.

He caught a glimpse of Bentpin turning a corner ahead, but when Leo turned the same corner there was a small splintering of glass and he was enveloped in a tar-black cloud that swirled slowly around him. Leo felt his throat lock up.

Howls and screeches filled the hallway behind him. The Throtrex had destroyed the rest of the trapdoor and were inside.

Leo thought he was going to die. His lungs were burning. Mucus flowed fast out of his nose and he was virtually blind from the pools of hot, salty tears in his eyes. He weakly crawled forward out of the swirling, black cloud, hacking and wheezing.

"*Chokesmoke!*"

Leo knew it was a Throtrex that had spoken; he recognized the creaking-metal-and-out-of-tune-piano-key tone he had heard back in the children's valley. The Throtrex were now behind the black cloud they called *Chokesmoke*, waiting for it to dissipate.

He forced himself to his feet, still coughing and blowing mucus, trying to suck air down his windpipe, which now felt like it had contracted to the diameter of a strand of hair. Throtrex barked and howled impatiently behind the *Chokesmoke*.

Leo stumbled down the hall, still unable to see well. He saw a blurry dark shape moving somewhere ahead and he staggered towards it, thinking it was Bentpin. All he knew, all he could think about, was that he absolutely had to get back that small wooden box with Zechariah in it.

There was an escalation of Throtrex babble behind him. The *Chokesmoke* was starting to vanish.

Suddenly he heard Wilwell's voice nearby: "Leo, help us!"

Leo had lurched into the Chair Room without even realizing it. He clawed the tears out of his eyes and found Crawlsome Bentpin rolling on the floor with the wooden box clutched tightly under his right arm. Wilwell, Oddo, and Benjamus were clinging to his arms and legs and pummeling him with their tiny fists.

Bentpin hissed and cursed. "*Get off of me! Let me go! When comes the Dark Feast I will devour you myself...!*"

Right then the Balloon House reached its structural limits and came apart forever. One half of it was already a pile of burning wreckage, and the spreading fire had burned through the final mooring until it had snapped loose at last. The whole structure leaned sharply, sending everyone rolling. The two giant, painted balloons holding up their part remained inflated, but the wooden beams and buttresses that connected it to the other half disintegrated. The Balloon House split in two. The burning half tumbled down upon the Tabletop in a heap, while the half with the Chair Room and Leo and the others sailed off into the night sky, two rounded sections still held together by long passages. It resembled a huge brown bone with a balloon on either end. Propellers were mounted on the outside, but there was no one piloting them.

The floor swayed beneath his feet, but Leo drove himself, zigzagging, towards Bentpin.

166

Screeching sounds made him glance back towards the hallway, where he saw the Throtrex making their way to the Chair Room. There were eight of them.

Bentpin lay upon the floor, watching Leo's inexorable approach. He hissed furiously, and from another pocket he produced a glass jar, wrapped in cord, with a cap stabbed full of holes. He unscrewed the cap and shook the wriggling contents at the wall behind him.

Oddo, who had recovered from the jolts of the Balloon House tearing apart, pointed at Bentpin indignantly. "Hey, those are our *Maggiore Termites*!"

Twenty-five fat two-inch long reddish-white termites gathered on the wall where Bentpin had tossed them and immediately they began to devour the wood. Each insect had more than one saw-like row of teeth and, making clicking sounds as loud as castanets, they burrowed into the wall like it was made of sand. In seconds they ate a man-sized hole in the wood and fell right through into the dark night air still clicking and chewing voraciously.

Bentpin scampered towards the hole. Clutching the wooden box with Zechariah in it, he pulled himself with his free hand to the rim of the opening and prepared to jump.

"Stop him!" Leo cried.

Wilwell and Benjamus leapt and grabbed hold of Bentpin's oar-shaped black shoes.

The remnant of the Balloon House was slowly spinning, rushing through the dark high above the island. The eight Throtrex coming up the hallway, though badly off-balance, had nearly reached the Chair Room.

Leo pounced and fell upon Bentpin. He locked his fingers around the wooden box and pulled, but he couldn't make the scoundrel loosen his green scaly fingers. The wind rushed past the gaping hole that the *Maggiore Termites* had made.

Suddenly Oddo joined the fray. He sunk his little teeth into the green flesh of Bentpin's hand, making the orange-eyed creature squeal.

All at once the balloon on the other corner of the house deflated. Deprived of buoyancy, that section snapped off. The eight Throtrex who had been making their way up the hallway to the Chair Room fell backwards in a shrieking rabble of claws and fangs. The entire hallway disappeared, and Leo caught a glimpse of enormous segments of the Balloon House and ropes and gears and balloon fragments and wailing Throtrex falling into the pit of night. Now, all that was left of the children's marvelous house was the corner section with the Chair Room and the one last balloon that held it aloft.

Bentpin wrenched out from underneath Leo and the boys with a power born of sheer desperation. There was a tear of fabric as he launched himself over the rim of the termite hole and into the blowing winds and the darkness. As he reached the apex of his leap he pulled the cork from another bottle.

Benjamus pointed and shouted, "*Snowball!*"

A massive globe of snow, twice the size of a Blue Whale, encompassed Bentpin in an instant. It fell in silence.

The remains of the Balloon House—just one cracked section, with a single painted balloon holding it in the air—sped on rushing winds farther into the dark. There was no way for Leo or the children to see where they were going or stop their flight, and they all screamed when their poor craft crashed suddenly through the tops of trees, one after another after another. Something broad and solid brought them to a final halt, slinging them against the wall. Dead silence followed.

Twenty

Leo felt pain.

It pinched the nerves up and down his body and pulsed in his joints. His face was hot. When he finally opened his eyes they were stabbed by rays of glaring sunlight pouring in through the hole that Bentpin's termites had made in the wall. Everything was quiet except for a whirring insect somewhere and a low, mournful breeze blowing through the shattered Chair Room.

Leo rolled over clumsily, groaning with the small shockwave of aches and pains that accompanied the movement. He stood shakily, and out of the other big hole in the wall he saw rocks and a small cliff, and a forest descending beyond it.

A pathetic croak drew his attention to the shadows of one corner of the Chair Room. Leo's eyes adjusted and he discovered Wilwell, Oddo and Benjamus lying in a heap, just beginning to stir.

"Boys…" Leo bent down and gently helped them sit up. "Are you O.K.?" There was dried blood on their faces and arms, but it looked like it was all from only minor cuts.

Leo stepped carefully over broken protruding planks and explored outside.

The air was warm and pleasant. The Chair Room and its surrounding segments and its flat, torn balloon lay upon a bare ridge. Green pine trees and oaks lay below but also above for a short way before thinning out, and farther up, rising like a tower, was the hollow mountain where Leo and Zechariah had first landed. The other, taller mountain stood across the valley, its peak still obscured by dense gray and white clouds.

Leo ducked back inside the Chair Room to check on the boys. "We've landed on the hollow mountain. The one where you guys first found me."

They were still sitting. Wilwell mumbled, "Mount Hollowchest. That's what we call it."

"Right..." Leo had started to feel a strange, mild elation all of a sudden, because they were somehow still alive, and because they had gotten closer to the Wayover and home, but now Wilwell's subdued tone caught his attention.

"Hey, are you alright? Is something hurting?"

The boys drew up their legs and began to cry. It was a sad, hopeless chorus of little sounds; Oddo sounded like a forsaken puppy, Benjamus like a heart-broken turtle, and Wilwell like a boy trying not to cry.

"Boys? What is it? What's wrong?"

"Everyone's gone!" whined Oddo, with tears dripping down his cheeks. "All the other boys! There's just us now...and first we lost our town... now our Balloon House..."

"And all the Waywobs..." Benjamus spluttered.

"...yes, the Waywobs!" Oddo suddenly became incensed and he smacked his thighs with his little fists. "Those stupid, awful Throtrex!"

Wilwell tried to speak, but only coughed. He recovered his breath, wiping his nose with the back of his hand. "And now Zechariah's gone, too! We

171

had been waiting for so long for him to come back, but as soon as he does he just disappears again!"

"Zechariah…" Leo began scanning the floor. He checked the area where he awakened a few minutes before.

Oddo stood. "What is it, Leo?"

"Here it is!" Leo bent and picked up something. He turned and proudly showed them the wooden box. It was half wrapped in black cloth. "Come here, boys. You should see this." He sat down so he could be on their level, and they gathered around him. Leo lifted the latch on the box and opened it.

The boys gasped. "Zechariah! He's been shrunk! Bentpin used *Smallsteam* on him!"

Oddo peered closer. "What's wrong with him?"

Leo put his fingers on Zechariah's tiny chest and felt the diminutive heart beating inside. "He's fine. He's just unconscious." He quickly explained what happened outside of the Balloon House the night before. "I just think his circuits got overloaded."

The boys stared at him blankly.

"I mean: his system shut down."

They still didn't comprehend, and he knew it was because his analogies were too modern for thirteenth century children. "Sometimes a person can't understand something, and it becomes so hard on them that their brains have to fall asleep." The boys nodded.

"So, how do we make him un-shrink?"

"With *Anti-Smallsteam Bigifier*," said Oddo. "But we don't have any…"

Wilwell cut him off. "It wears off, too, Oddo, remember? After thirteen hours."

Leo peered out at the sun. "Hmm. It's been thirteen hours, I'm sure."

Benjamus smiled his lazy smile. "He could grow back anytime now!"

Leo started to stand up again, and as he rose the black cloth that had been half-wrapped around the box fell to the floor. It landed with a heavy clunk.

The boys bent down and examined it. They turned it over and found that it had a pocket sewn onto it. Inside was a green bottle.

Oddo jumped up excitedly and handed it to Wilwell. "It's *Smallsteam!*"

They all realized that the black cloth was part of Crawlsome Bentpin's coat sleeve, and that it must have torn off the night before during the struggle for the wooden box.

"We'll keep this safe," said Wilwell proudly. "This could really help us later on, maybe." He searched the riff raff scattered around the room until he found a cloth satchel to put the *Smallsteam* in, then he turned to Leo. His small, pale face now glowed, having lost the despair it had been wearing only a few minutes before. "So, what is your plan, Assistant Protector?"

Leo pursed his lips. "Now, don't start that 'Assistant Protector' thing. I'm just Leo. And, I hate to break it to you, fellas, but I don't have a plan."

The boys all slumped their shoulders.

Leo cleared his throat. "What I mean is… well, I guess the first thing is that we need to find somewhere safe. Some shelter. Right now we're just sitting on an exposed ridge on the side of Mount… what'd you call it, Benjamus? Mount Hollowchest? Throtrex could attack us from any direction anytime they wanted. And we need fresh water. And food."

The boys' faces all brightened again. "Let's take a look and see where we are," said Wilwell, and they all tramped out of the Chair Room and onto the ridge. Leo followed them, gingerly carrying the box containing Zechariah's miniature body.

Wilwell scanned the valley. "Yes, I see where we are! You can't see Relm from here, but it's back there." He pointed in a roughly northwest direction.

"Good," said Leo, "Because we want to be as far away from there as we can. What are *those*?" He found himself stepping back to allow a swarm of bubble-shaped bugs go by. On the underside of each bubble were two blue dot eyes, and gossamer bodies with wide feet that they paddled to propel themselves through the air.

"Scumps," said Benjamus.

"What are they *doing* to you?"

Some of the Scumps had landed on Benjamus' and Oddo's exposed neck and forearms.

"Sucking the salt off us. They would do that all day if we let them." The boys casually brushed the Scumps off and batted them in the direction that the rest of the swarm had gone.

"The Fillwishing River is down there," Wilwell continued, pointing southeast, "going that way. You can see it there…" Leo looked, and there was indeed a silvery blue ribbon weaving among the trees of the forest far in the distance.

"Good again," said Leo, "There's fresh water. One important need down, two to go. How about some temporary shelter? Any ideas?"

Wilwell nodded enthusiastically. "Oh, yes. We could hide inside Mount Hollowchest."

Oddo's ears perked up like a puppy's. "Yes! We could get the Fishboat!"

Wilwell nodded again. "That's what I was thinking, too, Oddo. We could use the Fishboat to go downriver and find the Hair Coat."

Leo glowered at them. "Get the Fishboat to get the Hair Coat? What is this, a Dr. Seuss book? What in the world are you guys talking about?"

Wilwell explained that farther downriver was an area the boys called 'the Tunneltrees'. It used to belong to the children, of course, but had been overrun by Throtrex in Zechariah's absence. In fact, it had been claimed exclusively by Crawlsome Bentpin as a kind of private fortress.

"So, why would we want to go there?"

"Because that's where we left the Hair Coat." The boys stared at Leo as if he now had all the information he could possibly need.

"What is a Hair Coat?"

Benjamus' eyes grew very wide and serious. "It's a coat...made out of hair!"

Leo stuffed one hand into his pocket and rubbed the side of his face, trying to remain patient. "Thank you, Benjamus, I'm fairly sure I could have guessed that much myself, given enough time. What do we want a coat made of human hair for?"

"Not human hair," Oddo corrected him with an upraised forefinger, "The *Protector's* hair! It cannot be burned! Anyone who wears it is safe from fire— even the parts that aren't covered, like your head and your legs."

"Right," interjected Wilwell. "And we'll need that when we face Kak."

Leo winced. "What?! Face Kak? What are you talking about? Why would we do that?"

"To get Zechariah's Spear back!"

A distant high-pitched roar rose from the trees somewhere to the northeast, causing everyone's heads to snap in that direction.

"Throtrex," grumbled Leo. "They may have spotted the Balloon House wreckage. We should go."

Before he could move there was a snap.

Zechariah instantly inflated to normal size in Leo's arms, crushing the box and causing Leo to double over and fall to the ground.

Leo struggled to pull his arms free while the boys cheered and crouched down around Zechariah. They shook his shoulders and called to him, but he remained unconscious.

Leo, standing again, looked concerned. "I kind of wish he could have stayed shrunk for just a little while longer. I don't know how far I can carry a big guy like that, and I'm worried the Throtrex will catch up to us. Why won't he wake up?"

"Well," said Oddo, "We do have more *Smallsteam*. We could shrink him again."

"We shouldn't waste it," said Wilwell. "I have another idea." He led them back inside and ran to a corner of the Chair Room where he found lying on its side that for which the room was named: the large chair with royal red padding that had always stayed reserved for Zechariah. The other boys helped him lift it upright.

Oddo whistled approvingly. "Oh, I see what you're thinking..."

Wilwell stood beside the chair with his hands loosely folded in front of him. He closed his eyes.

Leo cocked his head to one side. "What are you doing, Wilwell?"

"Shhh," said the other two boys.

Another Throtrex howl sounded from the slopes of the mountain, still distant but—Leo could have sworn—closer. "What's he doing?" he whispered.

"Asking for Life," whispered Benjamus.

Leo heard more Throtrex calls. Apprehensive, he darted outside, his eyes skimming down the mountainside.

A mournful cry in the air caught his attention. Nearly a hundred yards above, a thick flock of the white and blue creatures with feathered jellyfish bodies were drifting by, their tentacles writhing gently beneath them.

Leo sighed with relief. "Never mind," he called to the boys. "I think it's just those... Billodriffs..."

A snarl and an answering snarl came from the forest. And another roar. *Definitely Throtrex*, thought Leo. *Definitely coming this way.*

"Boys, we have to go!" Leo burst into the Chair Room, only to be shushed by Oddo and

Benjamus again. Wilwell continued to stand quietly with his eyes closed.

"No, boys, we have to go *now*!"

Oddo grabbed his arm. "Wait, please! It's taking longer than usual, I suppose because Zechariah is not awake. But Wilwell is good at this...much better than me, I'm *terrible* at it, I can *never* do it..."

Benjamus sighed. "He can't do it at all..."

"Benjamus, you don't have to *say* it!"

"I only said it because *you* said it..."

Leo derailed the conversation, shoving Oddo and Benjamus out of the Chair Room.

Then the chair jumped. Leo froze, staring in disbelief. It didn't merely lift into the air as if in response to a tremor in the ground, but its four legs actually bent and propelled it upwards.

Wilwell opened his eyes and let out a long satisfied breath.

The chair took one timid step forward with its front right leg, testing the floor.

And it had eyes now, Leo realized. Two dark, oval eyes on the front of the seat, with an expressive brow to go with them.

The chair trotted forward confidently, experimenting with movement. Finally it turned to Wilwell, staring anticipatively with its dark eyes.

"Excellent, Wilwell!" shouted Oddo. "Its not just a chair anymore! It walks with us—it's a Conambulator!"

Benjamus, who had been clapping, stopped and frowned. "I can't say that. Let's just say 'Walkchair'."

Wilwell smiled up at Leo. "He can carry the Protector!"

For a few seconds Leo stood with his mouth hanging open in mute shock, snapping out of it only when the terrible sounds of the approaching Throtrex rattled through the air. "We," he stammered, pointing his finger at Wilwell, "are going to talk about this later…" Then he ran outside to fetch Zechariah.

"It's like…trying…to move…*Hercules*…" grunted Leo, as he dragged Zechariah inside and on to the Walkchair. It took nearly a full minute of sweating and pulling, while the howling and snarling sounds from the forest grew closer. Finally, they had Zechariah reliably strapped on with fragments of rope pulled from the wreckage.

"But how fast can it go?" said Leo, gesturing to the Walkchair.

"Run!" commanded Wilwell. The Walkchair scuttled at high speed onto the sunlit ridge. "But we shouldn't say 'it'. We should say 'he'."

The boys, looking like three elves in their dirty brown and reddish wool clothes with the yellow stitching, sprinted across the ridge and onto the forested slope. Leo went last. As he ran, he stared in wonder at the chair. It didn't run like a dog, but like a bug, except with four legs instead of six. It was faster than any of them, though not as agile. It was still made of wood, and yet the wood was somehow pliable, so that the legs could bend adequately and send it hopping over small obstacles and around tree trunks.

A hellish choir of grunts and yowls went up from the ridge behind them. The Throtrex had found the Balloon House wreckage. Leo wondered how good they were at tracking. Did they have a keen sense of smell?

Speeding in and out of Leo's field of vision was a gallimaufry of life-forms that would be heterochthonous anywhere else on earth: oval-shaped things with propeller wings on their heads that made cooing sounds as they passed; turtles with long arms growing out of the tops of their shells; trees with branches that looped and burrowed into the ground; spotted rodents with legs like stilts and ropey tails; shuffling, furry blobs; birds that changed colors. There was no time to pay attention, and even if there had been Leo was not sure he would have wanted to.

The trees flew by, and the ground kept sloping downward at a moderate angle. They were even on the remains of a trail, Leo realized. "Where are we going?"

"We are trying to find the secret entrance to the mountain!" Oddo shouted back.

"There are many of them," said Benjamus, panting laboriously, clearly not the best runner. "But only one on this side."

The barking of many Throtrex could be heard distinctly behind them.

"Where is it, Oddo?"

"It's close!"

Limbs smacked Leo in the face as he ran. He was not going at full speed, although he certainly wanted to; he forced himself to stay at the rear. Throtrex sounds seemed to fill the forest.

The ground began to level out. The trees had begun to change, as well, with fewer pines and oaks and more tropical-looking plants: breadfruit trees and philodendrons and spongy vines.

Leo glanced over his shoulder anxiously, expecting to see oily black figures in pursuit. He didn't see any, but he was definitely hearing them. "Where's that secret entrance?"

"It's close!" shouted Oddo.

"You said that already!"

"Oddo remembers," said Wilwell. "He'll find it!"

The Conambulator was now hopping as much as running since they had entered a low-lying area pocked with little pools of water and slow-moving streams. Benjamus slipped on a muddy bank and fell hard to the ground. Leo helped him up, but it was an agonizing use of precious seconds during which Throtrex noises grew noticeably louder.

Oddo suddenly stopped. His face was red with fury and he raised his stick-shaped arms to heaven. "I can't find it! Where is that stupid secret entrance?!"

Leo motioned him on frantically. "Don't stop, Oddo! It's O.K.! Just keep going!"

All at once the trees cleared and they found themselves surrounded.

Twenty-One

Leo halted abruptly and stood perfectly still like a statue, his hands raised conciliatorily. Wilwell shouted for the Walkchair to stop, and it did.

A large, gray colored pond took up most of the space in the clearing. Congregated around it were tree frogs—tree frogs that were three feet tall and standing on their hind legs like talking animal characters from some eighteenth century English children's book.

Leo stood directly beside one of them. He had almost smashed into it. It stood staring up at him with bright green goggle eyes.

Leo reflexively winced, and a thrill of terror went through him. He could only think of stories he'd read of Amazonian reptiles that spat poison, or did something horrible with projectile teeth…

It croaked, and the sound was almost deafening, as if a gargantuan cicada had made it. Leo cried out and stumbled back with arms up to protect his face from projectile teeth.

When he lowered his hands, the tree frog stood watching him.

"Gollyplox!" Oddo jumped high into the air, grinning as if the circus had come to town. He ran to the tree frog creature beside Leo and gave him a loving embrace around the neck.

"These are Cheevilnids, Leo! We haven't seen them in ages!"

Wilwell was grinning, too. "We didn't even think they were still alive!"

Branches were snapping farther up the slope of the mountain. Throtrex noises were getting louder by the second.

"Gollyplox!" said Oddo. "We can't find the secret door, and the Throtrex are coming. Please help us!"

The creature, Gollyplox, responded with a loud croak and a *crick-crick-crick cheeeeep*. The other Cheevilnids straightened up like a quiver full of little green arrows, then burst into action.

They leapt, and Leo had never seen anything leap like that. He had seen kangaroos hop and dogs jump for Frisbees. He had visited a wildlife preserve once when the park ranger told him stories of a red wolf jumping to the top of an eighteen foot high fence in order to escape. These were nothing compared to the Cheevilnids' leaps. Clear across the pond, or from the ground to the tops of trees—the equivalent of jumping to the chimney top of a two-story house—the Cheevilnids made it with ease. They hopped in the direction of the oncoming Throtrex, and met the fearsome dark monsters just as they came smashing through the brush.

The Cheevilnids swarmed around them, letting them chomp at them and swipe at them with their spidery, multi-jointed claws, but never getting close enough to be struck. The Throtrex became frenzied.

"*Eat frog!*" "*Can't catch, can't catch!*" "*Into my mouth, juic-y frog!*"

Gollyplox patted Leo on the leg and chirped, then hurtled over the boys and the Walkchair in a direction leading away from the Throtrex.

"Come on!" shouted Oddo. "Follow him!"

They all bolted through a mat of ferns and mushrooms and into a grove of mossy trees. Leo looked over his shoulder to see the entire tribe of green, rubber-limbed Cheevilnids pestering the Throtrex and goading them into pursuing them deeper into the forest. The Throtrex were livid, but couldn't seem to get their claws around a single Cheevilnid.

Leo stumbled over a root, and then nearly collided with a fallen tree draped in vines. He regularly caught glimpses of the Walkchair scuttling along with Zechariah bobbing in the seat, or of the boys chasing along behind the preternaturally agile Gollyplox, but there was no doubt they were moving into the wildest deeps of a jungle.

How could Oddo be so sure that this tree frog man really knew where the secret entrance to the mountain was? Was there really even a secret entrance?

Oddo, he remembered all of a sudden, seemed given to bold, unsupported statements. Maybe all they were really doing was just getting themselves permanently lost.

The jungle air was bristling with the harsh racket of squawking Throtrex and croaking Cheevilnids and of undergrowth being crushed beneath their uproarious brawl, which was really just a lethal game of cat-and-mouse.

Then the Walkchair and Zechariah disappeared from view. Leo craned his neck as he ran, but he didn't see them.

Next, Wilwell vanished.

Leo caught up to where he last saw him just in time to find Oddo clambering down a small cave in the ground. Gollyplox stood beside it, rocking on his spindly legs and waving everyone in. Benjamus stumbled in next, and finally Leo. The rim of the cave, as he passed into it, was decorated with swirls etched into the stone and little bits of colored glass similar to the kind used on the Rainbow Crown.

They crawled on hands and knees for a long time through a dark tunnel, like a parade of moles. Leo felt cold puddles of water soaking his trousers or fat insects being squashed beneath his palms.

"We're here!" It was Wilwell's voice, somewhere ahead in the pitch black.

Leo felt himself moving out of the tunnel and into a wider space, but he could see absolutely nothing. He heard the boys breathing and clearing their throats, and the Cheevilnid chirping, and all of it echoing softly around him.

He heard Wilwell again, this time a little farther away, say, "Wake up!"

A sudden gentle burst of light illuminated the space they were in. The milk-white, globe-shaped flowers that Leo remembered so well were glowing upon a mat of green vines climbing the walls of a damp cave with a wet sandy floor. The boys smiled and exhaled with relief, though their faces were dirty and bloodstained.

Wilwell led them up a passage, and every few yards he called to the flowers—'lampflowers'—to wake up. The ground slowly rose and became drier, until finally they rounded a bend and entered another cave. This one was roughly furnished. It had colored wool blankets on the floor for rugs, several chairs, and a fire pit in the middle hung with cooking equipment. It felt like a boys' secret clubhouse.

The cave opened up to a much wider area, from which Leo could hear the sound of flowing water. He ventured out curiously.

"That's the Fillwishing," said Oddo, and his words lit up lampflowers hanging along the walls beside a dark, wide river. "It cuts through the mountain here."

Leo looked up, and somewhere very high above him in the dark he saw sunlight. He was disoriented for a few seconds, but finally he realized that the light was coming from the doorway, thousands of feet up, that Chog had smashed through the day before, when Leo and Zechariah were on the platforms and beginning to descend on the elevator.

"Unbelievable…" he breathed. He said it before he knew why. It was the expression of a mix of wonder, and terror, and relief at being temporarily safe, and doubt that he would ever enjoy normalcy again.

The boys were quite pleased with things for the moment. They knew this place well, and how to survive in it. They had a warm fire going soon, and they pulled the chairs up to it. They contentedly meandered back and forth to the banks of the river to drink water or to wash themselves. Leo quietly joined them. The river water was cold, but it felt good to clean the grime off of his face and the back of his neck. It stung various cuts that he did not realized he had suffered, and the water that he splashed on his forehead and chin turned a cloudy red at first.

Benjamus made a turtle-y moan and rubbed his flat belly. "I'm hungry."

"Me, too," said Wilwell.

Leo realized the boys were looking at him again. "Right. I'm pretty hungry, too. I'm so hungry I could eat a *Throtrex*..."(this made the boys snicker, which Leo found gratifying) "...Maybe there's fish in the river? Do you have fishing poles somewhere around here?"

"Well," said Oddo professorially, "There's some excellent food right out there!" He pointed towards the main cavern, where there was a flitting of shadows near the river and an indicatory sound of leathery flapping wings.

Leo's face contorted. "Ugh. I don't really want to eat a *bat*."

"Oh ho, I forgot about them," said Benjamus excitedly, "It isn't a bat, Leo! We made it up..."

He led them back out by the river and called more lampflowers to life. Wobbling clumsily back and forth through the air on stubby, bat-like wings were round-bellied creatures with reddish plumage. Their faces were flat and unattractive, with yellow beaks and bright red wiggly blobs on their heads.

Oddo cackled, so gratified was he to finally have on the Island someone new who could appreciate the children's zoological inventions. "It's a chickenbat!"

"Juicy," Benjamus murmured deliriously.

Leo shook his head, but laughed in spite of himself. "How do we get them? They're way out over the river…"

There was a sudden sound, like a bullwhip had been cracked. Within the space of two seconds Leo caught a glimpse of Gollyplox's tongue stretching out seven yards from his little green head to snatch a chickenbat from midair and snap it back to his mouth, crushing its neck in the process. He waddled over and deposited it at Leo's feet.

Leo wrinkled up his face in disgust at the trails of saliva stretching from the dead creature to Gollyplox's gaping mouth, but Wilwell politely asked the Cheevilnid to grab a few more. The boys showed a practiced skill at quickly de-feathering the things and then cooking them on spits over the fire.

Leo could not remember the last time he had eaten anything so delicious. Swallowing the last morsels, he lounged contentedly in a chair by the fire and savored the taste and the warmth of his full belly. With a mixture of amusement and bemusement he let his eyes wander over the disparate bunch to which his very life had become linked:

The three boys, bedraggled and skinny and indefatigable, in spite of so much loss ("Watch what I can do," Oddo said to Benjamus, and he stuck out his tongue, then sucked it in quickly and made an exaggerated swallowing sound. "It's like I ate it."

Benjamus giggled and did the same thing, and soon all three were doing it)…

Zechariah, still unconscious, in his ill-fitting gray and black Edgar Allen Poe outfit, strapped to a living chair that toddled passively among the children. It gave all of them looks of affection with its black, oval eyes, or glanced uneasily at the fire, from which it constantly kept a safe distance…

The Cheevilnid, Gollyplox, gnawing the end of a chickenbat bone. The fingers that held it were long, with fat nodes on the end. His huge eyes bulged. He was narrow in the waist, colored lime green, with dark yellow and splotches of red on his child-sized chest. He seemed friendly, but he repulsed Leo on some irrational level—he smelled strange, for one thing. He struck Leo as being just a subhuman savage, in spite of his obvious intelligence, a primitive alien that, if provoked, might decide to throw its excrement at you…

"How?" Leo exclaimed.

The boys stopped swallowing their tongues and everyone looked at him.

"How what?" said Benjamus.

Leo laughed. "I don't know. I have a million questions, I think. What is this Island? Who is Zechariah, and what's wrong with him? There are all of these…*creatures* here that I've never seen outside of a Hieronymus Bosch painting, and apparently you *made* them? And what's with all of these crazy potions that Bentpin has? And where did the Throtrex come from? And who is Kak?" Anxiety was beginning to increase in Leo's chest, and the volume of his voice rose with it. *"And how do I get back home?"*

The boys looked crestfallen.

"Sorry, boys," Leo said humbly. "I'm just a little on edge. Remember me talking about Zechariah's circuits being overloaded? How sometimes a person has to deal with too much at one time, and it makes their brains tired? I feel like that." Leo immediately regretted bringing that up, because now he could see the boys were worried that he was about to fall unconscious like Zechariah. "No, no," he quickly added, "I'm going to be fine. Forget it. Just...help me understand some things. Where in the world is this Island we're on?"

"We don't know," said Wilwell. "I don't think anyone knows. It's hidden. Ships cannot find it, even if they were looking."

"And you made these creatures? Chickenbats and..." He gestured towards Gollyplox. "Kermit?"

"*Gollyplox*. And lampflowers and Tabletop trees, yes."

"And Throtrex?"

The boys were stunned at the suggestion. "Oh no," Wilwell retorted. "Of course not! They are Throtrex. Bentpin is one of them, too. And Kak... well, he is a leader, an Archthrotrex. Throtrex are an evil race that have been around for a very long time, almost since Zechariah was born."

"O.K. so forget them for a second, then. Go back to the other creatures. How did you make them?"

Oddo made a raspberry sound and casually waved away the question. "Awww, we cannot make a

190

thing! It's really Zechariah. Protectors can give the Life. They just can't make anything up on their own. They need humans to do that…"

Leo interrupted. "You guys keep saying that. Isn't Zechariah a human, too?"

"No, he's a Protector. They are much more powerful than humans…"

"…And," said Wilwell, "If we ask, we are allowed to use that power to make up new animals and plants. That is what we did when we first came to the Island…"

"From thirteenth century Europe? I mean, you boys actually were part of the Children's Crusade? You marched off to liberate Jerusalem…"

"And Nicholas, our leader, sold us to Kak. He opened a Wayover and brought us through and dumped us right on to the top of Mount Hollowchest. Here, you need to read this…"

Wilwell went to the Walkchair and pulled a tab on the side of the seat. From a hidden compartment he withdrew a thick black book. He brought it to Leo.

"What's this?"

"It's Zechariah's Journal. The Watchdog could have destroyed it, but he left it with us, so that's something to be thankful for! Read it. It will tell you much of what I think you want to know."

Leo took the tome in his hands, and his fingers seem to immediately sense they were touching something staggeringly old, something unearthly.

He opened the cover, and saw words that made no sense to him at all. The letters were not like any he had ever seen, yet seemed to combine every written language at the same time: the swirls of English calligraphy; the careful flourishes of Chinese; the elegant strokes of Arabic; the stoic lines of cuneiform; hieroglyphics; Mayan logograms; Roman numerals.

And then Leo found he could read it all.

It started with an electric tingle in his eyes and in his chest, and the words became standard modern English.

The children smiled and left him alone to read.

Twenty-Two

An hour had passed before Leo slowly closed Zechariah's Journal. He hadn't read all of it…that would have been impossible, and not merely because the volume of words was unfathomable, but because the content was, as well. Mysteries of mankind and the universe lay within the pages with the familiarity of stacked dishes or folded laundry, all of it taken for granted. If it was to be believed, Zechariah was not just ancient. He was timeless. But how could that be? Leo could once again only sidestep the profound and put his focus on what needed to be addressed now, in this moment.

"Wilwell is right," he announced to the boys. "You have to get Zechariah's Spear back."

Wilwell's face beamed. "I was right! I knew it! I remember Zechariah talking about his Spear once. He said: 'Wilwell, it isn't like a man and his sword, with the sword being just a tool he uses and throws away when he wants, or replaces with something else'…"

"It's a part of him," said Leo. "You can tell from the things he describes in his Journal. To take away his Spear would be like…I don't know, taking a man's brain out of him. Or his soul. It's…a *soul spear.*"

"Right," said Wilwell. "They are meant to go together."

"It's incomplete without him, and he's incomplete without it. And the Watchdog stole it? Because Kak couldn't?"

"Protectors cannot be killed, and Kak could never defeat him in a battle. But Protectors must sleep once a year in a pool of water—that is how they renew themselves. Zechariah's Sleeping Pool is inside his palace, at the top of his mountain, the tall one next to Mount Hollowchest. Zechariah had a tradition of choosing one of us to help him…"

"Why not these Oblates he writes about? Couldn't they?"

"No, they sleep when he sleeps. They receive their power through him. The last time, Zechariah chose Walwich Herstog to preside—the one who became the Watchdog. Zechariah felt sorry for him, I think. Walwich was angry and suspicious and had left our town in the valley to be alone on the southern part of the Island. That must be when Kak got to him. Kak promised him he could be a permanent grown-up with great power and beauty, if he would only steal the Protector's Spear during the Sleep."

Leo exhaled and thought for a few seconds. "Tell me about Bentpin. He's not mentioned in the Journal. He's just another Throtrex?"

"Yes, but much more clever. He has acquired heaps of knowledge during his many journeys from the Island to the Rest-of-the-World."

"Yes, he has all those potions…"

The children all jeered.

"No!" Oddo blurted. "He would like to be that smart, but he is not. Those potions are like the animals we made, with power only because the Protector gave it to them. We would spend *hours* dreaming them up, and then Zechariah would let us make them real! But, after the Protector was taken and the Throtrex invaded our town, Crawlsome Bentpin raided our houses and gathered up all the potions, pretending they were *his* creations. That giant snowball he made when he jumped out of the Balloon House last night? We invented that. We used to jump off the side of Mount Hollowchest inside them—you can fall a long way down and still not be hurt, because you're safe inside the snow!"

Leo rolled his eyes. "Great. So he's still out there somewhere. And Kak—he's the worst, obviously?"

"Well, not the *worst*," said Wilwell. "The Corpse is the worst. He is the ruler of all Throtrex. He likes to be called the World King, even though he isn't that at all. But he isn't on the Island. We have never seen him before."

"Alright, so then Kak is really the one you have to worry about. Kak is your Darth Vader."

"Who?"

"Never mind. He has the Spear. He can't beat Zechariah, but he's obviously pretty formidable. He can breathe fire?"

"Yes. And that is why we need the Hair Coat!"

"Which you made out of Zechariah's hair, which is pretty gross, I might add."

"He let us keep it!" Benjamus said with a chuckle. "He always cuts his hair before a Sleep. We had been saving it for a long time, and eventually we had enough to make a coat."

"And it would be an *excellent* idea," chirped Oddo in his Junior Scientist tone of voice, "if you had that on when you sneaked into Kak's palace to steal the Spear back!"

"Boys…" Leo looked at them imploringly. "I can't do that."

"But you are the Assistant Protector!"

"No…there's no such thing as an 'Assistant Protector'. I'm not *him*," Leo pointed to Zechariah. "I'm just an ordinary man. I can't protect you."

"But you already *are* protecting us!"

"There isn't much time," said Wilwell. "We need to get to the Tunneltrees, downriver, because that's where the Hair Coat is. Bentpin lives there now, but he's probably still out looking for us, so I believe we can get in and out of the Tunneltrees before he returns. But to make the journey in time we'll need our Fishboat, which is here inside the mountain. We get the Fishboat, we travel to the Tunneltrees and pick up the Hair Coat, then continue on to Kak's new palace on the southern end of the Island. We sneak in, and we steal back the Spear and give it to the Protector so he can be himself again and save us from the Throtrex!"

"Easy!" shouted Oddo, smacking one little fist against his palm.

Leo looked at them with a dead expression. They looked back, with hope glinting in their eyes like fireflies and energy coursing through their malnourished bodies. Leo hung his head and laughed loudly. "Boys…"

They started to plead with him, but he stopped them. "Boys, just let me think. I need some time, alright?"

He handed the Journal back to Wilwell, who reverently returned it to the hidden drawer of the Conambulator. Leaving everyone standing beside the fire pit, Leo ambled out by the river with his hands folded behind his back and his head cloudy with some of the darkest thoughts he had ever had.

"Alright, Leo!" Oddo called out to him. "We will go upstream a bit. The Fishboat is very close. We will get her ready, and you come find us when you are done having your time alone!"

Leo did not respond.

···+·+·+·+·+·+·+

Chog was still at the top of Mount Hollowchest, sitting near the edge of the peak with one enormous fist resting against his lower jaw, looking like a bizarre version of Rodin's *The Thinker*. In fact, he was doing very little thinking because (although he did not realize it) his transformation into a towering behemoth had included a reduction in the size of his brain. Neurons now popped and fizzled only occasionally within the squashy wrinkles of his much-diminished gray matter.

He wondered when Crawlsome Bentpin would return. The top hat-wearing imp had promised to go and apprehend Leo and Zechariah and bring them right back to Chog here on the mountain. That's what Bentpin *said*. It seemed like a deal Chog could not pass up at the time, but he was just now, over fourteen hours later, beginning to suspect foul play. In fact, it *might* be the case that Bentpin had wanted Chog to stay here only to keep him out of the way while he—Bentpin—captured their prey and earned all the glory…

What was that smell? Chog felt supremely smug about his enhanced olfactory capability. It was so acute that it was as if an entirely new dimension of living had been opened up to him. For instance, he could detect the spicy muskiness of the Billodriffs whenever a flock of them happened by. He could still smell Zechariah's distinctive cedar-and-rosemary aroma on the rocks around him, and the scent of Von Koppersmith's soap and of the detergent from his clothes.

But there was a new odor now. What was that? It was faint and smoky.

It smelled *good*.

Freshly cooked chickenbat?

···+·+·+·+·+·+·+→

Leo found a high bridge spanning the Fillwishing, along a spot where three steep waterfalls dropped noisily into darkness. Crossing over the bridge, he told some nearby lampflowers to wake up.

He knew where he was going, even though he did not want to admit it to himself.

Enough pale flower light reached the central part of the cavern to show thick ropes hanging from high above. They reached down to a wooden platform with pulleys, gears, and levers.

Leo knew what this must be: the base of the elevator.

Chog did a lot of damage up at the top, Leo well remembered. *It probably doesn't even work anymore.*

Leo tried a couple of levers. Gears began spinning, and the ropes began to be pulled automatically. It was not long before Leo was able to see the elevator, still very high up, but slowly descending. Most of its housing was smashed to bits, but the floor part was fine. It could easily bring Leo back up to the top.

Not that I would do that, of course.

Couldn't leave three little kids completely alone like that.

So much rope and lumber at the top, though. With just a little bit of ingenuity a person could construct something on the mountain peak that would enable access to that invisible opening and the Wayover.

Those boys don't understand. They are seriously, seriously overestimating me. There is nothing I can do to help them against fanged monsters and fire-breathing demons. They already have a superhuman guardian who's been around since the beginning of time! What do they need _me_ for? Zechariah could wake up anytime, and he's the one who is supposed to be looking out for them, not me! It's ridiculous.

The elevator was closer now.

He marveled at how perfectly the whole mechanism was working. Once it fully lowered, Leo would step on, pull the lever, and be back up top in no time. Then, up to the peak…pile some debris, make a grappling hook or something…back through the Wayover, and home in time for dinner. Dinner with Mom, and Anselm. He had already spent so much time away from home. *Yes, time to go home...*

The elevator lowered onto the platform in front of him with a few rattles and a clunk.

Here it is. My ride back home.

He put one shoe on the elevator. He paused. He looked back across the river, which was a cold path of faint glimmers on a deep black surface, and he could see the warm light of the fire pit in the boys' cave.

They'll be fine. They've done perfectly well without me for eight hundred years on an island of perpetual youth. I'm the one with the curse, not them. I have to protect myself. Time to go.

He put his other shoe on the elevator and reached for the lever.

Twenty-Three

Far above Leo, near the top of the cavern, the light streaming through the shattered doorway flashed and flickered, and then became blotted out altogether by an enormous shape.

A powerhouse roar blasted throughout the mountain.

Chog.

Had he seen Leo somehow, even though there was so much distance between them? The shadow flowed through the doorway, and soon Leo heard tiny snaps and the falling of bits of rock.

He's climbing down.

Leo leapt off the elevator and ran for the bridge.

⸱⸱⸱+⸱+⸱+⸱+⸱+⸱+⸱+⸱→

Returning to the little cave, he found Benjamus sitting extremely upright in his chair beside the fire pit. His eyes were wider than ever. "What was *that?*"

"We have to get out of here, Benjamus! Can you tell the Walkchair and Gollyplox? You have to show me where Wilwell and Oddo went, *quickly!*"

Benjamus was a slow runner, but he led them all as fast as he could go, upriver to another cave. No lampflower vines grew here, but somehow Wilwell and Oddo had acquired lanterns that lit the place with bobbing orange light. The boys were up to their ankles in water.

"Leo, you're back!" said Oddo with a pleasant smile. "Good! Can you help us find the Fishboat, please?"

"There's no time for that," snapped Leo. "We have to get away from here!"

"There have been rock slides since we were last here," said Wilwell, stretching his lantern in random directions. "I cannot tell where we are…"

"No, see!" Oddo stepped into a part of the cave where the water came up to his knobby knees, and he drew a sharp breath between his teeth. "It's cold!" He kept muttering about the frigidity of the underground ponds even as he forced his way through sloshing waves to a farther bank. "See! Here she is! Here!"

Wilwell followed him, and they both stood facing a mound of rubble dotted with moss and mushrooms.

"Boys, the Watchdog is coming! Only he's not the Watchdog anymore—he's Chog. And he'll be here any minute…"

"Oh no!" Oddo looked dismayed. "But we can't just leave now! We found her!"

"And we really need her, to make the journey to the Tunneltrees," said Wilwell. "Please help us free her, Leo!"

Leo could now see, shining dimly in the lantern light, a reddish-brown shape within the mound of rubble. Oddo began peeling off chunks of rock; Wilwell pulled on a bigger stone and let it tumble down into the waters with a deep ker-plunk.

Another roar echoed through the mountain.

Leo, Benjamus and Gollyplox rushed forward to help clear the remaining stones. They tore the skin off of their fingers as they clawed at the rocks and cast them away, to the sounds of devilish snarls playing throughout the recesses of the hollow mountain.

Everyone suddenly leapt back as the rock pile collapsed with a rush and snapping of stone and a cold boil of splashing. Leo dove to avoid a jagged rock that was as big as a bear.

Lying in the shallow water he heard the boys chattering excitedly. He turned to see Oddo leaping in place with a huge grin on his face as Wilwell's lantern cast its golden light over what the collapsing rocks had revealed.

"This is Kulapa," Oddo explained to Leo with a grin. "She's a Fishboat."

It was a boat, certainly, thought Leo, and (he supposed) a "Fishboat" because of its shape. Enormous smooth wooden pectoral fins thrust out on each side, and the rudder was in the shape of a massive tail fin. Mounted upon the back deck was a large tube that looked like some kind of gun.

"Help me push, boys!" Leo shoved his shoulder into the vessel's stern, and everyone quickly joined him. The water was just deep enough so that the Fishboat was buoyed slightly, but parts of the bilge still scraped roughly against the pond floor.

"This is crazy!" grunted Leo in between pushes. "I just thought of something: even if we can get this thing onto the river before Chog gets here, I'm the only one of us strong enough to row, and that won't be fast enough! We'll be sitting ducks in the water. Why don't we just make a run for it now while we still can?"

"You won't need to row, Leo!" squawked Wilwell. "She already has the Life. We just need to wake her back up."

"Oh…so, *can you just do that now?*"

"She's a *Fishboat*. She can only live in the water…"

"We're in water!"

"*Deeper* water. She needs the river!"

The prow jutted through the opening of the cave. The banks of the Fillwishing were only about three yards away, but it was three yards of sand-covered rock. Farther beyond, Leo could see the smattering of glowing lampflowers that grew near the elevator. Into their aura a mammoth shape was descending.

"*Push!*" Leo snarled savagely as he dug his shoes into the cave floor and forced the boat forward over rock.

"*Again!*" His face was blood red. The boys were giving it all they had. The Fishboat slid arduously across the rugged surface.

Chog had now reached the cavern floor. He let out a thunderous roar and his close set burning orange eyes began greedily scanning his surroundings.

Leo's legs were quivering. He knew he didn't have the strength to continue this.

He slammed his shoulder into the back of the boat one last time, feeling blood vessels bursting beneath his skin. There was another harsh scraping sound, and then the stern tipped up. Gravity had now become an ally, tugging the Fishboat the rest of the way down the sloping banks and into the flowing river.

Wilwell gave the Walkchair a sharp command and it hopped on board. Leo and the boys followed. Gollyplox was last, making the jump effortlessly.

The current was slow here; they floated along sluggishly, while farther into the cavern Chog's dark shape shuffled back and forth, searching, searching. Leo began looking frantically for an oar.

Wilwell knelt and closed his eyes. He held his hands to his head, frowning, as if he had a headache. He took a deep breath. He brought his hands together for a second and gently opened them again, palms facing the deck.

Oddo drew close to him, clapping his hands eagerly. "Do it, Wilwell! Wake her up! Would you like me to do it? Well, no, you better do it..." He frowned at himself. "You're much better at it than me, Wilwell...I'm *terrible* at it, I can *never* do it..."

Benjamus patted Oddo's arm. "You can't do it at all..."

"Benjamus, you don't have to *say* it!"

"I only said it because *you* said it..."

"*Boys!*" Leo barked. "Help me find the *oars!* We have to get downriver fast or..."

Chog spotted them. He smelled them first, but now his orange eyes were on them, sizzling with hatred.

The boat shuddered. Its fish-shaped wooden body took on that same bendable quality as the Walkchair. Leo, standing by the starboard side, caught a glimpse of big, round dark eyes blinking sleepily at first and then becoming alert.

Chog bellowed and ran at them. His huge hands were outstretched, hands with the kind of crushing power that could quickly reduce Leo's body to the consistency of peach preserves and make his eyeballs pop out of their sockets and dangle like Halloween decorations...

Kulapa's huge tail fin convulsed, and she propelled forward at a speed that sent everyone on board tumbling backwards and clinging to the stern rails for dear life. Chog reached for them but was much too slow, and they swept quickly downriver.

Leo ducked to avoid hitting his scalp against the bridge, which immediately reminded him of...

"The waterfalls...wait...!"

His words inflated hundreds of lampflowers and their light unfurled upon the precipice Leo had seen before. He gripped the rails with white knuckles and shut his eyes as Kulapa whisked them all over the edge...

Twenty-Four

Streamers of sunlight fell through the thick, moss-robed branches that hung in dark bowers over the Fillwishing. Cheevilnids reclined upon the boulders beside the cave where the river flowed out of the mountain, casually using their long elastic tongues to pick off fat, silver bugs that wriggled along the muddy banks.

Kulapa burst out of the cave with a furious splash of green water that sent the Cheevilnids leaping away in terror. The reddish-brown prow plunged deep into the river and quickly resurfaced. Kulapa's wooden fins reached out, steadying her course, and her tail-shaped rudder began to swish evenly with the flow of the Fillwishing.

Leo cautiously stood, wiping water out of his eyes. He did a quick headcount: no one had fallen off. Everyone was wet and shaken up, but unhurt. Within a minute the boys seemed to have forgotten all about their latest brush with doom and were skipping cheerfully around the deck.

Wilwell climbed on top of the cabin, laid back, and sighed. "I missed Kulapa. It's so nice to be on the river again…" Gollyplox crouched by his side and croaked happily.

Benjamus tightened Zechariah's restraints and carefully wiped wet smears of dirt from the unconscious man's cheeks. "I wish the Protector would wake up."

Leo glanced inside the cabin. There were clasped cabinets and a barrel with a tap on it, and several rows of cots.

He looked over the side. It was difficult to get used to the idea that the boat was moving itself —herself—with fins. He stared into one of Kulapa's soft, dark eyes, and found it mildly unsettling when the eye turned and looked back at him. His disquiet quickly passed, for in Kulapa's gaze he could see only the gentleness of a mother.

Oddo bounced over to the gun-like tube mounted near the stern. "The crossbow is still here! Can I go fishing, Leo? Please?"

Leo shrugged. "Uh…sure, I guess."

Oddo chirped and pulled a switch that caused two narrow wings to flare out from the side of the tube, instantly creating a bow. "I am an excellent shot," he proclaimed as he dug around in a nearby trunk and pulled out an arrow that was longer than his own body. He loaded it deftly onto the bow. He turned a handle that was connected to sturdy, clacking wooden gears to pull the bowstring back.

Benjamus trotted over eagerly and began scanning the river. "Look! There's one! Hurry, Oddo!"

Oddo twisted the crossbow in the direction that Benjamus was pointing and then scampered on to a little stepstool to aim. The bowstring vibrated as he stared with one eye down the length of the arrow. He pulled the trigger.

With a snap so loud that it made Leo wince, the bow's missile plunged into the water trailing a thin rope behind it. The boys cheered and Gollyplox ribbit-ed as they rushed to pull the line back in.

There was a spray of river water all over the deck when they finally grabbed hold of the arrow and hauled in their catch: a fat, squirming fish with goggle eyes. It was clear to Leo that it was yet another Island original, designed by the boys. It was as big as an armchair; it looked like an inflatable toy. Its scales were dark blue, except for enlarged markings on either side of its body. Both markings were an orange-silver that glowed brightly even in the sun, and each was exactly the shape of an enlarged "X". Buried right in the center of one of them was Oddo's arrow.

"O.K.," said Leo, smiling suspiciously, "Where I come from, we call that 'cheating'."

Wilwell shrugged, looking embarrassed. "The first fish we put in were too hard to hit."

Leo laughed, but the sound was soon smothered—first by a mild surprise at the fact that he had briefly forgotten the danger they all faced, and then by a bitter pensiveness. *I almost made it. The elevator was ready, the kids were all busy doing other things…I could have sneaked back to the top of that mountain and found a way back home—I could be back home right now, except for stupid Chog…*

Leo watched as the boys wrestled their furniture-sized, orange-silver "X" fish into a compartment below the deck, where it would remain until dinnertime. *Great,* thought Leo sarcastically, *and what will they eat for dinner after that? And after that?* There was no plan here—not for survival. Not for the realities of life. Whether from the thirteenth century or not, they were just *kids*, bumbling along day after day, blundering in and out of the jaws of death.

And why? What had led them here? The answer kept coming back to Leo like a bad aftertaste. Nicholas had mentioned it in his letter: they were innocent. Leo remembered, back in his college days, listening in class to a Western Civilization course instructor musing over this historical peculiarity. Certain medieval people, disappointed in the failures of princes and counts to win back the Holy Land, decided that innocence was what was lacking in the Crusades. Children were innocent; they could do what the powerful could not: destroy evil. Apparently this foolish concept just made sense to some people at the time, but the harsh consequences were right here in plain sight: three half-starved forgotten kids. Innocence had been kicked right in the teeth. That's what happens in this world when someone like Nicholas is given trust and responsibility. When you get right down to it, does *any* man deserve that sort of trust?

A low fleet of thunderclouds had begun to sail in from the northwest. They did not blot out the sun, but they were close enough to open their dark gray hulls and cast a thin, sparkling rain upon the Island. Thunder rolled over the trees, but only occasionally, and in deep, gentle rumbles that Leo and the boys found comforting.

They jumped at what they thought at first was a sudden, harsher peal of thunder. White birds with long, floppy ears took flight from a pounding and crashing in the jungle that grew more and more violent until, at last, the trees fifty yards upriver bent sideways and Chog emerged. He waved his enormous fists at the crew of the Kulapa. With his mouth open like a huge tear in his chest he emptied himself of one long crunching-coal-and-foghorn roar and dove into the river after them.

"Good thing we're in a Fishboat," said Leo. "Wilwell, can you tell her to go a little faster, just in case?"

The boy let Kulapa know what was behind them, since she had almost no posterior view. Her body shook in acknowledgement and her tail fin swept the water with fast, powerful strokes.

Everyone watched as Chog's wooly legs beat the water until it boiled. Soon his body dwindled to a lump of tangled hair that looked like a huge dislodged beaver's dam skimming over the water. Within seconds he was pacing them.

"Faster!" yelled Wilwell.

"He's catching up to us!" cried Oddo. "That's impossible!"

A rumple of deep furrows trailed off behind Kulapa and broke in wet tatters around Chog's furry, rushing top portions as the distance between them narrowed.

"Oddo!" shouted Leo. "Load the crossbow!"

His legs churning the water into foam, Chog reached up and his leathery fingers closed along the back of the vessel.

Suddenly he lunged over the stern, wet and bellowing. Like a boulder on a seesaw, his weight drove down the entire back of the boat, lifting the prow out of the water. Gollyplox clung to the cabin, but Leo, the boys and the Walkchair all tumbled over and slid towards the stern. Chog hauled one leg into the craft, which sunk it even more and sent river water surging over the deck.

Leo found himself flailing desperately in the murky pond that had formed along the stern of the boat. He could smell Chog's fetid breath and the grime of his unkempt fur, and he could feel the glinting orange eyes fixed upon him.

"Kopp'smith...."

Chog opened his massive mouth to bite off Leo's head and swallow it like a bearded melon.

Gollyplox's tongue snapped sharply across the deck and stabbed into Chog's left eye. The monster jerked back; he partially lost his grip on the stern and sunk halfway into the water.

The boat rocked in Chog's throes. It was still tilted back, and the boys were all squirming against their attacker's matted fur, screaming and trying to claw their way back up the deck. Chog ignored them, keeping his eyes on the Walkchair who, like a poor beetle, could not right himself and slowly inched closer to the waterlogged stern.

The Protector was the prize. Chog must not let himself forget that. Zechariah was the one and only key to getting back into good graces with Kak and stabilizing the career he had enjoyed for centuries.

Wilwell gave a gremlin war cry and threw himself between Zechariah and Chog's grasping hand. He wasn't strong enough to push the Walkchair up the sharply slanted deck, so he tried to shove it sideways.

The palm of Chog's hand smacked down on the boy. It was hardly more than a lightning quick pat, similar to a housecat batting at a tiny bell, but Wilwell didn't move again. Chog reached for Zechariah...

"Chog!"

The goliath's eyes glanced up at the sound of his name. Leo had loaded the crossbow with another arrow and he stood behind it with his finger on the trigger. He squeezed hard and the bowstring released.

With a rush of sound the arrow fired into Chog's open mouth. It struck with such force that it made the monster's upper body whiplash back. He toppled off the boat and into the river. Kulapa's prow fell back to its proper place with a splash, and she hurtled forward with a sweeping of her fins.

Chog paddled bunglingly to the riverbank, gruffling and snorting, trying to pull the arrow out of his throat. Kulapa quickly left him behind, and it wasn't long before they turned a corner and lost sight of him completely.

Oddo hugged Leo tightly around the waist and began to cry against his trouser leg, but he stopped suddenly.

Wilwell was lying pale and still in a puddle of murky river water. There was no color in his lips. Everyone crowded around him.

"Oh no!" shouted Oddo. "Is he...? He's not...?"

"He's alive," said Leo, his ear pressed against the boy's mouth.

Oddo wrung his hands. "Yes, but only a little!"

While Benjamus set the Walkchair upright, Leo gently patted Wilwell's cheek. "Come on, wake up," he whispered. He became irritated at the cloudy green water sloshing around Wilwell's face. "Can we bail this out?"

Oddo looked in the cabin, but there were no buckets on board, so Gollyplox began to suck up the water one mouthful at a time and spit it back into the river.

"Wilwell," said Leo, still patting the boy's face. "Wake up. Can you hear me?"

All of a sudden the boy's wide blue eyes snapped open. He gave a stifled shout of pain, clutching at his side.

Everyone squeezed in close and tried to placate him, but he cried out again and said, "It hurts!"

Leo calmly but firmly made him explain what, exactly, was hurting. Soon he discovered areas on the boy's right arm and on his left side that were red and swollen. "I can't breathe…" Wilwell's chest shuddered as the boy tried to fill it with air.

"Can you sit up?"

Wilwell started to wiggle into a sitting position, but almost immediately he yelped in agony and flopped down on his back again.

Leo sat back and rubbed his chin, his eyes heavy with concern.

"I'm no doctor, but those are broken bones. The swelling…the difficulty breathing…"

Benjamus looked at Leo with his big, gaping eyes. "How do we fix broken *bones*?"

Leo stood and began slowly pacing the deck. Though he didn't want to say it out loud, he knew this was serious. If it was only the broken arm he would have been reasonably confident about creating some kind of splint, but clearly Wilwell's ribs were broken, as well. Leo had no idea what to do about them. Worse, he knew that if a rib is displaced at all, it could puncture a person's lung.

Wilwell let out a scream when Oddo and Benjamus tried to move him into the cabin. "Boys, don't!" shouted Leo. "Just leave him!"

They quickly let go of Wilwell and apologized to him repeatedly, gently petting his hair.

Leo began to feel panic gnawing at his stomach. They were in the middle of a jungle— there was nowhere safe to go, and no way at all to treat serious injuries. *Wilwell's just a kid. We don't even have painkillers.*

He isn't going to survive.

As Leo crouched beside Wilwell, he became aware of Gollyplox's long green fingers slowly feeling their way across Wilwell's chest. The Cheevilnid's breath came in calm rhythm, and his eyes were closed.

Leo glowered. "Hey, look, Kermit, just give him some space, O.K...?"

The Cheevilnid ignored Leo. Delicately, the nodes of his green fingers explored the swollen areas of Wilwell's rib cage. They made their way from there over to his broken arm, to the whispery cadence of Gollyplox's breathing.

"*Chirp creeeek crik crik…*" Gollyplox bounced to the top of the cabin and crawled down the hull to Kulapa's left eye. He chirped and croaked something to the Fishboat, then hopped back to Leo, chittering up at him and gesturing.

"What is he saying?" said Benjamus.

Leo shrugged. Gollyplox leapt back to the top of the cabin, and began scanning downriver with his enormous eyes.

"He wants us to stop somewhere," said Oddo. "You have an idea, don't you, Gollyplox?"

The Cheevilnid waved his rubbery green arms and croaked.

"Look, he's pointing to that cliff—that overhang, there, with the Stikkin tree…"

Leo had seen Stikkin trees before: they had elegant, lean branches that arched away from their trunks and buried themselves neatly into the ground, giving an appearance of multiple huge croquet hoops. The one at the top of the cliff at which Gollyplox was pointing was particularly immense.

Kulapa paddled into a small, calm, shaded inlet at the base of the cliff.

From somewhere farther upriver came Chog's roar. It did not sound close, but it was close enough to make Leo wince in fear.

Gollyplox hopped into the river and disappeared beneath the water with barely a ripple.

"Hey, where did he go?" Leo went to the rail and gazed into the deep green of the inlet.

The Walkchair and the boys gathered beside him. "Did he get scared when he heard Chog?" said Benjamus.

They waited. The Cheevilnid did not resurface.

Oddo clutched Leo's arm emphatically. "Help him, Leo!"

"Help him? What do you mean?"

"I think he's afraid! Maybe he's hurt! You have to go down and get him!"

"Look, I think he probably just wants to hide and not come out. I can't say I blame him! But right now, Wilwell is badly hurt, and we have Chog on our tail, and Throtrex all over the place…"

"Gollyplox would never just leave us like that!"

"Why not? He's just an animal, trying to protect himself…"

"Gollyplox is not an animal!" Benjamus growled. "He's a Cheevilnid!"

Oddo grabbed Leo's shirttail in his small fists. "Please, Leo—just go look! I don't want to lose anyone else!"

Leo stared into Oddo's pleading eyes and surrendered. Kicking off his shoes, he put one leg over the rails. A flash of regret passed through him, which the boys seemed to sense.

"Please, Leo. Find him!"

He took a deep breath and dropped into the cold water.

Visibility was very low beneath the surface. He swam along the base of the Fishboat, thinking he might discover the Cheevilnid clinging to the hull, but instead found only softly waving water plants and "v" shaped bugs that propelled themselves along by pinching the two segments of their bodies together and quickly releasing them again.

Leo splashed back to the surface. "Nothing," he reported to Oddo and Benjamus, who were watching eagerly from the rails.

"Try again!" they shouted.

Leo frowned. "O.K. But we can't do this all day, guys…"

He took another gulp of air and submerged. He swam a short distance away from the boat this time, towards the cliff.

He nearly let out an underwater shriek when Gollyplox materialized from out of the murky depths. The Cheevilnid grabbed his forearm and began to pull. Leo tried to ignore him and swim back to the surface, but Gollyplox only squeezed his arm more tightly. Together, they swam deeper under the river, until the only guide Leo had were faint glimpses of Gollplox's wide, flapping webbed feet.

Leo was confused about the direction in which they were headed, but he felt fairly sure that they had passed into some kind of underwater niche in the cliffside.

All at once they were in almost total darkness, and Leo could not see Gollyplox's feet anymore. His lungs were starting to burn for lack of air.

He felt a hand on his shirt collar. Something was pulling him upwards. Out of fear he partially resisted, but at the same time he decided that it must only be Gollyplox pulling him and, either way, "up" is where Leo wanted to go.

With a rush of bubbles and swirling water, he burst into cool, open air. With relief, he filled his lungs, and his flapping arms found a stony embankment.

"Gollyplox!" he called.

A wreath of lampflowers responded, revealing a subterranean grotto. Lampflower vines grew along most of the walls, and the floor curved up to a doorway in which Gollplox stood waving eagerly at Leo.

Leo shuffled gawkishly out of the water, his hair and beard dripping and spikey. "What is this place? Some kind of underwater cave…"

"*Chirp chirp chirp creeeeeeeeek!*" Gollyplox gestured for Leo to follow him through the doorway.

He doesn't understand that we can't hide from Chog down here. We can't move Wilwell…I don't know if I could drag the Walkchair with Zechariah all this way…and what would Kulapa do…?

The doorway was small and low; just right for a Cheevilnid, but Leo nearly had to get on his hands and knees to pass through.

"Gollyplox, we need to go back…"

Lampflowers lit up another cave around him. When he got to his feet, he discovered a second Cheevilnid. It was slightly smaller than Gollyplox and a lighter-colored green. The two of them were nuzzling each other's faces and making purring sounds.

"*Igwish,*" said Gollyplox. The word came out as a long, whirring croak, almost a burp. He looked at Leo when he said it, but indicated the other Cheevilnid. "*Igwish.*"

Leo suddenly understood. "Oh…this is Igwish…" Embarrassed, he nodded and smiled clumsily.

Igwish *crik-crik-creeeeked* in reply, and something in the tone and the delivery made Leo realize with a start: *Igwish is a female.*

"*Podnids*," croaked Gollyplox. He pulled Leo by the trouser leg farther into the cave. Lampflowers hung on the walls, but the ceiling was covered in damp moss. Ferns and mushrooms grew in thick, low walls around a greenish-brown pond in the center of the cave. The whole place smelled like an aquarium.

"*Podnids!*" called Igwish, in her distinctly feminine-sounding Cheevilnid voice. "*Podnids! Crik creeeek crik crik crik!*"

Suddenly there was a frenzy of splashes in the pond. Gollyplox rushed to the edge and was smothered in hugs and kisses by more than a dozen tiny Cheevilnid bodies, each only a foot long. They only came halfway out of the water: their lower halves were just dark brown squiggly fish bodies, because they were still young. With a croaking chorus of what sounded like the word "Poppa," they eagerly reached for Gollyplox with elfin arms and held on to him tightly with their diminutive toad hands. Their heads, all piled together against Gollyplox, looked like a bushel of green apples.

Gollyplox laughed and exchanged gibbers and crik-criks with all of them. They seemed to be telling him all kinds of exciting things, but it was unintelligible Cheevilnid-speak to Leo.

Regardless, it all made Leo feel unexpectedly self-conscious. Until now he had regarded Gollyplox as only a non-human *thing*, equivalent to a pet monkey. It all came crashing down upon him that Gollyplox was every bit a rational being as himself. On top of that, he was a *husband*—and a *dad*. Leo had previously thought of himself as superior to Gollyplox; now he saw that they were equals...*equals, at least*, said a small, discomforting interior voice, *but perhaps he's a better man than I've ever been...*

"I'm sorry," Leo blurted out. Gollyplox faced him, and Leo felt embarrassed again. "You have a beautiful family..."

Gollyplox stared at him blankly, then let out a piercing croak and snapped up a passing slug with his long tongue.

Leo tried to urge him to return to the Fishboat, but Gollyplox was not ready to leave. Instead, he brought Leo to the far corner of the cave and showed him a pile of moss. His long fingers grasped the edges and peeled off the top in a single sheet.

Underneath were small boxes of live crickets, creeping restlessly over and under each other. Beside the boxes was bric-a-brac that only a Cheevilnid could appreciate: small, fat stones, mushrooms, rolled up leaves.

Gollyplox pushed them aside and withdrew a bundle wrapped in more moss.

"*Wilwell*," he croaked.

Inside the mossy package was a bottle. It was opalescent; it reminded Leo of the sea, but also of the many potions that the boys had created with Zechariah.

Gollyplox pressed the bottle into Leo's hands.

"*Wilwell.*"

...+·+·+·+·+·+·+

When Leo and Gollyplox at last returned to the surface of the Fillwishing, Oddo and Benjamus shouted and stretched out their arms toward them in a near panic.

"We didn't know where you went!" cried Benjamus.

"How is Wilwell?" said Leo, heaving himself back on board the Fishboat and splashing water across the deck.

"Hurting badly!" Benjamus replied.

They all gathered around Wilwell, who still lay flat. His face had become a whitish-green, and his blue eyes had lost their gleam. Small, pitiful groans of pain steadily issued from his mouth.

Leo showed Oddo the opalescent bottle. "Do you recognize this?"

Oddo and Benjamus gasped. "*Fixmender!*" They were flabbergasted, and Leo explained how Gollyplox had the bottle hidden in his under-the-river home.

"He must have sneaked in and taken it from the village sometime when the Throtrex weren't looking," said Oddo. He beamed a huge smile at the Cheevilnid. "You must have been saving this for a long time!"

Gollyplox proudly puffed out his yellow and red-spotted chest. "*Wilwell!*"

"So," said Leo, still afraid to hope, "This is some kind of medicine?"

Oddo smiled and winked. He opened the *Fixmender* and splashed a sparkling, clear liquid that might easily be mistaken for artesian water over the swollen places where Wilwell's bones were cracked.

Wilwell gave out a cry of relief. The bottle was soon emptied, and Oddo carefully sprinkled the last drops liberally over Wilwell's whole body.

The boy sat up. He smiled at all of them, and his eyes glimmered.

····◆·◆·◆·◆·◆·◆·→

They left the shaded spot under the Stikkin tree and were swept back into the steady currents of the Fillwishing. No one had seen or heard from Chog since Leo and Gollyplox first jumped into the river, which gave them a faint hope that he had abandoned the chase—or perhaps even succumbed to the wound made by the arrow?

The sky was now covered in gray. As rain began to fall more steadily the river's surface became a long, green stippled canvas, and Kulapa an impressionist painting.

"Look," said Wilwell, pointing downriver and conspicuously enjoying the feeling of being able to extend his arm again. "I can see the Tunneltrees! We're almost there!"

Rising above the jungle Leo saw dark, smooth cylindrical shapes curving around and

223

beneath each other like a huge life-size sculpture of brontosaurus necks. The boys grew excited, explaining how it had been their idea to turn what was once an ordinary grove of bamboo growing naturally on the Island into a vast play place. With Zechariah's indispensible help, the bamboo stems were made immensely wider, then interconnected and twisted in all directions. The boys used to slide through them on rainy days, riding the rushing streams of water inside of them for hundreds of yards before spilling out into pools dug in the ground.

"You made a water park," laughed Leo. "I guess it doesn't matter what century they're from, kids just want a water park."

A scream erupted from the Tunneltrees. Not just a scream: a scream stuck to a howl, the unmistakable cry of a Throtrex.

Twenty-Five

Leo's hair stood on end and his heart seemed to jump into his throat.

Another Throtrex cry answered the first.

"Do they know we're here?" said Benjamus, his angst oddly misrepresented by his slow, deliberate voice.

Kulapa drifted with the current. Everyone listened, hardly daring to breathe.

Minutes went by, but no more Throtrex sounds were heard. The tension began to lift.

The Fillwishing conveyed the Fishboat around another bend and under leafy vaults dripping with rain. Beyond, they came to a muddy outcropping and a short path leading into the Tunneltrees.

Oddo looked annoyed and heartbroken. "Look what those stupid Throtrex did to the place!" He remembered a wonderland: the winding soft-colored trees they had invented, exotic flowers, clear swimming pools garnished with lily pads and cat-o'-nine-tails, he and his friends flying on their backs feet-first through watery tubes for hours on warm summer days. All that had changed since Crawlsome Bentpin had made the Tunneltrees his domain. The bark of the trees had turned black, and everything was untended and gloomy and silent. It looked as if Kulapa was paddling towards a nest of gigantic snakes.

From the center of the Tunneltrees, roughly half a mile in, rose a hill, a jagged, blurry trapezoid under the dripping rainclouds.

"That's where the Hair Coat is," said Wilwell. "There are tunnels and rooms inside that hill. They used to belong to us, of course, but now it's all Bentpin's."

Leo, the boys and Gollyplox—the Hair Coat search party—gathered hooded cloaks and lanterns from the Fishboat's trunks and cabinets. Before disembarking, they untied Zechariah and laid him carefully on one of the cots inside the cabin. The Walkchair stretched his legs with relief and then stood beside the Protector's cot to await the search party's return. Kulapa was instructed to hide in a stand of tall rushes a little farther downriver.

"Remember," said Wilwell from under his hood as he led them all up the rain-soaked path, "Bentpin probably isn't here. But we know Throtrex are around, so we need to be very careful. Once we make it inside the Hill we will be safe."

"How do you know?" said Leo.

"That's Bentpin's House now. The other Throtrex are afraid of him. They will keep out."

"All I'm worried about now is the Glusskreep," muttered Oddo. Benjamus made a grunt of anxious concurrence.

Leo looked at them sharply. "Glusskreep?"

Wilwell shook his head and groaned. "No, no, there's no such thing as a Glusskreep."

"I don't know, Wilwell," said Oddo. "You remember the stories."

Leo slowed his pace. "What stories?"

"After the Throtrex chased all of us out of our homes and we retreated to the Tabletops, there were some late-comers—boys who had been in the Tunneltrees when Kak first took over the Island. When those boys finally joined us on the Tabletops, they had some stories about a monster they called the Glusskreep that Bentpin had put inside the Hill."

"It's true!" said Benjamus. "I remember them describing it!"

"Yes, but the more I think about it," Wilwell continued, "The more I think they didn't really see what they thought they saw. I think it was just a trick Bentpin played on them."

"Well, *I* think it's real," said Oddo.

"*I* don't think so," said Wilwell. "Bentpin can't make things like that." Seeing that Leo was staring at him dubiously, he added, "It's alright. It's just a story. There's no such thing as a Glusskreep."

At the threshold of the Tunneltrees, Leo felt a surge of awe. The smooth, massive trunks wound upwards almost a hundred yards. Many of the curvatures were not very steep and provided ideal walkways. "It will be good to be up high, in case we are spotted," said Wilwell. "We should be able to find our way to the Hill without ever touching the ground."

They climbed onto the nearest Tunneltree and walked lightly up the smooth slope. Soon they had a helpful view of things, about midway from the very tops of the forest. Huge black tree trunks curved all around them like massive serpents from some Nordic creation myth, and the wet bark glowed softly in the low light of the rainy afternoon.

Below, Leo could see several places where Tunneltree trunks opened like spouts and let out cascades of rainwater into an oozing brown swamp.

As they made their way towards the Hill, Leo suffered flares of acrophobia. He was careful not to look down very often, but more than once they had to step across to another tree if the one they were on suddenly curved up too precipitously or plunged downwards. The distance they had to step was never more than two or three feet, but Leo despised it every time.

Gollyplox suddenly put a long, green finger to his lips and pointed below. They all looked and spied a dark figure shambling through the gray foliage at the base of a tree. Three more followed him.

The Throtrex argued about something with a flurry of guttural yipes, stopping only when they heard a sharp noise. Their orange eyes scanned everywhere, and Leo knew it was impossible that they wouldn't look up, any second now, and spot him and the others…

But they didn't. They continued along their meandering way, grunting among themselves.

The rain stopped, even though the clouds stayed just as thick in the sky and the thunder kept growling. It had become too warm, and the air was cloying. A sauce of sweat clung to Leo's underarms, and schools of fussing gnats clogged the air among the sweeping black tree branches.

The limb they were following had begun to grow thinner. They toddled cautiously through a curtain of mist and were surprised to find that they had reached the Hill.

The branch ran right up against it. As they stepped off, Leo looked into the limb's dark opening and heard the sounds of their movements reverberating down its long throat.

A nearby path took them farther up the Hill, through thick, pulpy undergrowth and under the boughs of small trees heavy with moss.

As the incline became sharper the trees began to thin out. Gollyplox skipped ahead and leapt from one part of the slope to another with ease, but Leo and the boys, with their hair hanging in greasy strands and their clothes almost soaked, stumbled wearily on rocks and had to grab at vegetation to steady themselves.

"Here we are!" said Wilwell, breathing a sigh of relief.

They had reached a small cleared plateau. The rest of the Hill rose up before them like a wall, in the center of which was a large red door.

Out of habit the boys hurried towards what was, for them, only the entrance to their old, beloved hideout. They slowed down when they saw that animal skulls were now hung around the threshold like macabre decorations. Suspended from thick rusty nails on decaying strands of twine, they stared vacantly at the approaching visitors.

The image of a smiling gold sun had been painted upon the door originally, but now filth was smeared over its rays and claws had cut a pattern on its face:

me
me
me

"I know those markings," said Leo. "The Watchdog had the same tattoo on his forehead, back when he was still...human. What does it mean? Some kind of code of selfishness? 'Me me me'?"

"Oh, those aren't letters," said Oddo guilelessly as he opened the door to his lantern and adjusted the wick. "Those are numbers. They are always twisted around like that."

"It's the sign of the Corpse," said Wilwell. "The 'World King'. If something belongs to him, he likes to mark it, and he considers everything on the Island to be his now. Three hundred thirty-three—twice."

"What does *that* mean?"

The boys shrugged. They had lit their lanterns and pulled back their hoods.

"Let's go get the Hair Coat!" said Benjamus excitedly.

Wilwell nodded and looked at Leo. "I'll lead the way. This shouldn't take very long. I remember right where we left it: in the Treasure Room!"

He pulled open the red door and led them under the gruesome wreath of skulls.

A smell of dust and decay drifted out to meet them. Everything was dark. The doorway slipped away behind them and became only a pale swath.

They moved carefully down a bare passageway that was wide but low. Sounds were muted. The air was dead.

"Smells bad," grumbled Oddo. "You can tell Bentpin lives here."

The passage ended in an oval-shaped room that was empty and dry as dust. The trembling fingers of lantern light pawed weakly at the smooth, curving walls.

"This is just a big room we called the Gatehouse," Wilwell explained to Leo. "Nothing here, though. The way continues through the arched doorway on the other side, over there..."

The Gatehouse was not a large room, but the ceiling was high—at least twenty feet, rising into blackness, and it caught Wilwell's words and sent them tumbling: *over there...over there...*

They took a few steps in, and susurrus echoes, mimicking their footfalls and their clicking lanterns, sounded like assassins in the shadows.

Everyone flinched and drew back rapidly.

Hanging in midair in front of them was a dead Cheevilnid. Gray and desiccated, it hung from its neck by a cable that stretched up into the darkness. It swayed slightly with a low, chilling creak.

The boys gasped when they spotted another one hanging a few feet away from the first. And a third one next to it.

Chill bumps rose along the back of Leo's neck, and his breath came in shallow gulps. "Some kind of warning, I guess. From Bentpin. A 'Keep Away' sign."

"Leo," whispered Wilwell with a catch in his voice, "Could you take them down, please?" Leo looked around at the boys and they all had the same look of horror on their faces. Gollyplox squatted behind Wilwell and made nervous croaking sounds.

"Sure. Of course," said Leo. He did not really want to, but he could see how perturbed everyone was.

He stepped closer to the first Cheevilnid body. The head was cocked sharply to one side, and Leo's lantern cast lurid shadows over its pinched, staring face.

As he reached out, the grisly corpse suddenly shook like a living scarecrow and dropped to the floor. Everybody lurched back, and Oddo squawked involuntarily.

The body lay in a crumpled heap on the stone floor and did not move again. The cable from which it had hung was twisting and vibrating like a rubbery snake, and Leo could see now that there was no noose at the end, but a wart-ridden, swamp-green hand, twitching eagerly at the end of its long slender arm like a spider on a strand of silk.

Leo stood in blank shock, staring at the long, ropey arm hanging down from the ceiling. The hand somehow knew where Leo was, and its cracked yellow nails drew towards him.

He cried out when he felt a cold prickle on his cheek and he whirled to see that another rope-shaped arm had descended. The thick, black hairs of its hand felt like cockroaches on his skin as its fingers sought out his neck.

The other two Cheevilnid cadavers fell like broken dolls, and all around Leo more than a dozen arms were draping down in response to the group's movements, reaching hungrily like tentacles from the opaque blackness above.

Everyone dropped to the ground and scrambled in all directions.

As Leo rolled and squirmed, one of the ghoulish hands enveloped his face, the palm crushing against his nose, the yellow nails beginning to dig into his forehead and cheeks. He shouted and struck at it with his lantern. Flames scathed the pebbled skin and the arm retreated.

Then, as if enraged, it lunged forward again. It struck quickly like a viper, snatching the lantern in a vise-like grip and squeezing it tightly, *eagerly*. Another arm swept towards the lantern, wanting the prize for its own, and Leo threw himself backwards and left the two arms grappling with each other. The flame blinked and was suddenly doused.

Everyone was in a panic, swatting the hands away and crawling on their stomachs or tumbling randomly. Within a few seconds, every lantern had gone out, leaving Leo and the others all fumbling in the dark and shouting as dozens of disembodied arms swayed and clawed after them.

Leo scurried blindly on his hands and knees as meandrous limbs twisted at the edge of his blackened vision, haunting whatever direction he went. Someone fell against him; someone else—he thought it was Benjamus—cried out in pain. Creeping hands brushed Leo's trouser legs and ruffled his hair. He knew with a fatal certainty that any second now he would be snatched up and hung with his neck snapped like a convict in the gallows.

Then it happened. Fingers closed around his arm.

Leo yowled and choked the assailing wrist with his own hands.

A loud *crick-crick cheeeeep* brought him to his senses.

"Gollyplox!" Leo released the Cheevilnid's spindly arm. "Sorry about that." They had somehow escaped the Gatehouse, he realized, and made it to the other side.

A lantern sputtered to life, and Wilwell lifted it. Leo could now see that they were all piled just across the threshold of the arched doorway, panting and gasping for air, their backs against the walls of a corridor.

Wilwell waved the lantern among them with concern. "Where is Benjamus?"

They all jumped to their feet and Wilwell shone the light into the Gatehouse. Benjamus's twitching body was being hoisted up, a dark green hand crushing his neck. Other hands grabbed at his arms or tore at his legs.

The boys and Gollyplox shrieked but could only watch helplessly as Benjamus choked to death.

For the ragged edge of a split second, time froze for Leo and then reversed. He was a little boy again. The person hanging before him was not Benjamus. It was Leo's father. Staring with wide eyes and a joyless mouth. Then it was Benjamus again.

Leo howled and rushed back into the room. He leapt up and grabbed Benjamus by the waist and

234

used the boy's body as a rope. "You aren't taking him!"

Leo clambered up until he was holding the green hand by the wrist.

"You *aren't taking him!*"

He shoved his fingers between Benjamus's neck and the hand's choking grip. The other hands had already sensed Leo's presence and were grabbing him by the hair. Leo only snarled and tried to rend the warty fingers off of Benjamus's throat.

"He's...not...*yours!*"

Wilwell and Oddo were screaming. Leo kept bending the green fingers back, as if he was prying up old nails.

"He's...*mine!*"

Benjamus suddenly dropped, and immediately Gollyplox leapt and grabbed the boy's ankle to pull him to safety. Leo dove back down to the floor, losing clumps of hair and strips of skin to the disembodied hands.

They all huddled in the corridor, gasping and crying and hugging each other. Benjamus buried his head in Leo's arms, and Leo could see that the boy's neck was rubbed raw.

He gazed back into the Gatehouse, where the dim lantern light revealed an eerie sight: arms curling soundlessly back up into shadow one by one, folding up like spider legs.

Oddo patted Leo on the shoulder and nodded approvingly. "Assistant Protector."

They re-ignited all of the lanterns. Wilwell began to lead them down the corridor, but Leo gently held him by the shoulder and stepped into the lead.

Twenty-Six

A flight of steps took them down deeper into the Hill. On walls and in corners there were several shiny, black, fist-sized beetles that trapped luckless spiders or roaches with a kind of cap and then secretly munched them. ("Lerms," whispered Wilwell.)

They followed another passage that turned and led through an arch into a large room. Everyone instinctively bent low and scanned the high ceiling for more arms.

"The coast is clear, fellas," said Leo to the boys. He smiled at the resulting puzzled expressions on their faces. "That means it's safe."

This was the Big Hill Hall, Wilwell explained. Four thick, blue columns reached to a high ceiling. There were colorful rugs on the floor, trunks full of wooden toys, beds and couches, and tables with bowls of fruit and nuts. An enormous fireplace was built into one wall, with a massive cobblestone mantle lined with figurines that various children had made from dried mud. It was all just a big rec room, Leo realized, built by Zechariah and his Oblates, yet another creature comfort for the poor, lost children of another age.

Things had changed for the worse, of course, as it had everywhere else on the Island. Dirt and cobwebs covered the toys and couches; the fruit had long since turned rotten, the fireplace was dark and cold. Mice crept in and out of the folds in the rugs.

"The Treasure Room is this way," said Wilwell. He led them to a doorway with a set of dark stone stairs spiraling down.

Their lamplight filled up the stairwell as they descended, casting silent, leaping shadows over the cool walls.

A wide archway was at the bottom of the stairs. A curtain of beads colored yellow and green hung within the threshold, obscuring what lay beyond.

Leo felt uneasy as he led them all through. The beads were cool to the touch, and they clicked and rattled like rabbit bones as each person passed. Gollyplox chirruped anxiously, ready to spring away if any greenish arms came creeping.

...+·+·+·+·+·+·+

Outside, dark gray clouds gathered for another rainfall.

The trees and foliage on the lower parts of the Hill cracked and bent. Chog heaved himself onto the cleared plateau in front of the red door and the sound of coal and old foghorns being crunched together rumbled out of his mouth. His thick, tangled fur was wet and matted with mud and leaves. The inside of his mouth ached badly from the arrow wound he had received from the Fishboat's crossbow.

He stared down at the red door from his twenty-foot high vantage point, but it was his dilating nostrils that told him where to go.

He reached over and pulled off the door. Pale dusty sunlight toppled into the entrance passage. Chog had to get on his hands and knees to make his mud-caked bulk fit through, scraping away loose rock in jagged chunks.

When he reached the Gatehouse he could stand up. Right away he felt a hand grip the hair on his shoulder.

As he turned to look at it another one clasped his other shoulder.

Irritated, he reached up and grabbed the two dangling arms, which made him resemble a man on a trapeze. He began to tug.

A third arm swung down, its squirming fingers reaching towards Chog's face. He leaned forward, opened his terrible mouth, and bit the hand right off the arm, letting it fall wriggling to the floor.

He went back to pulling against the first two limbs, and they gave way with a popping noise and a glimmer of greenish light from the blackness above. They squirmed upon his back like severed lizards' tails for a few moments, then relinquished their weakening grasp and fell.

More arms came, but ultimately all Chog lost were some handfuls of hair and a little bit of time. As he crawled into the next corridor, he knew the chase was almost over now. Behind him, in the Gatehouse, a defeated scattering of arms wriggled like a nest of snakes.

····▶·▶·▶··▶·▶·▶·▶

239

"This was our Treasure Room," announced Wilwell, and it was immediately apparent what kinds of things were treasures to the boys.

There were hundreds of stones gathered from the riverbanks, of all different colors, some flecked with slivers of crystal that twinkled in the lantern light. Displayed on tables were more mud figurines like the ones from the fireplace mantle upstairs, only these clearly carried greater significance to someone, however esoteric might be the standards by which such things are judged. On shelves sat dozens of shells plucked from the beaches around the Island; some were enormous spiraling conchs, others were as small as coins. There were bowls of moss and pinecones. Piles of dried flowers. Bright, iridescent dead beetles. Snake skins. Driftwood. Everything was arranged proudly along the walls. In the center of the room was a wide, round black carpet.

"That carpet is new," chirped Oddo, "But everything else is still right where we left it!"

"This is all your stuff?" wondered Leo. "Bentpin didn't destroy it?"

"He thinks he can use it, I think." said Wilwell. "That is why he has not gotten rid of it yet. He thinks we kept it down here because it does something, or has some power, like our potions."

Leo nodded. "So, where is the Hair Coat?"

"It's over there," said Wilwell with a satisfied smile. "Hanging from that hook beside those walking sticks…"

An alarm sound had been growing in Leo's mind. It had begun as a seemingly irrelevant buzz, but had quickly swelled. "Wait…"

"I'll fetch it!" Wilwell hurried across the room.

Leo was seized by his interior alarm. '*The carpet is new*', Oddo had said.

"Wait!" Leo cried out and snatched Wilwell by the arm just as the boy took his first steps upon the round, black carpet. The material sunk beneath his shoes and into a deep, rough-edged pit. Leo was suddenly on his belly, straining to pull Wilwell back up.

Farther down, at the bottom of the pit, something moved.

···▸··▸·▸·▸·▸·▸·▸

Chog stood in the threshold staring into the Big Hill Hall. They went this way. Their smells were like incandescent waving flags forming a path through the room to a doorway on the other side.

He turned his shoulders and looked back the way he had come: one way in; one way out. His eyes searched the hall. It was a large room, filled with shadows and innumerable places for hiding—he realized he might walk right by his prey and they would escape. To even go in would be to let his present advantage slip through his thick fingers. He stood and thought, and his putrid breath came and went slowly like a cracked bellows.

···▸··▸·▸·▸·▸·▸·▸

Leo cried out and pulled Wilwell from the cragged pit.

Everyone scrabbled back against a wall, watching as a shivering, squirming Thing began to rise from the darkness. It was black, like a Throtrex, but with four slimy, tentacular arms and four pinched red eyes. It was the size of a rhinoceros. It opened its mouth and gave a wet, high-pitched squeal, showing teeth like awls.

Benjamus held tightly to the back of Leo's shirt and screamed, *"Glusskreep!"*

···+··+··+··+··+··+

At that precise moment in the Big Hill Hall above, Chog stepped forward and, with crushing force, he struck one of the blue columns. Stone shattered like eggshells, and shivers ran throughout the room. The ceiling groaned as Chog drove the pillar across the entrance. It smashed through the posts and lintel and brought down the entire threshold. A cloud of smoke billowed out into the hall. There was no way out now.

···+··+··+··+··+··+

Below in the Treasure Room they heard and felt the concussions caused by Chog, but there was no time to consider their significance.

As it crawled out of the pit, the Glusskreep lashed with oleaginous tentacles at the boys, who cried out and leapt in all directions like grasshoppers.

"Get to the stairs!" Leo shouted.

"Leo," Wilwell implored, "Get the Coat!"

Leo jumped over a swiping tentacle. "I will! Just go!"

The boys fled through the green and yellow bead curtain and up the staircase. Gollyplox stayed behind and made himself an infuriating distraction for the Glusskreep as Leo hurried around the edges of the pit.

"I got it!" Leo exclaimed. He plucked the Hair Coat from the hook, hastily bunching it up and tucking it under one arm like a football.

A tentacle swept around his ankle and tore him off-balance. He struck the floor painfully, nearly breaking his ribs.

A second tentacle slithered after the Hair Coat.

Leo and Gollyplox locked eyes and seemed almost to read each other's minds. Leo hurled the Coat over the pit and the Cheevilnid met it in midair.

The Glusskreep shrieked and grabbed desperately for the bounding frogman, but was always half a second behind. Gollyplox jumped from wall to wall, sticking briefly with its long fingers and toes splayed against the cold stone, then hopping to another spot, constantly trying to escape through the doorway. Whenever the monster got too close, Gollyplox threw the balled-up Hair Coat back to Leo, who ran with it as far as he could before throwing it right back to Gollyplox.

At last one of the Glusskreep's tentacles caught Gollyplox hard on the chest, swiping his little green body across the room and leaving him reeling deliriously against a wall. Leo had the Hair Coat again, but without his amphibian teammate it was only seconds before a tentacle whipped around Leo's neck and began to squeeze.

As Leo fell, struggling to break the grip around his throat, more tentacles tried to wrench the Hair Coat out from under his arm.

Right then Wilwell, Oddo and Benjamus came running back into the room, screaming in terror.

Sounds of battering and chips of flying stone followed them. The bead curtain tore away. Chog entered, shearing off chunks of the doorway.

The Glusskreep screeched at the hulking invader. It let go of Leo and bounded towards Chog, moving like a kind of giant reptilian insect on multi-jointed black legs. It locked its four tentacles around him and sunk its icicle-shaped teeth into the side of his face.

Chog snorted and grabbed it in a crushing embrace. A windstorm of roars and shrieks shook the walls. The two behemoths tore at one another and pummeled and bit.

Leo ran.

Clutching the Hair Coat, he scooped up the still-delirious Gollyplox and chased the boys up the stairs, shouting like a mad man. When they reached the top they heard what they knew were the last sounds the Glusskreep would ever make: a long, strangled shriek, followed by the crunching of bones.

With their lanterns bouncing wildly, the boys led the way across the Big Hill Hall to the next flight of stairs that would take them back up to the floor where they had started and then they could dodge their way past the creeping green hands and out the red door into fresh air and…

Everyone came to a sliding halt and gathered in a stunned knot.

The way back up was no longer there. That part of the room was submerged beneath tons of rock and splintered wooden beams. Chog had caused a cave-in. The group was trapped.

From below, a bestial roar sounded.

"What do we do?" shouted Oddo. They all began poking their heads into the nooks in the cave-in, vainly searching for some narrow escape route. Benjamus staggered around with his head craned back, gazing longingly at the high ceiling.

Chog squeezed out of the Treasure Room. For the first time in two days he felt in control. He had Von Koppersmith—not Zechariah, obviously, but that was alright. He would squash Von Koppersmith's body parts until he revealed the Protector's location. Sweet control…it pulsed in Chog's organs like a sugar rush.

"Leo!" cried Oddo. "*The fireplace!*"

Oddo was standing in the sooty recesses of the hall's huge fireplace, his eyes wide and white as he peered up into the musty blackness and gestured frantically.

"This way! Follow me!"

He scooted up the chimney hole until only his skinny legs showed, and then only his shoes, and then nothing. His head reappeared upside down and coated with black ash. "Come on, come on!"

Gollyplox, fully conscious again, leapt out of Leo's arms and followed Oddo. Benjamus was next.

Chog slowly realized his oversight. He shook the fur of his head like a bulldog and began lumbering towards the fireplace.

Leo and Wilwell broke into a dead sprint.

Chog's elephantine footfalls and outraged roars thundered behind them, almost terrible enough to freeze Leo's legs.

Leo and Wilwell dropped and slid feet first into the fireplace.

"You go!" shouted Leo.

During the maddening seconds he had to wait for Wilwell to climb up, he looked out into the Hall and watched Chog rushing at him, his matted fur shaking like trees, his little round eyes orange and hateful, his long, snarling mouth bellowing, his giant arms thrust forward like two battering rams.

Leo shot into the chimney and did not care that Wilwell's shoes scraped the sides of his face. His fingers quickly found handholds and he hauled himself up. The walls of the airshaft were tight, and as he bent his arms he got stuck. His feet still dangled in the fireplace. He thought he could already feel Chog locking onto a shoe and pulling…

"*NO!*" he cried and he heaved upwards furiously. The threads of his shirt tore and the skin of his ribs peeled off, but he rose. He drew his feet up just as a huge peltry hand plunged into the shaft, the giant fingers swiping in the dusty black and scraping the chimney walls. By pure chance it slapped against Leo's right shoe, but when it tried to grab hold Leo had already moved farther up.

246

He kept climbing; ash stung his eyes and choked him, and the rough stone tore his fingers. In the gloom high above he could see a dirty yellow light—a way out, surely—but he did not know if he had the strength to reach it.

Twenty-Seven

From the chimney's vent at the top of the Hill, Oddo emerged coughing and spluttering, his little face black. He crawled weakly off to the side of the vent and lay there under a fresh wave of rainfall.

The others quickly began to surface, as well. Leo was last, grit falling like hourglass sand from his hair. They were all bloody and bruised and covered in soot.

Deep inside the Hill, Chog howled.

"We don't know how long it will take him to dig out," gasped Leo. "Everybody up! We need to get back to Kulapa."

Even in the rain they could see the Tunneltrees sprawled below, dark and tangled up around the Hill like a huge Medusa's head.

It was a muddy but unchallenging climb back down the slope to where the red door used to stand but which now lay in pieces. Meanwhile, the rain had become a deluge, almost an island-wide waterfall.

Through the sheets of rain, several pairs of orange eyes stared at them. Indistinct, dark phantoms drifted up the hillside onto the plateau. More orange eyes materialized.

"Follow us, Leo!" said Wilwell in an urgent whisper. "There is a quick way out of here!" With a burst of speed the boys and Gollyplox led Leo back down the hillside path, away from the plateau. The Throtrex loped after them through the rain.

The run down the path quickly became a wet, muddy skating fumble. They came to the Tunneltree that had carried them to the Hill but, this time, instead of climbing on top, Gollyplox and the boys dove feet first right inside the gaping interior and disappeared.

Leo climbed in, but hesitated. The smells of wood and wet soil filled his nose. Rainfall pattered on the roof of the tunnel. The inside was as slick as fresh paint, and a cold stream flowed quickly down into impenetrable darkness. Once Leo launched himself, there would be no climbing back up.

Furious, screaming Throtrex rushed up behind him.

Leo plunged in to the Tunneltree, like a raw oyster down a giant's throat.

Through complete blackness he rushed, at bobsled speed. He saw nothing, but felt water whipping around his face and up his trouser legs. Butterflies in his stomach turned to marbles as almost all sense of equilibrium was obliterated; he only sensed vaguely that he was flying down, and then back up, and then into hairpin curves and even complete loops.

Light broke in upon him like an incendiary grenade. He swept out of the Tunneltree and his feet sort of found the ground all by themselves and began springing wildly over muddy ground. Leo recovered his balance and slowed himself down to a wobbling trot, then to a stop. He bent over, sure he was going to vomit.

"Leo! Over here!"

The boys were standing along the banks of the Fillwishing. Kulapa was paddling over to them, her deep dark eyes full of sweetness and felicity. The Walkchair was standing with its front two legs perched on the side, rocking back and forth with a kind of canine delight.

"The Throtrex won't slide through the Tunneltrees after us," proclaimed Wilwell, "They don't like losing control. Let's get going!"

...+·+·+·+·+·+

Kulapa's cabin had a little stove. They cooked the huge X-marked river fish they had caught earlier and Leo proclaimed it to be the best fish he had ever eaten. He was reminded of *Tom Sawyer* and its description of how superior fish tastes when it is fresh from the water and cooked right away; Leo had never had that experience until now, and it was supremely satisfying.

Zechariah was still unconscious. The boys were disappointed, but Leo had not expected anything else. He was certain now that this was going to remain the Protector's state—a kind of a coma, really—until his Spear was returned to him.

Evening was falling. The rain had passed, leaving broken trails of black and red clouds upon a deep blue and gray crepuscular sky. Pelicans drifted by overhead on their way to the seashore.

Lanterns were lit and hung inside the cabin as Leo took off his shirt and pulled on the Hair Coat.

It was thin, and not too tight or too loose. Naturally it was the same dark color of Zechariah's hair, because it *was* Zechariah's hair.

"It's no coat on you," said Benjamus in his mild, turtle voice. "You're too big!"

Oddo laughed. "It's more of a Hair *Shirt* on you!"

"It itches," Leo said with a grimace. "I'm going to go crazy if I wear this too long."

Benjamus scoffed. "You'll get used to it."

Leo pulled his old shirt back on over the Hair Shirt. "I hope so. And I hope this thing works."

"Of course it works!" Oddo cheeped. "Try it!" He opened the little door to one of the hanging lanterns and enthusiastically pointed his thumb at it.

Leo closed his fingers and extended his hand towards the lantern's flame. He paused when he suddenly remembered the sizzling meat of the fish they had cooked on the stove a few minutes before.

The boys all mocked him good-naturedly. Leo laughed out loud at himself and then gave it another shot.

When his knuckles were less than a finger's length from the hissing tongue of flame in the lantern, he realized that he couldn't feel the heat. The little hairs on his knuckles should have withered by now, but they were just fine.

At last, he gently slipped his hand all the way inside.

The fire wreathed eagerly around it, but the strongest sensation Leo felt was something like little breezes puffing upwards to caress his skin.

"I told you!" said Oddo, and they laughed and rubbed Leo's back.

"We'll be at Last Landing soon," said Wilwell, peering downriver through the cabin windows.

"Where our trip ends, I presume?" said Leo.

"We will have to walk a little from there to get to Kak's palace. But not very far."

"Well, walking's not bad! But it certainly has been good to have the Fishboat to take us this far."

"Yes," said Oddo, his professor's voice re-emerging, "But we definitely wouldn't want her to take us past Last Landing, that's for sure!"

Leo eyebrows lifted. "Oh? Why's that?"

"We would all go down the Sink!" said Benjamus, eyes round and earnest.

"The Maelstrom," said Wilwell, more calmly than Benjamus.

" 'The Maelstrom'?" said Leo with a snort. "That sounds a little melodramatic, fellas."

"Yes, *very* modoromatic," said Oddo. "It's a huge whirlpool…bigger than any you have ever seen, I can tell you that! It was already on the Island before we arrived. Anything that goes into it is *doomed*. You would spin around like a bug a couple of times, and then: sucked down, drowned, and torn apart."

⋯✦⋅✦⋅✦⋅✦⋅✦

Zechariah was hoisted back onto the Conambulator and tied down with long white cloths that held his head and torso and limbs more securely than the ropes they had been using. Their whiteness glowed softly in the twilight, and they reminded Leo of burial cloths.

Last Landing was a rough, simple pier, but surrounded with tall, floppy bushes of purple and yellow flowers that swelled and deflated in gentle rhythm, as if they were breathing.

Meandering among them were beetles ranging in size from peas to grapes, and colored bright yellow with red spots. They traveled on top of each other in two and three foot high towers, with the biggest ones on the bottom. The boys called them Monchpibs.

Crude wooden signs were posted a few yards beyond the pier, showing skull-and-crossbone shapes and whirlpool pictures and what Leo guessed were variations of "nicht", the German word for "not."

"I'm bringing the last bottle of *Smallsteam* this time," announced Wilwell as he hopped onto the pier and adjusted his satchel over his shoulder. "I wish I had brought it to the Tunneltrees. Chog would have ended up no bigger than a furry baby!"

While Oddo and Benjamus helped the Conambulator waddle over the side of the Fishboat's rail, Wilwell looked up at Leo with a frown. "I've been thinking, Leo. Where did Bentpin get the Glusskreep? And those Creeping Green Hands?"

Overhearing the conversation, Oddo turned with his fists on his hips and his eyes gazing thoughtfully. "That's right! What about that? Bentpin can't really make anything! He just steals from us."

"You're sure about that?" Leo replied.

"Yes, completely sure," said Wilwell. "Zechariah taught us that about Throtrex a long time ago, before we had ever even seen one. They can't make things up. The only one who can make anything is the Corpse, and even *he* can't do it without the cooperation of humans."

Leo nodded. "Like an evil version of Zechariah and you guys." He thought for another few seconds and then exhaled loudly. "Well, if Bentpin can't make things like Glusskreeps himself, then they must have been given to him by the Corpse. Doesn't Bentpin work for him? The Corpse is kind of his boss, right?"

"But, then, who is the human who helped the *Corpse*?" wondered Benjamus.

Oddo looked thunderstruck. "Who would *do* that?"

Leo considered that it might have been the Watchdog, but the theory didn't seem quite plausible. All accounts pointed to the Watchdog only interacting with Kak, and never with the Corpse or with Bentpin. Besides, the Watchdog had left the Island almost immediately after the betrayal, and would not have been around to help design monsters for anyone.

The sun was close to setting. Soft, clean winds blew over the river, tousling the purple and yellow flowers as they gently breathed in and out. ("We made those up!" blurted Oddo, as if Leo needed to have that explained anymore. "We call them 'Breezebreathers'.") Bubble-bodied Scumps paddled by in small clouds.

Gollyplox rested on his haunches and rubbed his belly with his long nodular fingers. Zechariah was as secure in his Conambulator as they could make him. Everyone was ready, Leo saw, and they were all looking at him with unalloyed trust.

"We go that way, right?" He pointed to the only path there was. It led away from the pier and down a slow incline covered in tall grasses and small trees.

Wilwell nodded. "It will take us very close to Kak's new palace. We can sneak in. You have the Hair Shirt—Kak can't burn you! You can get the Spear away from him and give it back to the Protector."

It was the stupidest plan Leo had ever heard, but he didn't say that, and not only because he didn't want to dash the children's hopes. He *shared* their hope, he realized all of a sudden. He had been bumbling along from one freakish situation to the next for over two days now, sure that everything had gone completely out of control and was tumbling into an existential abyss. Now he saw that things had actually *gone* somewhere; it all seemed to have a point. He recognized that he was in this moment feeling more alive and more purposeful than he had felt since…he was a child? No, since he had *ever* felt.

He led the way on to the path, and his small crew followed him.

And, from behind a distant grove of trees, Chog appeared.

Twenty-Eight

"He must have gone east from the Hill to cut us off!" said Oddo.

"Well, he's here now," muttered Leo. "Everybody back on to Kulapa!" Everybody skipped and scrambled in response, and Kulapa sidled up as close to the pier as she could and leaned over to let everyone on.

"He's coming this way!" shouted Benjamus.

Leo was still standing on the pier, and an idea flashed through his mind. "Wilwell! Hand me that *Smallsteam*!"

Wilwell pulled the green bottle out. His hand shook nervously, and it fell off the side of the Fishboat.

Leo caught it. He turned and faced the path. Low vibrations were pulsating below his shoes as Chog stomped up the grassy slope.

Chog's close-set eyes burned like soup bowls full of lava. *Won't get away this time. Won't.* Zechariah was here. He would be Chog's, again, and that would be the end of this exasperating interlude in his life and he would be back on top again.

He saw Von Koppersmith poised on the pier with something in his hand. Some kind of trick or trap…Chog had been a sucker too many times, lately. He was done falling for tricks. He smashed his fists together and broke into a dead run. The ground shook.

Kulapa turned and began to back off from the pier, slowly swishing her fins. The boys shouted for Leo to get on board.

"Wait!" called Leo.

Chog was building to a startling speed. Coal and foghorns crunched in the depths of his throat.

Leo hurled the bottle.

It smashed upon the ground at the head of the path and the green vapors of *Smallsteam* wafted up.

Chog bent at the last second and jumped over it. Leo felt a low rush of wind as two shaggy feet flew by.

Chog's hands raked Kulapa's prow and his legs smashed the water into a wet, blue-green explosion. The repercussions made everyone topple over.

Kulapa whirled around, but with Chog clinging to her prow she couldn't see very much. His weight lifted the stern so high that her tail fin flapped uselessly in the air, while her pectoral fins swept the water into foam.

Leo leapt off the pier. He caught the Fishboat's rails and pulled himself up. He eyed the big crossbow, but it was obvious that the cabin would block any shot fired at Chog.

They flowed past all the "Nicht!" signs and skull-and-crossbone drawings.

A sudden lurch knocked everyone flat as Chog heaved his whole body on board the Fishboat.

The river swept down a decline, picking up speed. Kulapa still couldn't propel herself very well and could only manage sluggish pirouettes.

A sound of rumbling water grew steadily louder.

"There's a waterfall coming up, Leo!" shouted Wilwell. "If we go over that, we'll be swept in to the Maelstrom for sure!"

Leo followed Wilwell's pointing finger downriver where, less than fifty yards away, the Fillwishing spilled past a brocade of jagged rocks and over a cliff.

He began shoving everyone into the cabin, even as Chog was climbing over the top. Oddo stared in horror out of the window and cried, "We're going over!"

Through the glass of the forward windows Leo looked and saw…nothing. The river was gone. There was only air.

Time came to a halt. All sounds went mute, except for the slight creak of the hull. The stern left the brim of the waterfall and Kulapa stared into a colossal steaming water pit, swooping away underneath her.

Leo felt his guts rising; for a few seconds he hovered in midair.

Then came the monstrous, bone-numbing collision. Everyone had the breath knocked out of them. Sound and time returned as Kulapa's cabin windows shattered into dirty splinters. Water burst in through them and the sun itself was doused for long, hideous seconds.

When they resurfaced the steady rushing of the river filled everyone's ears. Kulapa, dazed, bounced helplessly along with the current. Leo sat in a murky pool at one end of the cabin, sprawled like a discarded marionette. He felt a heavy fluid dribbling down the side of his head and he realized that it was blood from a deep gash somewhere on his scalp.

He forced himself to his feet, and for a few moments he could only lean against a shelf numbly and listen to the ringing in his ears. Gollyplox and the boys were scattered throughout the cabin, moaning and slowly recovering themselves.

"The Sink, Leo!" Benjamus said weakly. "We have to get off the river *now!*"

They all emerged cautiously from the cabin. The deck was ankle-deep with sloshing water. The crossbow had been ripped off.

Chog was still sprawled across the top of the cabin. The fall had temporarily disabled him; his usual coal-and-foghorn breathing sounds were labored, his movements torpid.

Towering above and behind the Kulapa was the waterfall, a huge, quivering gray and white monolith. Ahead, the river leapt along, white and tumbling. In another hundred yards it was all snatched up and set into whirling motion on a massive, bellowing vortex: the Maelstrom, an entire lake wildly spinning until it coiled up at the center into a dark, gushing hole.

"We need dry land quick, Kulapa!" shouted Wilwell.

The Fishboat paddled backwards ferociously to slow them down, but it didn't help much. Finally, she drove her starboard side against the riverbanks to keep from moving forward. The current continued to force her along, but only in fits and starts, which was just enough for her crew to make an attempt to disembark.

Leo practically threw Benjamus off Kulapa and onto the banks; Wilwell jumped; Gollyplox followed with his customary spectacular agility.

Chog, regaining his wits, discovered that Kulapa was letting everybody escape. With a defiant roar he shoved his fist into the roof of her cabin, ripping it wide open. Essentially, it was a punch through the top of her head.

She spasmed painfully. Unable to cling to the riverbanks any longer she was shoved along by the frothing river.

Leo, Oddo and the Walkchair backed up towards the stern as Chog dragged himself the rest of the way over the cabin. The Maelstrom grew louder and closer, but Chog didn't care anymore. Murder was the only impulse left in him.

Kulapa chose that moment for a tremendous, intentional convulsion. It knocked everybody over. Chog lost his balance and his legs fell into the cabin, his massive feet crushing the cots and the cabinets. Before he could climb out again, Kulapa stretched the wood of her cabin walls in a way that was obviously beyond the normal limits allowed by the Life that had been bestowed on her. As thin cracks roved across her decks, Chog was pinched between the massive folds of the Fishboat's cabin walls. It was a supreme irony: the very wound he had caused her had become a trap for him. His arms and torso were still free, but he could not pull his legs out of Kulapa's grip.

With another wild starboard turn Kulapa ran herself along the riverbank again. Leo and Oddo and the Walkchair scrambled to safety.

Chog swiped at them but missed. He pummeled the Fishboat, but she would not let go, and when she was satisfied that her children were safe she thrust out into the leaping white river again.

Leo watched with paralyzed dread as Kulapa and Chog were swept into the Maelstrom. The Fishboat seemed tiny and pathetic as the fearsome carousel steadily dragged her toward its awful core.

Chog looked like a wooly jack-in-the-box, his hair-laden bulk plugging up the center of the Fishboat like a cork. He squirmed and roared and fluttered his arms above him in panic.

Finally reaching the inescapable center of the Maelstrom, both boat and beast were ripped beneath the water. In an instant, there was simply nothing left to see of either.

Oddo's words suddenly came back to Leo: "*sucked down, drowned, and torn apart.*"

Oddo screamed in protest. He ran downriver to the edge of the Sink, calling for Kulapa. He nearly dove in, and Leo had to restrain him.

The Walkchair shuffled up beside them. They all stared out across the spinning, churning Sink as the sun hid behind the trees and the night began to slump over the Island. Stars, cold and distant, had already begun to come out in the east.

A spray of water not far from the bank caught their attention. It was soundless compared to the never-ending churn of the Maelstrom.

Oddo's body tensed up when he saw it. He broke out of Leo's grasp and charged farther down the banks. "Kulapa!"

She was swimming with all of her might. Chog was gone for good, so she was no longer burdened by his weight. For two full revolutions she was carried by the Sink's current, slowly inching her way towards dry land. At one point she disappeared below the water again, and Leo was sure she had finally run out of stamina. Oddo cried out. Then, almost miraculously, she resurfaced and got her front half on to the grassy, muddy banks.

Leo and Oddo ran to help her, with the Walkchair scuttling along behind them. They reached her and began to pull her the rest of the way out of the water.

"Kulapa!" Oddo was laughing and crying at the same time. "You did it! You killed him! Thank you! Thank you for saving us!"

Her deep, dark eyes were tired. Her body sagged and creaked and had very little power left to help Leo and Oddo get her to safety. When her stern finally left the water, she became rigid. Her fins froze and her eyes became empty.

"That's alright," said Oddo softly, "You sleep now. That's alright."

Leo remembered that Kulapa only came alive when she was in water.

"You'll be alright here, old girl," said Oddo, patting her hard, reddish hull. "We'll come back for you. Once we've gotten the Spear back and we're finished with everything, we'll come back and get you and make you as good as new…"

They left the Fishboat in the grass under the stars and the last wisps of daylight.

"Thank you," Oddo tenderly called back to her over his shoulder, "You sleep now. We'll be back for you!"

...➤·➤·➤·➤·➤·➤

There was no sign of Wilwell, Benjamus or Gollyplox. Leo called out for them, but no one answered.

"Where are they?" he wondered aloud. He led Oddo and the Walkchair on a search upriver, towards the towering waterfall. They did not find anybody.

The Island sloped up from the Sink on all sides, covered with tall bamboo groves. Leo heard sounds of movement farther in.

"That *must* be them," said Leo. He shouted out for Wilwell and the others to wait for them, and they proceeded through the bamboo, using the thick stems to help them up the rising ground.

Insects (Oddo called them 'Fings'), that looked a little like mayflies but with two plump eyes on antennas, had begun to spill from unseen burrows and cruise through the bamboo groves in quiet clouds. This last breath of twilight was their normal flying time, evidently. Waiting patiently for them were 'Bllbs': conical bugs with dozens of iridescent eyes living in thick clusters at the base of many of the bamboo trees. They were stationary, but each one had long, tiny arms that would dart out to grab a passing Fing for dinner. More of the

263

yellow and red Monchpibs wandered by, too, stacked one on top of the other in wobbling Monchpib towers.

It soon grew very dark. Leo, Oddo and the Walkchair began to stumble over bent lengths of bamboo and jutting rocks. They could still hear the sounds of other people moving around somewhere ahead of them.

Leo called for Wilwell. He breathed a throaty sigh of relief when the boy answered. They followed his voice to the top of the slope where the bamboo groves came to an abrupt stop and a grassy clearing opened up.

They could make out the faces of Wilwell, Benjamus and Gollyplox on the far end of the clearing, staring anxiously. Dark figures surrounded them, so dark that it took a couple of seconds for Leo to realize that they were Throtrex, holding the boys and the Cheevilnid captive.

There was a wooden click and a scattering of gray powder and the center of the clearing became a bonfire.

"*Instant Fire*," grumbled Oddo.

On his wide, oar-shaped black shoes Crawlsome Bentpin padded into the light of the fire. Shadows danced along the creases of his top hat. His orange eyes glimmered.

"*Caught you.*"

Part 3 – To the Palace of Kak. A Jail. The Protector's Spear.

Twenty-Nine

Two Throtrex grabbed the Walkchair's back and shoved him to the middle of the clearing, beside the crackling bonfire.

Leo and Oddo were forced onto their knees the same as Gollyplox and the other boys. Throtrex claws dug into their necks and crushed down on their shoulders.

Bentpin, with his scaly green hands clasped behind his back, shuffled slowly and pompously over to the Protector and stared.

"Much smarter than Chog, am I. Even smarter than Kak."

With a long stick of bamboo he began to draw a wide circle around Zechariah.

The Walkchair's wooden eyebrow was raised high and his dark eyes stared in terror, but the Throtrex held him firmly in place.

Bentpin stared away to the west to make sure that the last of the day's light had been swallowed up. He faced the circle he had made and clumsily drew: mɛmɛmɛ

Leo noticed how quiet the Throtrex had become. He didn't know that it was *possible* for them to be so quiet. When he considered the reason for it, he became sure that it was dread. They had all of a sudden become deeply afraid of something.

The glowing flames of the bonfire tossed and twisted.

Bentpin began to hum. It was an ugly, strangled sound. His orange eyes disappeared, because he had closed them, and the space within his high collar and under the brim of his hat became only a dark void.

His dissonant humming became words:

"O Terrible World King, O Mighty World King, O Supreme World King, I summon you!"

From out of the night a black vapor drifted into the clearing.

Bentpin repeated the formula.

The vapor grew thicker, like black blood, and flashed dimly like faraway lightning seen through a dirty window.

A sound formed within the blackness. It seemed almost like words being spoken, but also like words being rounded up and executed. Leo's hair stood on end and his skin crawled. He felt sick.

Bentpin spoke a third time: *"O Terrible World King, O Mighty World King, O Supr—"*

A popping sound and a petrifying shriek split the air. The firelight showed a fat-bellied, gangly-limbed orange body rushing upon Bentpin from out of a blue-black cloud above the nearby trees.

The glinting, black, liquid vapor Being that Bentpin had nearly finished summoning now vanished. Its terrible, sickening sounds collapsed in on themselves.

The creature with orange skin—not like a ripe orange but like a poisoned orange—held a long spear in one hand. With the other he caught the black-coated Bentpin by his neck and lifted him into the air like a toy. There was a rush of sound like a windblast churning up from a deep gorge, and Bentpin's body was overwhelmed by fire vomiting out of the orange creature's gaping mouth.

Leo was transfixed by the horrifying spectacle of the creature grinning maniacally and holding Bentpin in mid-air, watching him burn, watching him tremble and kick. Bentpin's screams diminished to piteous wails as, within a few seconds, he was reduced to a tattered, flaming scarecrow, then to freakish, wretched amorphism, an emblazoned parody of form, and finally to red ash, crumbling from the orange creature's grip to a black pile on the ground.

The few Throtrex that had given their allegiance to Bentpin had long since fled into the forests. Others, who were loyal to the orange creature, arrived with howls and grunts. They began throttling Gollyplox and the children. Leo jumped to his feet to intervene, but just as quickly he felt the smash of something to the back of his head and everything went dark.

Thirty

Leo awoke to the ache of the gash on his head, and he remembered the long plunge down the waterfall, then the Maelstrom, then Bentpin's agonizing death. He opened his eyes and saw, out over a dark ocean, the full moon.

Around him, fire flapped softly like bat's wings, on torches in black iron sconces and in coppery metal bowls, lighting a sand-colored ceiling above him, a wall behind him, and another to his side. The rest of the room was open, looking out over a surf-swept beach. Breezes, heavy with the taste of salt, blew in timid little dust devils that swirled sand and debris in the room's only corner.

Leo sat up. He was lying on thick, soft pillows that smelled like they had just been bought from a department store. He noticed tags with barcodes on some of them. Stacked against the wall were several black, polished chairs with rattan seats that looked like they might have just been delivered from Pier 1 Imports.

Am I home, somehow?

"No. Just trying to make you *feel* at home."

Around one wall came the creature with skin the color of poisoned oranges, and in the bright firelight Leo could see that it was knobbed in many places with sickening, rubbery, yellow warts. He was very tall and hairless. His stomach was as fat and bloated as if it was about to burst, yet his arms and legs were long and gangly. One of his eyes was nearly two times larger than the other; his nostrils were wide and flaring. His mouth was stretched into a huge, perverse grin made of variously shaped teeth. He wore no clothes. He had no fingernails or nipples or genitalia, almost like a clay sculpture that had been abandoned before being finished. In his right hand he clutched what Leo knew instinctively could only be Zechariah's Spear. The handle was made of a dark wood, inlaid with silver and green filigree; the sharp, metal tip was a lustrous black.

The creature stared at Leo for a few seconds. Then, without taking his absurdly disproportionate eyes off of him he reached back and grabbed one of the black rattan chairs. Deliberately he scraped it across the smooth floor until he was uncomfortably close. He sat and faced Leo.

"Kak," he said, indicating himself with his long, spindly fingers. "As if you hadn't guessed—right, Leo?"

Leo did not respond. He felt numbed by fear and revulsion.

"And, once again: no. You're not home. *But I am*! Welcome to my island palace! Not just this, of course, this is just one room. It isn't finished yet, obviously. There will be French doors here, leading onto a veranda, and stairs over there leading up to… well, I can give you the tour later. I think you'll be impressed. Oh, it isn't the Von Koppersmith estate, I grant you—but then again, which Von Koppersmith ever had his own *island*? So, you're here for the Spear, right?"

Leo gawked at the freakish, grinning face. It was disconnected from Kak's words, as if there was another mouth behind it doing the talking. It was disturbing, but even more so was the familiar, almost normal quality of the voice—it made Leo think simultaneously of a university professor and a sleazy salesman standing on the corner with fake gold watches under his coat.

Kak cleared his throat. "The Spear? You need it, right? To give back to Zechariah and restore his power and save the babies and all of that."

"Where are they?"

"The babies? Don't worry. The babies are in their crib. And, by 'crib', I mean a dark, sad, unsanitary pit."

Leo could no longer tolerate being so close to Kak. He stood abruptly and backed towards the wall.

"Let us go."

He didn't know why he said it. He did not have the faintest hope that such a request might be granted. He just wanted to say *something*, because he felt as though Kak's stare was going right through him and making him insignificant.

"*Go?* Let you and the squabs go?" The creature leaned back in his chair and pointed with his long pinky finger at Leo, and there was no way to tell to what degree he was serious or pretending. He looked over his shoulder towards the distant beach. "Just…go?"

Leo decided to continue, knowing it was pointless. "Well…sure. Why not? We can't hurt you —I think we've proven that. We can't get the Spear back. Why not just let us go?"

"'Us'! 'We'! Listen to all of this plural, community talk! Not just you, but you *and* the little children? So…what, after years of solitary globe-trotting without thinking of anyone's suffering but your own, now suddenly you're concerned with the well-being of *others*? Come on, Leopold, we both know that's not really your style. All you've been able to think about for two days is how you can get yourself away from here and back home to mommy. And that's *great*! Let people like Zechariah do the protecting. That is one thing you can say about Zechariah: he does love his little human monkey people. Ecchh! It's revolting. But that was always his Achilles heel. He would do *anything* for them. Even with those first two, way back at the very beginning, he was the eagerest beaver that could ever be, pro-tect-ing them and all that."

"Here's the thing that kills me, though: when the Corpse and I stole them right out from under his nose, does he get punished? A lightning bolt to the face, perhaps? An asteroid to the head? No, no, no! He gets an island paradise, undetectable to the rest of the world, with a palace on a mountain and an army of Oblates. There's no justice! Who repays their failed underlings with an ISLAND?!"

"Anyway, I made up my mind a long time ago that I would figure out a way to take his little tropical paradise for myself, and humiliate him even more! It took patience, I can tell you. The patience of Job. But I knew, I KNEW, when I saw those little Crusader babies, that the game was over. They were the key! I knew if I tossed them down the Wayover on to Zechariah's Island that he would absolutely go

272

nuts over them. And he did! Completely opened himself up. And—once again—with patience, I was able to coax one of the little rotten babies over to my team. That silly-looking humpback gimp-legged one. Of course Zechariah *would* have a soft spot in his heart for *that* goofy homunculus. But I got to him, yes I did! He was eating out of my hand! He accepted all the power I can give a guy and became the Watchdog, then Chog. You saw it, right? You saw what I can do for a person, if they only will it?"

Leo shook his head in bewilderment. "You *planned* all of that? Making the deal with Nicholas, being the Pied Piper, leading the children to the Island—it was all to get to Zechariah?"

Kak leaned back in the chair, tilting the front legs up, and burst into gales of eerie, high-pitched laughter that was disturbingly female sounding. He even clapped his hands in that short, quick way that little girls do when their mothers sign them up for pony-riding classes.

"Yes, yes, yes! And, wow, don't you provide the most wonderful segues, speaking of Nicholas and deal making! Your old forefather certainly knew a good deal when he spotted one, and he jumped on the opportunity. The Watchdog did, too, even if he did screw it all up for himself. But now it's *your* turn, my main man!"

"As you have come to discover for yourself, I can't kill Zechariah. Truth be told, it hurts if I so much as touch him. He and I just don't mix. Now, I've done all the heavy lifting already; I have his Spear. That's his Better Half, so to speak—he needs it or he's not fully himself. Again: all this is old news

273

to you. Here's the new news: I need a new Watchdog."

Leo blinked. Kak blinked back.

"Yes, yes! *You*, Leo! And you don't have to call yourself 'Watchdog,' of course. You can pick whatever name you like. You can *be* anything you want. You know I'm not lying. You saw the Watchdog—at least, before he decided to become King Kong. I made a god out of him! I can do that for you!"

Leo was dumbstruck. What Kak was proposing was overwhelming enough, but the way he proposed it made it an excruciating experience. That was because, Leo was slowly beginning to realize, Kak was not entirely tied to the world like the other Throtrex. He lived outside of it, too, in some kind of spiritual dimension that gave him access to other places and even times. Leo could not guess the extent of that access, but he was sure it included himself. He realized that even now Kak was probing him, sneaking invisible fingers into his mind and looking into places he had not been invited. Or had he?

"What do you want? Power? Wealth? That certainly worked for Nicholas, but after so many generations it seems to be running a little dry, wouldn't you say? Seems like you could use a little cash infusion, if you don't mind me saying so. No doubt your poor mother would appreciate it—you could finally *do* something for her, instead of always being on the take, and traveling around Europe leaving her alone to suffer in misery with nothing but memories of a clinically depressed suicidal husband to keep her company. Kind of heartless, aren't you, Leo? I mean, I'm not judging you, of course, but—wow! She couldn't have any other kids —you were her one and only pride and joy!"

"Well, anyway, maybe having endless sacks of money just isn't your bailiwick. You want super-strength, like the Watchdog? O.K.! How about the ladies? You like girls, right? Who doesn't? How about a harem of vestal virgins—you could arrange them by hair color and assign them each a different day of the week. You want good looks, washboard abs? You got it! Go ahead, be creative! I'll bet you could think of things even I haven't thought of! The point is: *whatever you want*."

Leo noticed the ambiguity of Kak's final sentence. He might have meant: *the point is, you can have whatever you want*, or: *the point is whatever you want the point to be*. Either way, it made Leo feel cold.

"Why me?"

"Why not you? Do you think Walwich Herstog was better than you? Do you think Nicholas of Hamelin was more deserving of my goodies than you are? Look at it this way: it's a win-win situation. I need someone back in the Rest-of-the-World to watch the Protector. Who better than you? Honestly, I think that was the problem with poor, old Watchdog. He tried, but he just couldn't fit in. But you: you're such a naturally easy-going fellow, aren't you?"

"You can't give anything. You can't make anything. How are you able to do any of this?"

"Ughh. You're getting a little hung up on details, aren't you? Alright, alright, it's true. You got me. I can't make anything. But the World King can! That's where I get this stuff."

"But he can't do it without a human."

"Oooh, you're good. And that human is...." He paused for effect. "...our ace in the hole. I'll give you a clue. Remember how there were, not just one, but *two* children's crusades? Nicholas led the one from Germany, and we know what happened to *that* one. But what about the other one? The one from France? The young man who led that one makes Nicholas look like *Saint* Nicholas, I assure you! We had him in the bag even before we had Nicholas, actually, and this dude is in *complete cooperation* with the World King! Yep. So, he's the one who helped the World King create the Glusskreep for Bentpin, and those freaky strangling arms...well, remind me to tell you all about it later. For now it's neither here nor there. I need a commitment from you. Be my guy, Leo! Get that ridiculous, failed Protector off of my island. Go bury him in a hole somewhere...I don't care where. The Himalayas. Do that, and I'll make you the god you deserve to be."

Leo was suddenly aware that he was perspiring. Sweat dribbled down his face, and beneath his saturated clothes the Hair Shirt became almost intolerably itchy. Even worse, there was now a mysterious pressure upon his sternum, as if an Olympic wrestler was pushing one knee into his chest. Kak was behind it all, somehow, and Leo felt an overpowering hatred for him, because he knew that he was being manipulated and deceived. He wanted to lunge at him and tear his eyes out. And yet....

"But Nicholas…he needs me to set things right. My father needs me…"

"You don't have to be your father's son, anymore, Leo—the sad empty child of a sad, empty child in a chain of cursed men. I'm offering you a way to break that curse. What does Nicholas of Hamelin have to do with you, anyway? What does *any* man have to do with you? Take your life back! Beat the curse on its own terms!"

Leo felt knotted up in barbed wire. He walked in slow circles, sweating, shaking his head. Kak's words lingered in his mind: *You don't have to be your father's son…*

"But I *would* be my father's son…if I let down my boys. They aren't really mine—I know that. But…they *are*. They were Nicholas' boys, centuries ago, and Nicholas betrayed them. You're asking me to betray the exact same boys, the boys I've struggled with and risked death for. And they're innocent! I didn't know anyone could be so innocent, and so free. If they knew I had allowed this conversation to go even *this* far, they would look up at me with those big, innocent eyes and their hearts would be broken. I won't do that to them. I don't want anything from you. I want everything for them."

"Alright, alright, don't wet your pants," grumbled Kak. "So, it's a 'no', then?"

Leo was trembling with excess energy. He didn't answer, but stood with clenched fists.

Kak shrugged. "Fair enough." He stood, and dragged the chair back to its spot. He smacked his bloated belly loudly and then rubbed it, breathing out deeply as if he had just enjoyed a nice snack.

"Well, sayonara, Leo Von Koppersmith. Someone will be along shortly to kill you." He turned and began to walk away.

"Wait! What about Wilwell? And Oddo and Benjamus? What will you do to them?"

Kak stopped and giggled girlishly. "Well, *they're* not going anywhere. Not them or any of the others."

Leo looked at him sharply. "The others?"

"Four hundred fifty-one, *in toto*—well, minus the Watchdog, that is. Yes, they're all here. We've been saving them."

"Saving them? What do you mean?"

"The World King wanted to take some time to see if we could turn any of them. No luck so far, I regret to say. The Watchdog was the only one from the whole lousy bunch interested in making a deal. All we're waiting for now is to see what you will do. Either way, tonight's the night. In just a couple of hours, in fact, it will be time!"

"Time for what?"

"The Dark Feast! You know, you can't keep kids too long; they start to go bad…lose all their flavor. Gee, isn't it stupid how you declined my offer for the sake of a few mite-infested kids who will all be dead in two hours?"

Kak exploded into more peals of high-pitched laughter. "Now I bet my offer is starting to look a little more appealing! Tell you what: I'll check back with you in a few and see if you'd like to reconsider."

He snickered and mumbled to himself on his way out of the room. Leo sunk to the ground, holding his face in his hands.

Thirty-One

Two Throtrex entered, with arms so long that their claws nearly scraped the floor. They dragged Leo to his feet and forced him out of the room and along an outside path that paralleled the beach.

Leo now had his first view of Kak's palace. It was a colossal joke; it was so badly constructed that it was as if a one-eyed dyslexic comedian had been the architect. Towers hung out at steep angles and were supported by meshworks of beams and tree branches. Stairs ran up the sides of walls and then suddenly ended. There were more rooms with insufficient numbers of walls. Scaffolding clung to huge sections; one corner of the palace looked as though it had recently collapsed.

Leo was shoved under an arch and down a long alleyway, away from the ocean, to the back of the palace. The forest came up nearly to the walls, and there beneath the branches of an enormous oak tree was a small, simple cube-shaped building set apart from the palace. It had one thick, metal door; it was opened and Leo was roughly tossed inside.

One of the Throtrex locked the door and, after making a crude sound of disdain for Leo, went and sat down at a table. He hung the key on a nail protruding from the table's edge.

Leo watched him through a small square window cut into the door. He wasn't facing in Leo's direction, but was turned towards a huge, raised area lit with dozens of tall torches. Throtrex had begun to gather in it, wandering in the tremulous firelight and snarling at each other.

Leo looked around at his cube-shaped prison. There were no other windows. The dirt floor was littered with leaves and acorns that had fallen through the ceiling, which was only a network of thick, crisscrossing metal wires.

He jumped up and grabbed hold of the wires. As he hung he kicked at them like a chimpanzee, but it did no good.

With a metallic clack, someone unlocked the door and opened it. A dark figure slipped inside.

"Oddo!" Leo dove forward and scooped the boy up in a powerful hug.

Throtrex came in behind and rudely pushed them aside so that they could drag in the Walkchair. Zechariah still sat tied down, his eyes closed, looking as peaceful as he did the day Leo found him in Nicholas' grave. The Walkchair's little dark eyes peered out cautiously from the edge of the seat. Once he spied Leo he scuttled over like a chair-shaped beetle and leaned affectionately against his leg.

The Throtrex left, and Kak entered, holding the Spear. He drifted just above the floor. He was now dressed in a thick black and silver robe with a pattern of angular designs down the chest. It looked like a priest's chasuble.

"So, I'm aware of the way you humans tend to form sentimental bonds with your animals." He looked sidelong at Oddo. "Just remember: ultimately they're all only fit for slaughter. But, in the spirit of negotiation, I'll let you keep this one. This, and whatever amazing gift you'd like, e.g., wealth, money, power, *et cetera, et cetera.*"

He gestured towards the Walkchair without looking.

"There is Zechariah. He will be entirely your responsibility, and I do not ever want to see him again. That's it—my final offer. You have exactly thirty minutes to decide. If you agree, my Throtrex will help you back up the mountain and into the Wayover tonight. You could be eating Cheerios and Poptarts for breakfast in your own kitchen by dawn."

He left, and the door was slammed shut and locked again. He turned back to look at Leo through the door's small square window, which framed his leering smile and his eyes.

"Thirty minutes. And, this time, when I come back, if you aren't at this door shouting 'yes, yes!'…"

Kak's face intensified; the one big eye seemed to grow just a little larger, the little eye became like the tip of a knife.

"…*then I will stab you to death with my pinky finger.*"

He held up his long, orange fourth finger and gave it a lick with his tongue.

When they were alone again, Leo knelt down in front of Oddo. "Are you alright?"

Oddo nodded glumly. His cheeks were dirty and his eyes were red from exhaustion and crying. "They have Wilwell…they have everybody, so it's good to know we're all still alive. But I'm afraid that…" His small chest heaved a couple of times like he was about to sob, but he got control of himself. "I'm afraid that we aren't going to make it out of this."

"Don't say that." Leo looked deeply into his eyes. "*Don't say that. We are going to make it.*" He rubbed the boy's greasy hair and went to look out the door's square window.

The Throtrex had grown much more numerous. There were at least a thousand of them now, crowding the edges of the torch lit area. There were so many pairs of orange eyes that it looked like a sea of fireflies.

Kak drifted into their midst, causing an excitement among them that steadily grew.

The silver of his chasuble faintly glowing, he floated to a white stone altar around which the Throtrex had begun to gather. Their fingers moved in all directions at the ends of their bony, lanky arms, wriggling with expectancy.

Kak held the Spear sternly in one hand like a shepherd's staff, and with the other he produced a large, quivering burlap sack that inspired hoots and chortles among the Throtrex. He reached in and began drawing out all kinds of living animals: long, twisting snakes, kicking rabbits, turkeys and tortoises. He began flinging them into the crowd like Mardi Gras trinkets.

The Throtrex chomped the wet fangs of their long mouths and fought furiously among themselves for whatever they could get their spidery claws on. Any animal grabbed was instantly swallowed whole, and could sometimes be seen still writhing under the Throtrex's tar-black skin for a few seconds before being mashed between teeth.

Kak, no longer able to stay in character as a stern priest, cackled loudly and raised his long, orange arms. "Hors d'oeuvres, they are only hors d'oeuvres! Something to whet your appetite…for the Dark Feast!"

The Throtrex erupted into squealing, squawking, snorting, roaring, growling and ululating.

Oddo clapped his hands over his ears to block out the deafening noise. Leo stared through the window longingly at the key dangling from the table.

"What do you say we have a look at the main course, shall we?" cried Kak, earning another wave of riotous ovation. There was a grinding of stone as some of the Throtrex began moving something— Leo could not see what it was, at first.

He soon realized that there was a huge, heavy slab on the floor in front of the altar, and it was being pushed and pulled from its place to reveal a shallow, grimy pit. There was more savage, cheering exaltation as the Throtrex gathered around.

Hundreds of small, fear-stricken faces stared up from the pit. All of the crusader children were here, huddled together. Most of them were thin as rails from near-starvation, and many of them were feverish. Their reddish brown clothes were filthy and the yellow stitching hung in torn, frayed strands. There was Wilwell, holding in his arms Gollyplox, who looked exhausted and nearly unconscious… there was Benjamus…and Albert, the copper-blond-haired boy whose normally sturdy frame was now wilted…Leo spotted the others whose names he never properly learned: the black-haired boy with freckles…that white-blond kid…the fat kid…they all looked as though Death had half-swallowed their souls. Pale and wide-eyed, they sunk down in terror under the avalanche of Throtrex shrieks; some began to weep.

Leo gasped. Tears rolled down the front of his face. His blood ran cold.

Then it boiled.

"We are getting out of here, Oddo." He struck the door. He wasn't concerned about attracting attention; the Throtrex that had been sitting at the table had long since left to join the gathering, and all attention was on Kak and the children in the pit.

Leo pounded at the door. "We are getting out of here…" He got a running start and smashed the door with his shoulder. It rattled on its hinges but didn't give, not even one centimeter.

Oddo's face grew red with outrage and he shook his fists.

"I just wish Wilwell was here! He could think of something…make something come to life…"

Leo had started to take another run at the door but stopped in mid-stride.

"Oddo…that's it! Zechariah's right here…do that thing you guys do and make something come to life! Make this jail come to life and let us out!"

Oddo frowned. "I don't think we can do that. It can't be a building, or a rock or metal—it has to have parts from living things. Or things that used to be alive, anyway…"

Oddo's train of thought was interrupted by a surge of emotion. "But it doesn't matter! I can't do it—I told you that before! I'm a failure!"

Leo turned back to the window, because he could hear Kak shouting over the din. "Attention, Throtrex! Pay attention!" He waved his long arms and repeated his command with all the august severity of a Roman statesman, but the Throtrex were over stimulated.

"SHUT UP, YOU NITWITS!!"

The hullaballoo abated.

"Good. Now, let's hear the Credo."

The entire multitude of Throtrex assumed the most formal poses that they could muster, and they chanted enthusiastically along with Kak as he led them all in a droning voice, using his forefinger as a maestro's baton:

> *"We have no head! We are bod-ies with no head.*
> *Our mouths are where our hearts are.*
> *Our hands are strong! Our claws are fierce!*
> *Our lust for all is forever and ever with-out end."*

They summed up the entire proclamation with a collective hack and spitting of black juice from their foul, gaping mouths.

Leo got down on one knee and he gripped Oddo's shoulders. "Wilwell, Benjamus...Albert...all those kids need your help *right now*, Oddo. And Gollyplox, too. We are the only chance they have. Any minute now the Throtrex are going to..." Leo couldn't make himself finish the sentence.

Oddo closed his eyes. "I can't do it. I've never been able to. I'm a failure!"

Outside, Kak was giving a speech, describing to his audience in detail the range of his powers and successes.

Leo put his hands gently on both sides of Oddo's face and smiled, not knowing exactly where the smile came from. "Oddo, you can do it! I know you can. You're just a little afraid. But now is the time to be brave—braver than you've ever been before, maybe. We need to get that key that's hanging from the table just outside. I'll bet you can think of something that can go and get that key for us!"

Oddo's face relaxed, and behind his eyes thoughts were clicking together.

He began scanning the ground, and it was not long before he spied what he was looking for. He grabbed it and showed it to Leo: an acorn.

Leo watched as the boy cleared a patch of dirt on the ground and placed the acorn in it. "I need sticks!"

Leo was puzzled, but he picked up the biggest branch he could find and held it out to him.

Oddo shook his head. "No...*little* sticks!"

The boy had already found what he was after. He had gathered a fistful of tiny oak twigs no bigger than matchsticks and was snapping them into various lengths. He placed them carefully in relation to the acorn. Soon it was clear to Leo what the boy was doing: he was making an acorn man.

Oddo stood, staring down at the little figure. He glanced at Leo. "This is the hard part, of course."

Leo patted him on the shoulder. "You can do it, Oddo! I know you can!"

Oddo got down on his knees. He held his hands against his forehead and breathed deeply, as he had seen so many of the other boys do so often in the past.

Leo stared, glancing back and forth from Oddo to Zechariah. He could not have explained it to anyone, but he somehow sensed that the Protector, though completely unconscious, was nonetheless present to Oddo, cooperating with him.

Delicately, Oddo brought his hands together and then opened them again with his palms facing down.

The little figurine's parts hopped and vibrated like they were on a metal serving tray during a small earthquake.

He sat upright. He now had tiny dot eyes. He blinked. His acorn head rotated left and right on his sliver of a neck.

"It worked!" Oddo cried. "I can't believe it really worked!"

The Acorn Man stood. He looked down at his stick legs and wiggled them, feeling them for the first time. He pushed his acorn hat back and scratched his green-brown head with mirthful bewilderment.

"Hi!" Oddo said to him, grinning ear to ear. "Hello!" He then thought that something more formal should be said, but all he could think to do was spread his arms grandly and say, "Welcome!"

The Acorn Man had no mouth with which to smile, but his eyes seemed to twinkle happily, and he clicked his knees together twice. Taking off his acorn hat, he made a perfect little bow from the waist.

Oddo was practically quivering with happiness. He extended his palm, and the Acorn Man stepped on to it.

Leo drew close and marveled. "I knew you could do it, Oddo."

The Walkchair shuffled near, trying to catch a glimpse.

Oddo's eyes grew big. "He needs a name!"

"Later," said Leo, "We need to get…"

"No, no, it's important! We can't just call him 'Acorn Man'. Besides, what if I make more of them, then they definitely couldn't all be called Acorn Man because then how would they know which one of them I was calling for when I needed them?"

"My gosh, boy. A minute ago you were convinced you were a total failure—now you're talking about starting your own army."

"I like his little stick legs. Maybe I'll call him 'Sticklegs'. But I like 'Fred', too. That's it! His name is 'Fredlegs'!"

Leo felt like screaming. "O.K. *good*! But tell him to get the key, *quick*!"

Oddo explained to Fredlegs what needed to be done. As the tiny creature carefully listened, his little ink dot eyes winked. With one stick hand he pushed back his cap and he scratched his smooth, green head. At last he gave a confident nod.

He was easily small enough to roll under the metal door. Breathless, Leo and Oddo watched through the window as he skittered over to the table and shimmied up one of the legs. In a few seconds he reached the top.

The Throtrex jailor wandered by the table, having grown bored with Kak's speech. It snarled and chomped its jaws together.

Fredlegs became completely motionless.

The Throtrex stomped over to the metal door and looked in through the window at Leo and Oddo.

"*Go-nna eat you. To-night. Go-nna eat you both.*"

It hissed, but turned and left. It seemed that Kak was finally coming to the end of his speech.

Leo looked out of the window. Fredlegs had disappeared.

A jingling sound drew Leo's attention to the floor, where the diminutive Acorn Man was wiggling back in, dragging the metal key.

Leo reached out through the square window and turned the lock. Hardly daring to breathe, he, Oddo and the Walkchair crept out of the jail.

"Go hide now!" whispered Oddo to Fredlegs. "Hide among the oak trees, and hopefully we will see you soon!"

Fredlegs gave them a tiny wave good-bye and disappeared cheerfully into the forest.

In the torch lit area outside, over the white stone altar, Kak's voice had the singsong astringency of a preacher-turned-politician. "In closing, I would just like to say that I *am* indeed great, and I *am* powerful, yet I am also *frightening*. But that doesn't mean that I can't also be *ruthless*…" The Throtrex cheered automatically, if no longer enthusiastically, with each adjective.

"Now, before we indulge ourselves in this Dark Feast, we shall enter into a short period of meditation, during which I shall have my toes sucked!"

The Throtrex groaned.

"But when I return," Kak continued quickly, "Then we shall devour every last child and rid my island of them *forever*! Everybody say 'Kak'!"

In unison, every Throtrex shouted: "Kak!"

"Kak!" said Kak.

"Kak!" roared the Throtrex, like a cannon blast.

"KAK!" screamed the Archthrotrex.

His audience gibbered wildly and hopped in place.

"Konkubines, follow me to my chambers!" Kak snapped his fingers, and from among the Throtrex a group of short blood-red creatures toddled eagerly after Kak. Like Throtrex, they had glowing eyes and wide mouths in their chests. They had no fangs, however. Just fat, puffy red lips.

Every other Throtrex on the Island waited beside the pit. They licked their jaws, staring down at all of the children. Wilwell held Gollyplox in his arms, and tried to give strength to his friends, though he had little to give.

Crick chireeeeep crick, said Gollyplox, his pencil-thin green arms trembling as they clung to Wilwell's neck. He wanted to go look for help, but he knew even his best leap couldn't carry him out of the pit and beyond the reach of so many Throtrex.

"It's alright, Gollyplox," Wilwell assured him. "I don't know how I know that, but I *know* it."

Kak led his Konkubines impatiently through an archway and up a flight of stairs. With his silver and black chasuble flowing behind him he swept imperiously past a shadowy niche, where Leo, Oddo, and the Walkchair quietly watched and waited.

Thirty-Two

Most of Kak's enormous palace was dark, so the one doorway glimmering with red and orange firelight drew Leo and the others like timid moths.

They peered around the corner. Towards the center of a large room was Kak, reclining upon a lavish, padded throne, wheezing with pleasure. At his feet were his red-skinned Konkubines, greedily sucking his toes.

He had laid the Spear against one arm of the throne. His hands were folded loosely across the mound of his orange belly.

"Oooh, ladies…oh…we should stop…" Kak giggled. "Really now, we should stop. Everyone's waiting for me…we can't put the Dark Feast off anymore. And I'm *starving!* Oooh, well…when you put it that way, I suppose another few minutes wouldn't hurt anyone…"

Leo crawled upon his hands and knees into the throne room. He was approaching Kak from behind, out of his direct line of sight. Probably out of his peripheral vision, too. Probably. Those vile red things might spot him, but for now their eyes were shut tightly and they seemed sufficiently preoccupied…

"Stop!"

Leo froze at the sound of Kak's exclamation, until he realized it was only directed at the Konkubines. The Archthrotrex doubled over in his throne and squealed: "Ooh, stop! That tickles!"

293

Oddo and the Walkchair watched with terror as Leo softly shuffled forward a few more feet. Slowly, he was closing the distance between himself and the Spear. It's blade shone like polished hematite.

Soon he was close enough to hear the Konkubines' slurping. He could smell the acrid chemical odor of Kak's skin.

He could hardly believe it—his hand was reaching out for the Spear. As his fingers closed around its green and silver handle, he felt a ghostly, invisible energy…

Kak leapt up and whirled around, scattering squealing red Konkubines across the floor.

Leo jumped to his feet at the same time. He was petrified. He held the Spear at both ends, unable to decide what to do next.

Kak stretched his mouth into a cavernous yawn and he retched fire. Flames spewed out in a crashing torrent, toppling over Leo and drowning him in its withering heat.

Unscathed, Leo turned and sprinted back the way he had come. Oddo, crouching behind the Walkchair, threw up his arms and cried out with elation, *"The Hair Shirt!"*

Kak was incredulous. As the Konkubines fled the room, he screamed like a witch. He threw himself after Leo, catching his ankle and bringing him crashing to the ground.

"I'll snatch you up and SMASH YOU, Von *Kopperdoody!"*

Leo kicked and squirmed, but he could not get loose.

294

"I'LL CRACK YOU, SMEAR YOU, I'LL FEED YOU SNAKE EGGS AND GRAVESTONES AND DROWN YOU IN *SPIT!*"

With the butt of the Spear, Leo jabbed Kak's smaller eye. The Archthrotrex wailed and his grip untightened just enough for Leo to tear himself away.

Kak recovered quickly and pounced, locking his skinny orange arms around Leo's waist.

The Spear was knocked loose. It pitched into the air and landed squarely upon its point, making a high ringing sound. For one impossible moment it stood straight, balanced on its sharp, glossy tip, and then fell, landing with a light cuff in Zechariah's lap.

Kak dragged Leo to him like a spider reeling in a web-wrapped bug. Leo stared into Kak's terrible eyes, hearing the breath rushing in and out of the demon's nostrils, feeling the long fingers creeping around his neck like eels.

"I will *maul* you, human. I will start with stings and scratches, and end by desecrating every last inch of you…"

Leo closed his eyes.

He heard a sound like crunching stone, and he opened his eyes to see Kak's body striking the far wall.

The white straps from the Walkchair were lying in loose pieces on the floor. Zechariah stood beside Leo.

He had all the features Leo had grown used to since finding him in Nicholas' grave—the broad shoulders, the spear's point nose, the grizzled close shaven head—but it was as if an old, cloudy coat of

295

wax had been stripped off of them. He seemed taller, and the dark centers of his eyes were like polished black diamonds. The Spear was more lucent, too, now that it had come back to Zechariah. Together, they formed a perfect symmetry, exalting each other.

Zechariah extended his hand to the bewildered Leo and helped him to his feet.

"Rise, my friend," he said in a voice rich with strength. "Be witness to Kak's well-deserved annihilation."

There was a blood-curdling shriek as the Archthrotrex jumped to his feet, furiously breathing arcs of flame in all directions, setting furniture on fire. He barreled towards the Protector with hands outstretched.

In one swift movement, Zechariah cracked Kak's chin with the dull end of the Spear, sending him staggering backwards. He followed with a wide, powerful swing that brought the edge of the Spear's blade tearing across Kak's chest, ripping the poisoned-orange flesh and scattering a gush of blood.

While Kak stood staring at the wound in goggle-eyed outrage, Zechariah plunged the Spear into his stomach, marching forward until the tip ripped out of his back.

Leo, Oddo and the Walkchair watched with a mix of dread and fascination, of love and fear, as Zechariah lifted the Spear into the air with Kak impaled upon it. Zechariah looked up at the swiftly dying Archthrotrex and whispered something that only the two of them heard; to Leo it seemed like a condemnation.

Zechariah twisted and swirled the Spear, casting Kak into a burning pile of debris.

A strange hush followed. The only sound was crackling flames.

Zechariah turned to Leo and smiled warmly.

"Leo Von Koppersmith. Good to see you."

Thirty-Three

The throne room opened onto a balcony that provided Zechariah, Leo and Oddo with a surreptitious view of the altar area and the children's pit. There were so many round heads in the pit that it was like looking down on a nest of fish eggs. Snarling Throtrex leaned over the edges and shook their claws at the children.

"Get them, Zechariah!" urged Oddo. "Quickly!"

"Caution, Oddo. This is a somewhat delicate situation. As long as the Throtrex think that Kak is still alive they will not attack the children, but they certainly will the moment they know he is dead. There are so many Throtrex down there, I could never fight them off fast enough to keep at least some of them from hurting the children."

"What do we do, then? Create a distraction? Lead them away, somehow?"

"Better than that: we kill them all. But it has to be done all at once, with overwhelming force. For that, we'll need my army."

Leo watched as the Protector stepped away from the balcony and closed his eyes. Oddo's face lit up and he let out a sigh of understanding.

Zechariah turned towards the balcony again, staring intently northwestward, through the night and across the forests to where his tall, mist-topped mountain stood.

"Oblates! *Wake up!*" He did not shout the words, yet they left his mouth like invisible falcons.

"Now what happens?" said Leo.

"We wait for a little while. Not long."

Leo looked outside. Although the darkness of Throtrex bodies dominated the ground below, the darkness of night had begun to thaw into a nearly imperceptible glow as dawn trembled in the east.

···+·+·+·+·+·+

"*Hung-ry!*" The Throtrex was looking right at Wilwell and Gollyplox when he said it.

"*Can't wait no more, no more!*" shouted another.

The first one leaned as far over the edge of the pit as he could towards Wilwell, with his tarantula-leg claws clicking the stone. "*Kak wouldn't notice if me's just scooped up this one quick and, bloop, into the mouth!*"

"*Into the mouth, into the mouth!*" More Throtrex took up the chant.

···+·+·+·+·+·+

"Zechariah, they aren't going to wait much longer." Leo watched anxiously as the vast crowd of Throtrex began to squeeze in towards the pit, contracting like a gigantic pupil and chanting, "*...into the mouth...into the mouth...into the mouth...*"

"You're right." Zechariah strode onto the balcony. "It's time. All of you stay here."

Zechariah's feet left the balcony and he hovered in the air briefly. With a rush he flew into the Throtrex horde like a missile.

Leo's lower jaw fell open. "He can fly…"

Oddo jumped in place and cheered.

···✦·✦·✦·✦·✦·✦·✦

Throtrex bodies scattered into the air like dead, black leaves when Zechariah swung his Spear. Parts of them flew off in different directions.

Many Throtrex, seeing the Protector, caterwauled and fled into the forest, but many more rushed at him. The more opportunistic ones scrambled to the sides of the pit and reached for the children, hoping they could gobble up at least one before anyone noticed.

The hundreds of little faces in the pit had glowed like Christmas lights when Zechariah first hurtled out of the night, but now they screamed and ducked down as low as they could, trying to evade grasping claws. Benjamus, the tallest and slowest of all the boys, was the first to get snatched. As he was dragged by the hair out of the pit, he could see other boys being grabbed, as well. They kicked and fought, but they could not free themselves.

Zechariah smashed Throtrex on every side. They howled and climbed over one another to get at him, and over their shoulders he could see his boys being plucked like berries from the pit and dragged into the night.

"No!" cried Leo, staring down in horror. "We have to go down there, Oddo! We have to do something!"

Oddo grabbed him by the shirt and pointed. "No, Leo, look! Do you see?"

From the northwest a silvery-white cloud was descending upon the palace. As it approached, Leo realized that it was moving extremely fast, until all at once it poured like an avalanche upon the Throtrex. It was not until then that Leo realized it was a mass of moon-colored humanoids with hairless heads and large, pointed ears.

"The Oblates!" shouted Oddo.

Each one wielded a sword and wore a red-and-silver striped helmet that looked like a steel fez. In a silver cataract they swirled once around Zechariah and then poured out over the Throtrex in an omnidirectional tide.

In seconds, Throtrex perished by the hundreds. Some of them were able to swing their claws uselessly once or twice before their limbs whirled off through the air or their chests came apart. Most just ran as fast as they could. None survived.

···+·+·+·+·+·+→

In the light of morning, four hundred-fifty crusader children danced and sang and hugged the Protector.

His Oblates hopped around him, too, and rested their heads against him. He instructed some of them to gather food and water for the children.

Others were assigned to demolish Kak's palace, a task they accepted enthusiastically.

"Are they *people*?" asked Leo, watching as they darted like lightning around the palace and sent its already unstable towers crashing onto the beach.

Zechariah smiled. "No. They are loyal and affectionate, and very intelligent, too—but they do not have a human nature. You could compare them to dogs, I suppose. You can see how they obey my every command with all the love that is possible for them." He smiled around at the ones by his side, beaming with pride, and they smiled back and nudged him with their noses.

By noon everyone had gathered on the beach. The children built sand castles or swam in the sea or chased crabs. A huge fire burned in a sand pit filled with crackling logs, and they roasted fish on long sticks.

Zechariah played music. He sat with eyes closed, and melodies flowed out of his Spear accompanied by delicate, colorful auras. For anyone who stopped to listen, the song evoked a pleasant evening spent by a river, and the colors that went with it were gold and crystalline; sometimes it sounded wistful, and the auras melted into blue.

When he was done, he stood on a piece of rubble from Kak's palace and called everyone to him. It took a few minutes, but finally all were gathered close.

"Children! My little boys! I have been your Protector for such a long time, but now what has happened? You went and protected *me*!"

Everyone laughed.

"I am sorry you had to endure so much fear and suffering for so long. I hope you can forgive me for letting you down, for not being there when you needed me…"

The boys all gasped and shook their heads and loudly assured Zechariah that he had nothing to be sorry for. In gratitude and humility he hid his face from them for a few seconds before continuing.

"What makes me very happy is to know that, while we were separated, you had…an *Assistant Protector*, isn't that right?" The children burst into riotous cheering as Zechariah reached over and put one arm over Leo's shoulder and hugged him tightly. Leo grinned sheepishly.

"Leo Von Koppersmith was there for you. He chose you…"

Leo shook his head, wanting to blurt out details about how cowardly he was, how selfish he had been, how he only reluctantly ended up doing anything good for them and even then it wasn't very much.

"He chose you," Zechariah repeated. "And that, I think, is why you must choose him."

Leo looked up. The boys listened attentively.

"I am a Protector, and for a long, long time I had no one to protect—until you came along! For that I am deeply thankful. But the time has come for me to leave the Island. I am being called, in the way that only a Protector can know; called to protect others, who live elsewhere. I must go to them. And I go a wiser Protector than the one I was before! For centuries I was angry at myself, and sad, because I was positive that it was up to me and to me alone to protect; that everyone and everything relied on me! Isn't that foolish? All does not rely on me, even if I *am* a Protector. I, too, must remember to rely on the ones who love me, and on the One Who Loves Me. I think, now, that I will be a little better at what I do, knowing this—don't you agree?"

Some of the boys laughed in agreement; others smiled; others only stared. They understood what he was talking about only imperfectly, with their childish minds and their incomplete frames of reference.

"And I know something else: you cannot stay here any longer! I was so eager to protect you that I kept you here too long. I know now that this Island was always only meant to be a temporary home for you. The Rest-of-the-World is where you belong. You must grow up now! You must become men, and one who is already a man is the best one to show you how to do that!" He laughed and gave Leo another one-armed embrace.

Some crying began, having been building slowly. Many of the boys wanted to know if they would ever see Zechariah again. He assured them it was "very probable." They were encouraged, also, to know that they would be allowed to visit the Island from time to time, with Leo's permission.

···+·+·+·+·+·+

Before leaving, Oddo insisted that Kulapa be repaired and placed in the gentle currents of the northern end of the Fillwishing where she could swim in peace. He also went and found tiny Fredlegs and introduced him to everyone and told them how the brave Acorn Man had single-handedly obtained the key that made possible the victory over the Throtrex.

At the foot of Mount Hollowchest, Gollyplox, his wife, Igwish, and the entire Cheevilnid community gathered to give their beloved humans a froggy farewell—that caused a new wave of tears among many of the boys, but it helped to know they would see them again someday.

The elevator eventually got everybody to the higher reaches of the mountain, and then they began the winding climb up the stairs to the peak. Leo laughed at himself when he remembered his first experience there, when he was paralyzed by a certainty that any move he made would allow the wind to wedge beneath him like a spatula and toss him off the top of the mountain. Now there was no fear at all.

Leo stood next to Zechariah and watched the silvery-white Oblates lift the children one at a time through the invisible opening in the sky and into the Wayover.

"I don't even know most of their names."

"You'll learn."

"Do you really think I'll be able to take care of them all?"

Zechariah smiled. "You'll learn."

Leo laughed suddenly. "You know what I just thought of? It *worked*. The Children's Crusade of 1212. Nicholas wrote, in his letter, that the idea of using children to win back the Holy Land came from an idea that innocence could destroy evil. Everybody thought the idea failed. But it really didn't. It *worked*. Just not the way they had planned."

Leo watched as the Oblates carried the last few boys, including Wilwell and Oddo, up through a passing wisp of a smoky cloud, where they almost seemed to erase themselves as they climbed through the sky portal.

"I have something for you," said Zechariah. "A farewell gift."

Into Leo's hands he placed a flute.

"To open the Wayover."

Leo quietly marveled at it. It was not the warty, green flute of a Pied Piper but a small, brass polished pennywhistle that promised bright, clean sounds.

"That gets you *here*…though here is not where I will be. If you need me—and only if the need is extraordinary—you must go to my palace…"

He gestured over the valley, towards the gray white fog cloaking the peak of his mountain. "Inside is a way to summon me. The boys know of it. I will come when and if I can."

The two of them, man and more-than-man, shook hands. Leo nearly embraced him, but then the impulse felt awkward—until Zechariah overwhelmed him in a crushing bear hug. Leo was still trying to recover his breath when Oblates hoisted him into the sky, but he waved good-naturedly.

Zechariah stood and waved back, still wearing the gray and black Edgar Allen Poe clothes that had belonged to Leo's father and grandfather. Leo laughed at the clunky black shoes and the way the trouser cuffs failed to cover the bright, white socks, and he kept waving until the Wayover received him and the Island disappeared.

⋯⇢⋅⇢⋅⇢⋅⇢⋅⇢⋅⇢⋅⇢⋅⇢

Mrs. Von Koppersmith stood on her front steps breathing in the cold, December air. The sky was ice blue.

From her bedroom window, which had been replaced since the Watchdog's attack, she had seen them coming: little bodies, hundreds of them, toddling across the bright green rye grass meadows towards the mansion.

Anselm stood beside her. "Shall I call the police, ma'am?"

"No, Anselm. I see Leo. He's leading them—see?"

Anselm squinted and grunted with surprise. "So he is! Our Leo's back—again!"

There was soon an army of small boys assembled around the front steps.

Leo smiled mischievously at his mother. "I found them. They're going to be staying here for awhile."

Mrs. Von Koppersmith opened her arms, and when the boys went to her she laughed and cried.

Leo stood on the steps behind her and gave Anselm a fond handshake. As he listened to the children introducing themselves to his mother, his eyes wandered over the little crowd and there, standing behind everyone, was Nicholas.

His bony arms hung peacefully at his sides. As Leo watched, the ghost's black, snake-egg eyes cleared as if clean water was being poured into them. His clothes became new again. His teeth became straight and white and his body transformed from green and shriveled to beige and vigorous. He gave Leo a lingering, tender smile. Finally, he gazed upwards, and his body shot like a dart into the sky.

Even as his vaporous shoes left the ground, a new spirit appeared. Like Nicholas, he caused no disturbance to the grass or the dirt, but melted out of the ground in short, rhythmic increments, as if climbing a circular staircase. He was ghoulish and black-eyed, at first, but as he ascended he went through the same cleansing metamorphosis as Nicholas: the eyes cleared, the skin brightened, the clothes freshened. For a second there was a red and purple rope burn on the neck, but it disappeared. Leo saw the sleepy smile and the deep, kind eyes from old photographs and from the few memories in his mental shoebox.

"Dad..."

Mr. Theodore Von Koppersmith put one hand over his heart and then cheerfully extended it to Leo, right before speeding off in the same direction as Nicholas.

Moments later, more ghosts followed: all of Leo's male ancestors, father after father after father. They spilled out of the ground in a silent, joyful eruption, springing into the atmosphere with longing eyes fixed on faraway places.

Leo glanced at Anselm, who was seeing it all, as well. The loyal old housekeeper was dismayed, initially, but the longer he stared the more certain he became that something marvelous was happening.

When the last of the ghosts disappeared, Leo, Anselm and Mrs. Von Koppersmith helped the boys out of the cold and into the warm, old mansion.

THE END

The adventures of Leo Von Koppersmith will continue...

A note from the author:

This is the 5th edition of *By the Downward Way*, completed on March 11, 2025. I had pronounced the 4th edition to be the final, definitive one, but obviously I pronounced too hastily. For this edition, I added what I thought was some badly-needed depth to Mrs. Von Koppersmith and to her relationship with her son; I improved dialogue here and there; I also tried to make Leo's motivations more clear and intelligible, including making the death of his father an event that happened not when he was an infant but when he was four years old, instead—and an eyewitness, on top of it......I think all these changes make the book a more intense, dramatic, and ultimately more satisfying experience. I hope you'll think the same. Once again, to new and old fans alike: thank you for reading my books!

By the Author

-The Von Koppersmith Saga:
  Book 1: *By the Downward Way*
  Book 2: *From A Dark Wayover*
  Book 3: *A Fantastic Confluence*
-*Choosing Joy*

For more of Dan Lord's work, please visit:
ThatStrangestofWars.com

www.ingramcontent.com/pod-product-compliance
Lightning Source LLC
Chambersburg PA
CBHW070631260626
47161CB00007B/2661